I0635965

Fall Down Easy

Also by Laurence Gough

THE GOLDFISH BOWL
DEATH ON A NO. 8 HOOK
HOT SHOTS
SANDSTORM
SERIOUS CRIMES
ACCIDENTAL DEATHS

Fall Down Easy

LAURENCE GOUGH

M&S

This one's for the Rose sisters –
Gabrielle and Vicky

Copyright © Laurence Gough 1992

All rights reserved. The use of any part of this publication
reproduced, transmitted in any form or by any means, electronic,
mechanical, photocopying, recording, or otherwise, or stored in a
retrieval system, without the prior written consent of the publisher
– or, in the case of photocopying or other reprographic copying, a
licence from Canadian Reprography Collective – is an infringement
of the copyright law.

Canadian Cataloguing in Publication Data
Gough Laurence
    Fall down easy

ISBN 0-7710-3444-X

I. Title.

PS8563.084F3   1993   C813'.54   C92-095171-6
PR9199.3.G68F3   1993

Soon as I fell for you baby
Knew I was gonna take a fall
'Cause you got jailbird eyes
And you ain't sweet at all . . .

Lyrics to 'Fall Down Easy' courtesy the estates of Washer
Brown and Lincoln R. Powell, Long as Yer Arm Records and
UpBeat/BeatUp Music, Ltd, copyright 1948, 1991.

First published in Great Britain 1992 by Victor Gollancz Ltd.

Photoset in Great Britain by Rowland Phototypesetting Ltd.,
Bury St Edmunds, Suffolk
Printed and bound in Great Britain by
Butler & Tanner Ltd, Frome, Somerset

McClelland & Stewart Inc.
The Canadian Publishers
481 University Avenue
Toronto, Ontario M5G 2E9

1

The mini-blinds were broken. Several rows of the thin, pale green plastic slats had been bent and crushed as Greg nervously spied on a City of Vancouver blue and white that had, for no apparent reason, parked halfway down the block.

Greg'd told himself to relax, it was nothing. He went into the kitchen, grabbed a can of beer out of the fridge and drank it while the patrol car sat there, its idling engine polluting the atmosphere. Man, what were they up to now?

The canary chirped.

Greg hissed at it like a snake, and it dropped to the bottom of its cage and fell silent.

He killed another beer, snorted a couple lines of coke. Big mistake. Now he was really worried, more than a little paranoid. He used a whole roll of shiny black electrician's tape to fasten a sawed-off double barrel twelve gauge Purdy to a kitchen chair, taped the triggers together and tied them to the doorknob with a length of twine. He crouched behind the weapon and squinted down the short barrels, made sure it was lined up just right. He lit a cigarette, cocked both hammers and ran back into the bedroom.

The cops were still there. He sniffed a little more coke, honing that edge and keeping it sharp. The bed was littered with handguns. He snatched up his favorite, a Colt ·357 magnum. Too heavy. He couldn't hold it still, it'd break his wrist the first cap he busted.

His fingers plucked at the mini-blinds, twisting and turning. The cigarette burned his upper lip. He swore and spat the butt on the carpet. A light went on inside the patrol car. There were two uniformed cops in the car, someone else in the backseat.

He hurried into the kitchen, checked the Purdy and snatched another beer out of the fridge, ran back into the bedroom.

The cops were still there.

He turned his back on them and lit another cigarette, shielding the flame from his lighter with both hands.

When he looked up, the car was gone. Now what? He could phone Hilary, invite himself over. But was that such a good idea, when he was wired?

Not really.

He shoved his arsenal to the far side of the bed and lay down, found the remote and used it to turn on the TV, run up and down the channels.

Twelve hours later, the fat worm of sunlight that had slipped through the gap in the mini-blinds and spent all morning crawling across the tangled sheets made it as far as his right eye. Greg coughed, rolled over. A manic burst of laughter from the foot of the bed yanked him out of his dream.

Greg struggled to a sitting position.

Arnold Schwarzenegger was still chuckling. He'd made a joke, and Greg had missed it. Schwarzenegger's blocky, cheerful face overflowed the Hitachi's tiny screen. Greg turned up the sound. Arnold was denying that he intended to run for Governor of California. Greg flipped through the channels. He found a tennis match on TSN, Martina thundering around the court. Every time she struck the ball it made a sound like somebody ripping the tab off a frosty cold one.

Greg, still waking up, slowly became aware that the bedroom was hot and stuffy and that he had a terrible headache and an overpowering thirst. He turned the TV off and climbed out of bed, heading for the fridge with such single-minded purpose that he came within inches of overrunning the trip wire and blowing himself in half.

2

He gingerly lowered the Purdy's hammers, relieved the fridge of a liter of fresh orange juice and drank deeply. He continued drinking as he went to the door and opened it a crack. Cold juice trickled down his chin, on to his belly. He scratched himself.

The hallway was empty, deserted. He picked up his delivered copies of the three morning newspapers, shut and bolted the door. Back in the kitchen, he tossed the papers on the pale blue formica table and then poured six cups of bottled water into the coffee machine's clear plastic bladder, dumped a careful measure of his special blend of Kenyan and Dark French beans into a fresh filter and turned the machine on.

In the bathroom, he studied himself critically in the cheap full-length mirror screwed to the door. Then he turned on the shower, waited until the water ran hot, adjusted the temperature and stepped into the tub.

The heat lamps dried him while he flossed and brushed his teeth, smiled a foamy rabid smile. Hilary was crazy about his smile. It was what had snared her. He tried the smile again. Sweet kid. Too bad, what he was going to have to do to her. He spat into the sink, rinsed his mouth and spat again. She was the possessive type and, even worse, had an active imagination. He'd told her he was an out-of-work actor from Toronto and she'd bought it okay, but never stopped asking questions. Greg didn't like answering questions. It was too much like work, keeping track of his lies.

He used the dryer on his curly black hair, fluffing it with his fingers, trying for more body. The perm was starting to go, not that it mattered.

Naked, he wandered back into the kitchen, mixed a fresh batch of cinnamon and sugar and cut four thick slices of sourdough bread off a loaf and dropped them in the toaster.

By the time the toast popped he'd sunk half a cup of coffee and was starting to feel like a citizen again. He lightly buttered the toast and added a heaping spoonful of cinnamon, gobbled it down. He was drinking from his favorite mug. The mug

3

had a pattern of small black and white squares, like a chess-board, except the shape of the squares was distorted by the curve of the mug. That was the way he perceived people – simple but twisted.

He added milk to the coffee, stirred it clockwise with a spoon. He was fascinated by patterns of every kind – patterns betrayed you. If you followed a pattern the cops would pick up on it and use it to put you away.

Still naked, Greg drank his coffee and ate his toast. He liked to walk around the apartment naked on the day of a heist. He was no Schwarzenegger and didn't want to be, but he was proud of his body, the flat, taut musculature that he worked so hard to maintain. Being naked made him feel powerful. But at the same time, it made him aware of his vulnerability. There were mirrors all over the apartment, huge gleaming sheets of silvery glass at every turn. It wasn't vanity – the truth was more complicated than that – he loved to surprise himself, confront his image from unexpected angles, in varying conditions of shadow and light. The thought of seeing himself through the eyes of a stranger endlessly fascinated him.

He poured a second cup of coffee and went into the living room. The midday sun had turned the furniture into gold. He sprawled out on the sofa and browsed through the news-papers, read the crime news and sports section, columns and columns about the latest brain-dead stiff to make six million playing right field.

The telephone rang three times and fell silent. He counted ten and it started ringing again. He picked up.

There was a pause and then Hilary said, "Greg?"

Greg said, "Who is it?"

"Hilary. Can I talk to you a minute?"

"What about?"

"Tonight."

"You can't make it?"

Hilary said, "What? Don't be silly. I just wanted to know what you thought I should wear, that black satin dress I bought last weekend, or the red one I wore the night before last."

"Black," said Greg. "Wear the black."

"Not the red – you sure?"

"Black," said Greg. "It'll suit my mood."

Hilary said, "Greg?" Her voice was low, dripping with spice and musk.

"What, what?"

"Should I wear anything else, or . . ." Her voice trailed off. Greg waited, listening to the background chatter of somebody's keyboard. Finally Hilary said, "You're really awful, aren't you?"

Greg said, "Just wear the dress, baby. Remember what I said about keeping it simple?"

"You still picking me up at eight?"

Greg said, "Somewhere around there," and apologized real quick, before she could hit him in the ear with the phone. He lit a cigarette, blew smoke at the ceiling fixture, read the *Globe and Mail*'s comic section while she enthusiastically told him about a new perfume she'd discovered, that was going to drive him crazy. Finally he couldn't take it any more, told her there was someone at the door, and gently hung up.

He lit another smoke, his fourth or maybe fifth of the day. What right did he have to treat her like that? None at all. Creep. Was it her fault she happened to phone while he was lying around the apartment trying to get himself psyched up to pop a bank? No way. He sat up, snatched the phone off the coffee table, dialled her number. An older woman picked up. Greg didn't recognize her voice. He asked for Hilary and the woman said Miss Wainwright had apparently gone for lunch.

Greg finished his cigarette and then lay down in the middle of the living-room floor on the creamy DuPont carpet and did nine push-ups, because the gun he was going to carry that day was a nine-mil. He followed the push-ups with twenty-six sit-ups, because he was twenty-six years old, and then rolled

5

over on his belly and did his three-digit apartment number in hot, sweaty push-ups, sets of ten.

Finished, he glanced at the electric clock over the sink. One-thirty. Perfect. It'd take him at least an hour to vacuum, wash and wax the kitchen and bathroom floors, wash the dishes. By the time he finished he'd need another shower. Add at least an hour for makeup and another twenty minutes to choose his clothes and dress, ten more minutes to load and clean the gun, and he was right on schedule for his planned departure time of 4:00.

Greg knelt and reached under the sink for a can of Comet cleanser. The snout of a ·25 calibre semi-auto wedged into a bend in the drain was pointed right between his eyes. The day's first lightning bolt of adrenalin ripped through him, warming his flesh and tickling his bones.

Vacuuming was a breeze, something he almost always enjoyed. It took him a little longer than he'd expected to wax the kitchen floor, but when he'd finished the yellow linoleum gleamed like ice.

He showered again, towelled himself dry, splashed on a little cologne, slipped into a pair of loose-fitting dark green twill pants, brown socks and a forest green shirt, all of it bought by mail from L L Bean. Greg'd bought all his clothes long distance ever since buying a silk tie from an Eaton's clerk whose previous incarnation had been as a bank teller. Greg had caught the panicky look in her eyes, recognition and fear, and then the shutters came crashing down as she decided she was hallucinating, that Greg *had* to be a bad dream. He'd taken no chances, though. Paid with cash and gone straight home to bed.

He booted his rented Macintosh, dipped into the file called *Faces*. Today, feeling pugnacious, he was thinking along the lines of a broken nose, cauliflower ears, bulge of scar tissue over the eyes. Maybe an open cut or slash high on a cheekbone.

Greg believed in playing fair. The mask he fashioned had to fit his mood, present a kind of truth. He smiled, remem-

6

bering a classic description of a bank robber he'd clipped from a newspaper years ago. *He had a scar*, said the witness, *and a gun*. These two useless details were all the police could pull from a man who'd spent a full ten minutes with the bandit, staring uninterruptedly at him from the passenger seat of his stolen car.

A gun and a scar.

Greg could picture the robbery squad falling asleep over the mug books.

But the scar across the cheekbone was out, he saw as he tapped the keyboard, working his way through the file. He'd used the scar a little over a year ago, when he hit a Bank of Commerce. Studying the color screen, Greg saw he'd gone for a kind of Chinese look. He couldn't recall why. The teller hadn't been Chinese. What was her name? Greg had to look it up. Beverly. There she was. With the Brooke Shields' eyebrows and Streisand nose.

The scar tissue over the eyes would work just fine, though, and the mashed nose was great. The ears might be a little tricky; matching the skin tint. He could give himself a short diagonal scar that ran, say, across his chin up to the corner of his mouth. If he mixed a little red tint into the face putty, he could make the scar look inflamed. Then he could mix in a little bit of paper-thin, translucent sheet latex, give himself a secondary infection. Greg was getting into it now. His artistic side bubbling away, on the boil.

He scrolled through the file, staring at his previous faces as they drifted up the screen, seeming to levitate into the electronic darkness. Occasionally he stabbed at the keyboard, locked a face on screen and avidly studied it, devouring the details, memorizing every pore.

When Greg'd viewed all the faces and was confident he knew them all and was in no danger of repeating himself, he turned off the computer and went into the bathroom and began to go to work, transforming himself from stud to pug.

In twenty minutes, he added five years and a thousand body-blows to his age, dropped twenty points from his IQ.

7

Grunting, he brought up his fists, lowered his shoulders, feinted, and tossed a left hook at the mirror that caught his reflection flush on the jaw. His head snapped back and he shuffled out of range, grimacing in pain. He looked great – like a punched-out extra from one of the *Rocky* films.

Peering out from behind his eyebrows, Greg tried the actor's voice on for size. "'Dis is a stick-up. So stick 'em up!" He started laughing. A ridge of scar tissue sloughed away, hung from his lower lip like a dehydrated worm. He pressed it back into place, working the putty-like substance into his flesh. Nobody would believe a voice like that, even if they could understand what he was saying. He tried again, taking care to speak slowly, not rush his words. "This is a stick-up." No, hold-up was better. He made a fist and thrust his index finger at the mirror, cocked his thumb as if it was a hammer. "This is a hold-up. Gimme the cash or I'll blow your head off." Nah, too dramatic.

He tried, "Gimme the money or I'll shoot."

Yeah, that was a lot better. He waited a moment, got set and then took it from the top, walked up to the tiled counter, pointed the fist that was a gun, stared into the mirror with eyes that were remorselessly cold and deadly and said, "This is a hold-up, sweetie. Gimme the money or I'll shoot!"

Wowie zowie. Very scary.

He bulked up his stomach with a folded bath towel, wedged a pair of foam shoulderpads under his shirt. He looked pretty good, but not perfect. To add a touch of menace, Greg slid a cheap silver ring – a death's head with red glass eyes he'd bought at a biker shop for ten dollars – on his righthand pinky finger. Now he was a brawler with a belly, a fighter run to fat. Obviously past his prime but still not the kind of guy most people would choose to mess with.

For extra insurance, Greg shoved a spare clip and his favorite piece, a fourteen-shot 9mm Browning, into the side pocket of his moss green L L Bean windbreaker.

During his career as a bank robber he'd only showed his weapon twice. It was not a smart thing to do because if you

8

used a weapon you were looking at armed robbery – a heavy rap, maximum security, extra time.

But sometimes things got out of hand; you were forced to demo the ruthless side of your personality in order to control the crowd, settle down the rowdies.

Even if you didn't carry a weapon, the sad truth was that there was always a chance the prosecutor would sweet-talk or coerce your victim into remembering she'd seen a weapon. If the jury bought her lies you were dead meat, crispy on the outside and cooked all the way through. So the best plan was not to get caught in the first place.

The Secret of my Career as a Bank Robber – Don't get caught.

From time to time Greg wondered what would happen if he waved the Browning or Colt or Smith & Wesson in some guy's face and the dope kept coming. From time to time he wondered if he could take the guy out.

He had a mean streak, sure. But if it came right down to it, would he turn into a killer or take early retirement?

He just didn't know.

2

It was early, a little past four, but traffic was already thickening; moving into the meat and marrow of the rush hour. The Caprice's front end bounced as the tires hit the curb. Willows gave it a little more gas, pulled in behind a blue and white.

Claire Parker said, "You still get a kick out of it, don't you?"

Willows turned off the flashing red dashboard light, then the engine. He slipped the keys in the pocket of his leather jacket, got out of the car, locked the door and slammed it shut.

"Get a kick out of what?"

Parker shut her door, made sure it was locked. It was amazing, the circumstances under which people would steal. She said, "Out of parking on the sidewalk, Jack. After all these years, you still get a little surge out of parking on the sidewalk, don't you?"

Willows grinned, didn't deny it.

They were on Main Street, standing in front of the Rialto Hotel, located a convenient five blocks from the Public Safety Building at 312 Main and the roughly one thousand cops who called it home. They were within easy walking distance of a Sky Train station and a McDonald's outlet, the terrific architecture of the CNR terminus and eye-popping displays of the Science & Technology Center. A devious real-estate agent might have been able to make it sound like a wonderful neighborhood.

10

It wasn't.

A uniformed cop stood in the shelter of the Rialto's grime-encrusted doorway. The cop was young, looked like he still worked out. He was wearing non-regulation mirror sunglasses that reflected the pale blue sky, passing traffic. Willows couldn't read him. He had no idea if the cop was the type who'd take a moment to visit the Science & Technology Center, grab a little culture. But he was juggling a trio of bright yellow balls made of crumpled wax paper, so Willows was fairly sure he'd explored the wonders of french fries and cheeseburgers.

The cop finally noticed the two detectives. Rattled, he fumbled the ball.

Now the cop was staring at Parker. Willows couldn't blame him, but didn't like it. He kicked the balled-up cheeseburger wrapper into the gutter, brushed wordlessly past the cop and started up the stairs, into the musty, crumbling heart of this fleabag hotel.

Parker, right behind him, said, "Outside, I counted five floors. Body's on the fifth, right?"

Willows said, "It's all the climbing that gets you, in the end. Homicide detectives never die, they just run out of wind and take early retirement."

Parker started laughing. It wasn't all that funny, but she hadn't cracked a smile all day. Now she was laughing so hard she had to pause and catch her breath. Willows slowed his pace and glanced over his shoulder, smiled down at her.

"You okay?"

Parker leaned against a wall that was clearly out of plumb. She said, "Yeah, sure. I'm fine."

Willows was frowning, looking concerned. "You want to, we can go back to the main floor, take the elevator."

The chances of finding an elevator in a dump like this were about the same as finding a water cooler in the anteroom to hell. Parker started laughing again. After a moment, Willows joined in.

The only cars in front of the building were the blue and

11

white and Willows' unmarked Caprice. The ME hadn't showed up yet, and neither had the techs.

For a moment or two, the body could wait.

3

A wind that smelled faintly of iodine had kicked in from some-where out in the Pacific. The clouds were low, crumpled, moving fast across the sky. Sharp splinters of sunlight came and went. Greg was wearing a cheap throwaway raincoat but he regretted not bringing an umbrella. A downpour would wash the complexion right off his face.

He walked to a nearby Muffin Break restaurant, dropped a quarter in the pay phone in front of the shop, dialled Black Top and ordered a cab, went inside and bought a ham and pineapple and a takeout coffee. The Black Top dispatcher had said five minutes, and he was right on the money.

The cab took him to a three-story medical building with an underground parking lot that was only two blocks from the bank. Greg paid the fare, strolled in the front door, loitered for a few minutes in the lobby and then took the elevator down one level to the parking lot. The brown Ford Taurus station wagon was right where he'd left it, the brown paper bag containing his change of clothes still on the backseat floor.

Greg wandered around the lot, a set of keys dangling from his hand, whistling tunelessly as he pretended he couldn't remember where the hell he'd left his car. If there were any undercover auto squad guys in the parking lot, he couldn't find them.

He went over to the stolen Taurus and took a closer look at it. The tires still had air in them. The gas tank hadn't been drained. He opened the door and tapped the horn. The battery was still charged. Greg smiled. Maybe Ford really did have a better idea. He shut the door, dropped the keys in his pocket and strolled out of the building.

Time to case the bank.

One of the reasons he'd chosen this particular bank was because there happened to be a convenience store located directly across the street. Greg loitered at the magazine rack, a copy of *StreetBike* magazine clutched in his grimy hands but his mind on the bank, the ebb and flow of customers, pattern of pedestrian and automobile traffic. There were two easy ways to get busted. The best way was to tell a snitch what you were up to. The second best way was to loiter on the premises. Greg believed the cops had a response time of somewhere in the neighborhood of three minutes. One hundred and eighty seconds. He never allowed his visits to exceed half that time. Ninety seconds – that was his personal limit. After that, no matter how much fun he was having, *hasta la vista* baby, he was gone.

The biker magazine was weird. There were more nude women in it than you'd find in the average *Penthouse*. And fewer motorcycles. He put the magazine back in the rack and checked his watch. Twenty-seven minutes past four. Patterns were dangerous, but sometimes necessary. Banks were like donuts. Any time was a good time. But he favored the start of the lunch hour and also between four and six in the afternoon. Later was best, because when the streets were jammed it slowed the cops' response time, rendering their lights and sirens all but useless.

Not that Greg'd ever been involved in a hot pursuit. If he ever came that close, he'd have to take a long hard look at a career change – retail sales, something along those lines.

He walked down a narrow aisle to the freezer at the back of the store and pawed through the icecream. So many choices, so little appetite. He helped himself to a lime pop-sicle and then changed his mind and snatched up the last of the fudgicles. On his way to the cash register he developed a limp, dragged his left heel so it left a black skidmark on the linoleum.

The guy behind the counter saw how he was disfiguring the store and gave him a look that clearly said – If you were a horse, I'd gladly put you out of your misery, pal.

Greg asked for and was reluctantly given a dollar's worth of quarters in his change. Snuffling and shadow-boxing, he limped out of the store and went around to the side of the building where there was a concrete retaining wall he could sit on while he nibbled at his icecream and studied the traffic patterns a little longer.

He finished the fudgicle, lit a cigarette. It was 4:35.

He limped over to the phone booth and dropped the first of three quarters, dialled Black Top and Yellow and finally Checker Cabs. All three cabs were scheduled to arrive at exactly five o'clock. The Black Top would pick him up in front of the bank, the Yellow would arrive at the convenience store, and the Checker would pull up in front of a Bino's restaurant a few doors down the block.

This was a new thing, the multiple use of taxis. He hoped it would work out. If not, he'd yank some commuter fool out from behind the wheel and borrow his car; all he needed was something to get him to the Taurus stashed in the garage of the medical building. Or he could hop on a bus, steal a tri-cycle. Whatever, the idea was to get out fast. Because if they trapped you inside the bank, you might as well jump in the vault and slam shut the door, it was all over, mama, roll the credits.

On the other hand, Greg believed that the minute he hit the street, he was a free man. Because if there was one thing he was good at, it was thinking on his feet, the fine art of improvisation.

Given a little elbow room, they could drop a drift net over the whole damn city and never catch him. The thing was, they didn't know who they were looking for or what he looked like. And they never would.

Greg used the sleeve of his shirt to wipe his prints off the telephone. He lit another cigarette. He felt as if he was going to live forever – that's how slowly time was passing.

15

At 4:51 he started across the convenience store's parking lot towards the intersection, timing his limping gait perfectly, so he hit the corner at the exact moment the albino pedestrian appeared – a symbol of reassurance to all but the blind.

At 4:54 he elbowed open the glass door and stepped inside. There were only three customers in the bank; an elderly woman wearing a pink pant suit and a cheap straw hat decorated with artificial roses; a skinny blonde in her early twenties; and a pudgy bald guy in his forties dressed in white coveralls with the logo of a local cablevision company.

The blonde was the wide-awake-and-extremely-observant type, a good witness. She'd memorize everything about the heist and tell it to all her friends but never say a word to the cops because she didn't want to get involved. The cable guy got paid by the hour – he wasn't going to risk his ass to save the corporation's money.

That left the old lady, and it was the old lady that experience had taught him to worry about. She knew right from wrong and was proud of it, had lived long enough to think she was immortal, and probably swung a mean purse.

Greg decided that if he had to, he'd show her the Browning. If that didn't cool the old babe off, he'd put a bullet right between her eyes, turn that goofy straw hat into a gravestone.

Greg smiled at the cable guy. Just kidding, fella. The cable guy suddenly took an interest in the terrazzo, avoiding eye contact. The shy type. Where'd he get that tan? Hawaii, no doubt. The annual vacation, two weeks all included. Didn't somebody tell him about the deadly ozone layer thing, the deadly skin cancer thing?

Only two of the five teller's cages were open for business. The blonde was at the one near the window, and the old woman had the other – Hilary's – nailed down.

The cable guy shifted his weight from side to side, unable to keep still. Greg's smile seemed to have made him a little nervous. Well, that's what smiles were for. Greg tapped him lightly on the shoulder. The guy jumped. He was carrying a

16

shiny black briefcase and it seemed to Greg he might have squeezed the handle a little tighter.

Greg said, "How come channel seventeen's impaired?"

Without missing a beat, the guy said, "Maybe it ain't the reception – maybe it's you." He had a strong accent. Cuban or Mexican? The guy'd suddenly lost his shyness, was staring at Greg with dark brown, Rottweiler eyes. Greg gritted his teeth, resisted the urge to drop the mug with an overhand right. After what seemed like a very long time the cable guy muttered a word Greg wasn't familiar with, and turned his back on him. *Puta*, was that it, *puta*? Was that a nice thing to say, *puta*?

Greg didn't think so. He pictured himself screwing the Browning into the guy's ear, yanking the trigger and watching his head light up.

He sensed movement behind him, and turned and saw a woman who looked too old and frazzled and worn-out to even consider having children shove a doublewide stroller through the door. Greg counted two babies. Twins. Redheads. Tiny little things, but were they ever *noisy*. The one closest to Greg dumped its bottle overboard. The bottle skidded across the terrazzo and spun to a stop a few inches from Greg's foot. He gave it a kick, sending it back towards the stroller. The woman glared at him. She knelt and picked the bottle up and stuck it in the baby's screaming mouth. The other kid dumped *his* bottle. Greg let it lie.

The blonde's lips moved as she counted her money, slowly made her way towards the door.

The *puta* guy moved towards the teller's cage nearest the window. Which meant, hopefully, that Hilary's cage would be free next, and Greg could step right up and say hello. If it didn't work out that way, Greg'd let mommy step in front of him, crash the lineup.

The stroller jerked back and forth, back and forth.

Greg was very tense. In his stomach, the fudgicle had turned into a sludgicle. He felt like he'd spent most of his life in the damn bank. He checked his watch. One minute to five.

17

He glared at the old lady. As if in response, she snapped shut her purse so forcibly that it sounded like a maximum security cell door clanging shut. Then turned and walked right past him.

Greg limped up to Hilary's cage. She was watching him with those cool green eyes of hers, aware of him but completely uninterested. And who could blame her? The whole point of a disguise was being able to shuck what was memorable. Greg smiled at her, said hello in his throaty fighter's voice, then looked her over, made a slow pass with his squinty eyes. She wore a plain white silk blouse and a skirt with more pleats than the average accordion. She hadn't bothered with the top buttons of the blouse, giving the customers a peek at a frothy underlayer of pink silk and the rope-design gold necklace Greg'd given her. She looked terrific. Sexy, full of juice.

Greg passed her the note, which he'd labored over for almost an hour the previous evening. The note was in rhyming couplets. It needed a rap beat to do it justice but Greg was too shy to try. He watched as Hilary read the note, saw her begin to smile, the smile fade as the content began to sink in. She looked up, stared across the counter at the worn-out but kind of beady-eyed hulk who was trying to rob her. To Greg, Hilary looked tense, but not frightened, more like she was trying to remember what to do.

Greg picked up the lightweight plastic nameplate that had *Hilary Fletcher* engraved on it and slammed it down on the counter hard enough to make a dent in the wood. "Just give me the money, that's all."

Hilary stared at him.

Greg said, "Gimme the money, sweetheart, or I'll blow away the Bobbsy Twins and phone the papers and tell them I'm real sorry but Hilary made me do it."

She still didn't move. She was frozen, stiff as a brand-new icicle. Against his better judgement, Greg gave her a quick peek at the Browning. Hilary's head fell back. She opened his mouth so wide that Greg could count each and every last filling, then screamed with so much enthusiasm that the twins, awestruck, fell silent.

18

After that, several things happened at once. A man in his fifties wearing a dark blue pinstripe suit walked out of the manager's office with an expression on his face like someone'd turned the stereo up too loud. The twins started screaming again. The blonde, standing at the door with a fist full of twenty-dollar bills, did a little pirouette and stared open-mouthed at the scene. The old lady hurtled back into the bank. But what really got Greg's attention was the *puta* guy.

The *puta* guy didn't even turn around.

Greg reached over the counter and grabbed a handful of silk, shoved the muzzle of the Browning up against Hilary's forehead. She immediately stopped screaming and started pushing money across the counter.

Greg said, "That's the idea – now you're cooking!" He began to stuff his pockets.

The pinstripe veered away from Greg. His face was white, sweaty. The *puta* was no threat but the way he was holding the briefcase made Greg want to grab it away from him. Had to be something more valuable in there than a peanut butter sandwich in a brown paper bag.

Greg, acting on the spur of the moment, took a step backwards and said, "That's mine, pal," and snatched at the briefcase. The cable guy lost his balance. His arms windmilled. Greg shifted his grip on the briefcase and yanked hard.

Hilary started yelling again. Something about a hold-up. Thanks, babe.

Greg stomped on the cable guy's wrist, heard a bone snap. The high-pitched electronic shriek of the silent alarm filled him with pain. He stomped down again, the heel of his shoe digging into the guy's collarbone. The dude finally let go of the briefcase. Greg staggered back, hit the stroller. He was bleeding, could feel the blood streaming down his leg. He glanced down at himself as he went for the Browning.

He was standing in a puddle of warm milk. My God, he thought, I almost shot a baby.

Somebody behind him yelled, "Hold it!"

It was the cable guy, the *puta*. Back on his feet. He had

19

something in his hand – a small mirror. What did he think he was up to? Greg was a boxer, not some kind of fruitcake vampire! Greg started towards the door, the briefcase clutched tightly to his chest. Hilary, bless her heart, was still throwing money at him but he had a hunch it was small spuds compared to the briefcase. He held the Browning loosely in his right hand, pointed at the floor.

Suddenly the *puta* had a gun, was pointing a gun at him. The sound of his shot slapped Greg in the ears. He heard the bullet zip past just as the second round struck him in the chest, on the left side, just below his heart. Greg staggered, held his ground, squeezed the trigger as he began to raise the Browning. His first three rounds wailed off the polished terrazzo. The next three or four punctured the plate glass window in a diagonal line moving from left to right. An incredibly lucky hit took out the security camera next to the front teller's cage. Greg couldn't tell where the next several shots went, but the last time he pulled, he scored a direct hit.

Loops of arterial blood spun through the air. The redheaded twins suddenly looked as if they were molting. Mommy shrieked hysterically and fell across the stroller. The tubular chrome frame buckled under her weight. The twins started screaming again. Fair enough. The *puta* guy waved a limp hand, as if to signal defeat.

But he hadn't dropped his weapon, had he? Greg took a bead on him, shot out an eyebrow.

The *puta* guy got that plucked and de-boned look that meant he was dead on his feet. Gravity took him by the hand. He started to drop. Now the blonde was screaming, and so was the old woman in the pink suit. Hilary, always a joiner, was yelling her head off.

The *puta* hit the floor and did not bounce. His left hand fell open. Greg saw that the mirror was a goddamn badge. He picked it up. The metal was warm. There was a single drop of blood just above the word DETECTIVE.

Greg couldn't believe it. All he'd wanted to do was rob a bank, steal a little money and go home and have a hot bath and unwind, and here he was all of a sudden in the middle of an *a cappella* nightmare. He'd shot a cop. Shot him more than once, if you wanted to get technical.

Greg snuck a look. Spent casings littered the floor. The *puta* cable guy was dead, no question, lay flat on his back in the middle of a pool of blood so big they'd need a canoe to retrieve the body.

He glanced at his watch. Sweat blurred his eyes. He had to bring his wrist up almost to his nose before he could get the dial in focus, read the numbers.

5:04.

No way. Impossible.

Greg peered at the big electric clock high up on the wall at the back of the bank.

5:05.

He tried to think of some way to travel backwards in time, but his brain had turned into a hornets' nest, all abuzz and aswirl. What was the point of leaving when he had no place to go? Greg checked his watch – the date, this time. It was only the tenth, and his rent was paid through to the end of the month. Plus he could stay with Hilary, in a pinch. Couldn't he? The hornets vacated Greg's brain. He took that crucial first step towards the door.

Something clutched at his ankle. Mr Pinstripes. He was an easy target, but Greg'd had enough blood and gore for one day. He tried to shake him off, stumbled. His leg twisted beneath him. Suddenly it felt as if he'd been stabbed in the kneecap with a fondue fork. He lost his balance and fell. A thin ribbon of pain zipped down one side of his body and back up the other, exploded in his skull in a ball of rippling white light.

For just a second or two – about the same amount of time that it takes to tell about it – nobody moved.

4

The Georgia Viaduct was so close that anybody with a reasonably strong arm could hit the scummy brick wall of the Rialto with an accurately thrown hubcap. The window was wide open, and the throb of traffic was so loud that Willows, who was the soft-spoken type, had to raise his voice to make himself heard.

Not that the guy lying on the bed would hear him, no matter how much he cranked up the volume.

Willows studied the bloated body, the way the dark and swollen flesh bulged at the man's shirtcuffs, throat and ankles. The shirt had white piping and fake mother-of-pearl buttons, triangular silver points at the ends of an unfashionably wide collar, and was made of a shiny red material that looked like silk, but wasn't.

Willows walked around to the foot of the bed. The linoleum crackled underfoot. The woman sitting demurely in the corner followed him with her eyes.

The dead man's shirt was tucked sloppily into a pair of faded black jeans. His belt was wide black leather and had a heavy brass buckle depicting a stylized bucking horse apparently trying to throw its rider.

The cowboy motif went all the way down to the boots, which looked expensive – some kind of snakeskin, maybe – but were badly neglected, rundown at the heels.

The desk clerk had been told not to touch anything but had pushed open the room's solitary window as far as it would go. Willows wasn't going to give the guy a hard time about it.

22

The Rialto was the kind of place that made you feel like you needed a hot shower the minute you stepped through the door. Despite the pile of rotting garbage at the bottom of the window, the breeze drifting into the room smelled relatively sweet.

Willows said, "Three, four days?"

Parker nodded. Willows glanced at the woman, back to Parker. He went over to the window and looked down. A couple of men hunkered down out of the wind under the viaduct were sharing something in a brown paper bag.

Parker, speaking very softly, said, "Can you tell me when it happened, Honey?"

The woman, her back to the wall and her eyes focused on the ceiling, blinked twice, very slowly, as she thought about it.

Parker waited, impatient but not letting it show. The woman hadn't yet gotten around to looking directly at Parker, and Parker was beginning to doubt it would ever happen. Finally Honey said, "Wednesday. I think it was Wednesday."

"Any particular reason?"

Honey nodded. She licked her lips. "He made me go out and buy a lottery ticket. It was raining, pissing down. He knew I was gonna get soaked but he didn't care. Getting rich was all he cared about."

Parker said, "How old are you, Honey?"

"Nineteen."

"No, really. How old are you."

Honey smiled wistfully. A front tooth was gone and the rest didn't look too stable. She said, "Twenty-six, somewhere in there. On a bad day, almost thirty."

Thirty was the number Parker had in mind, but she let it go. "Is Honey your real name?"

"It's what real people call me. Got a smoke?"

Parker shook her head, no. A cheap black plastic purse lay like a dead crow on top of a battered highboy to the left of the window.

Parker said, "Is that your purse?"

23

"What purse?"

Parker went over to the highboy, picked up the purse and dangled it in front of Honey's bleary, deconstructed face.

"Yeah, it's mine."

Parker said, "You mind if I look inside?"

"What for?"

"Cigarettes."

Honey looked out the window. The sky had a bruised look. Punch a cloud and watch it bleed. She said, "Go ahead, do whatever you want."

Parker gingerly poked around inside the purse, found a crumpled pack of Export As, matches. She handed the cigarettes to Honey, helped her light up.

Honey inhaled deeply. "My favorite vice." She spat a shred of tobacco at the floor, sighed.

Parker said, "We'd like to talk to Chet, Honey. Ask him some questions."

"Such as?"

"The circumstances of his death," said Parker. "How he died."

Honey said, "Yeah, well . . ." A passing truck on the viaduct made the air hum and throb. Honey scratched her scalp, smoked.

Parker said, "But we got here too late, didn't we? I mean, by the time we arrived, he was long gone."

Honey flicked ash from her cigarette into the cupped palm of her hand, made a fist.

Parker said, "Will you help us, Honey? Will you fill in for Chet?"

"You wanna know what happened, that it?"

Parker nodded. She said, "You don't have to tell me, if you don't want to. But it would really help a lot if you did."

"Do I need a lawyer?"

Willows said, "I can get one for you."

"What do I need a lawyer for?"

Willows shrugged.

Honey said, "Just stay out of it, okay?"

24

Willows held both hands up, palms out. "Whatever you say."

"I mean, you mind?"

Willows said, "Sorry . . ."

Parker repressed a smile. Despite his age, Willows continued to add to his vocabulary.

Honey, her eyes on Parker, said, "Okay, go ahead." She waved her arm. Ash spilled from her cigarette. "No, hold it, wait a minute." She held a hand out to Parker. "What's your name?"

"Claire."

"Nice to meet you, Claire?"

They shook hands. Parker said, "I just want to be clear on this – are you waiving the right to a lawyer?"

"No doubt about it."

Parker said, "It's just a formality, but I've got to caution you that anything you say can and will be used against you in a court of law."

"Surprise, surprise."

Parker smiled.

Honey said, "So, go ahead."

"Why did you wait such a long time before you called the police?"

"Because I wanted to make damn good and sure that he was dead." Honey wiped away what might have been a tear. "Soon as I saw that he was cut, I knew it was hopeless, there was nothing I could do for him."

Parker glanced at Willows. He shrugged. She turned back to Honey.

"Why couldn't you help him?"

"Because the minute he got out of the hospital, he'd come looking for me. Beat me to *death*."

Parker said, "Tell me what happened, okay."

"You take a close look at him, you'll see right away what happened. He got a bellyful of knife and it didn't agree with him."

Willows was turning to look out the window, smiling.

Parker said, "What I want to know is, why was Chet stabbed?"

Honey lit another cigarette. Her hands were steady. She gave Claire Parker a wry smile, and Parker couldn't help wondering where she'd learned to smile like that, put so much into so little. Not plying her trade in the eastside, that was for sure.

Parker said, "Honey . . ."

"Beats me. I mean, I wish I knew. It's all kind of vague . . ."

Parker waited.

After a few minutes, Honey said, "It was the lottery ticket. I got him the wrong kind, he wanted a red and I got him a blue, and he got real pissed off, like he did sometimes when he'd been drinking or whatever. Anyway, he blew his top, came after me."

Parker said, "How do you mean, he came after you?"

"Thump me. He was gonna thump me." Honey reached out, lightly touched the hem of Parker's dark blue skirt. "Nice material. Where'd you buy it?"

"Somewhere there was a sale."

"There's a place over on Robson . . ." She closed her eyes, and for a moment Parker thought she was going to nod off. Then Honey said, "Chet used to take me there, once in a while, if business was good. He'd tell me to go ahead and choose something I liked, buy me something else. Take me back here. Make me get dressed in my new clothes.

"While I was getting changed, he'd go get Wendell, tell him he wanted to show him something."

Parker said, "Wendell's the night clerk, right?"

"I'd have to do some poses, get Wendell all hot and bothered so he'd give Chet a couple days free rent. Or if I was extra nice to him, a whole week, sometimes."

Parker said, "How long were you and Chet together?"

"Since about the middle of the summer. Late July, early August. Somewhere in there."

"When did he start pimping for you?"

26

"On day one." The question seemed to have taken Honey by surprise. "That was the whole idea – that he'd take care of me, cover my ass."

"What were you doing before you met Chet?"

"More of the same. Lots more. I was younger then. More of a downtown person."

Parker said, "Chet sent you out for a lottery ticket. You bought the wrong one and he beat you up, is that what happened?"

"Sounds good to me."

"Is that your knife in Chet's stomach?"

"I dunno. What's it look like?"

"All I can see is the handle. It's mother-of-pearl." Parker shuffled slowly through a dozen of Mel Dutton's crime scene Polaroids, found a close-up that wasn't too graphic.

Honey shook her head. "That's Chet's knife, not mine. All his shirts got buttons made out of that stuff. Like the one he's wearing. It's fake. Plastic. You pull the knife out of him, you'll see it's got a button that you press, makes the blade fly out. Mine's an ordinary paring knife, but extra sharp. It's got a wood handle with copper wire wrapped around it."

Parker said, "Do you know where your knife is, Honey?"

"Chet told me fingerprints couldn't stick to the wire, so if I had to cut somebody up, it was no big problem, nothin' to worry about."

"Do you know where your knife is?" Parker said again.

"In the purse, right down at the bottom, tucked away under a flap. You must've missed it, the first time you looked." Honey expertly flicked her cigarette butt out the window.

Parker tilted the purse to the light from the window. There could be anything in there. She went over to the highboy and carefully shook the contents of the purse out on to the cigarette-scarred top. The knife had a six-inch blade. The wooden handle was loosely wrapped with copper wire, and Chet was probably right about it not taking a print.

Honey's eyes were on the knife. She said, "My best friend."

27

Parker said, "You're serious about saving your life, try a condom."

"Tell it to Chet. You could die of old age before he stopped laughing."

Parker said, "Honey, can you remember what happened when Chet found out you'd brought back the wrong lottery ticket? You said he lost his temper."

"Never gonna find it, now."

Parker said, "No, I guess not." Honey slipped the Polaroid into her jacket pocket. Parker let it go, for now.

"He took a punch at me. Hit me in the breast and I started screaming."

Honey fumbled the last cigarette out of the pack. Parker tossed her the matches.

"Wendell must've heard the racket. He walked right into the room, wanted to know what was going on. Chet hit me again, and asked Wendell would he be interested in going a few rounds. Wendell said yes."

Parker said, "What time does Wendell come on duty, Honey?"

"Midnight. But if you're thinking about having a talk with him, forget it."

"What d'you mean?" said Willows.

Honey waved her cigarette at the open window, the air shaft. "He's just a little guy, but by the time he hit that pile of garbage down there, he was going real fast, and he just kind of disappeared right into it."

Willows and Parker exchanged a quick look. Willows leaned out the window. The two men were still cooling their heels under the viaduct. The pile of garbage was wide and deep. He couldn't see Wendell.

Parker said, "Did Wendell fall out the window, Honey? Or was he pushed?"

"Jumped. Chet's wrestlin' me around and the knife goes into him. Wendell's eyes bug out. I guess he figured he was next."

Willows heard footsteps on the stairs, in the hall.

28

Willows' inspector, Homer Bradley, appeared in the open doorway. There was a feather in his hat, a ten-dollar cigar in his mouth, a twinkle in his eye. He cocked a finger at Willows, disappeared back into the hallway.

Parker hesitated, and then said, "Honey, is there anybody else who was here at the time, that you haven't told us about?"

Honey nodded towards the highboy. "Take a look in the bottom drawer." Smoke leaped out of the gap that had been knocked in her smile. "Just kidding."

In the hallway, Bradley said, "Something wrong with your beeper, Jack?"

Willows said, "Battery must've died. I'll check it out when I sign off."

At the far end of the corridor, a door opened a crack. A short, bald man wearing a bright yellow plastic jacket peeked out at them.

Bradley pointed the cigar at him. "Get back in your room and shut the door."

The man said, "I worked all my life in the woods. I cut down trees taller than this building and never gave it a thought."

Willows said, "That's great. Now do yourself a favor and shut the door."

"You seen Brenda?"

Willows shook his head.

"You see Brenda, you tell her I been looking for her, okay?"

Willows nodded. The door eased shut. Willows turned to Bradley. "What's up, Inspector?"

Bradley smiled. "Nothing much. I felt like taking a stroll, catching a little air. Since you and Claire happened to be in the neighborhood, I thought I'd drop by. How's it going, you making any progress?"

"Just wrapping up." Willows led Bradley back to the room, knocked lightly.

Parker said, "Give me a hand, Jack." Together, they helped Honey to her feet.

She said, "You gonna charge me?"

Parker said, "We don't have much choice, do we?"

"Guess not."

Bradley, trailing a cloud of cigar smoke, led the charge down the stairs. On the street, Parker turned Honey over to a uniformed policewoman.

Bradley, watching, realized something was up. He turned to Willows. "Am I missing something?"

Willows told him about the pile of garbage at the back of the hotel, the vanished night clerk, Wendell. He and Bradley and Parker walked around to the rear of the building. Bradley took one look at the rotting mountain of garbage and started laughing.

Willows said, "What's so funny, Homer?"

"The perp, she's an addict?"

"Yeah, why?"

"Anybody report Wendell missing?"

Willows shook his head.

Bradley kicked a plastic bag. "We're going to need a garbage truck. An *empty* garbage truck." He kicked the bag again, and it rolled to one side, exposing a corner of a fire-blackened mattress. He said, "This look like a fire hazard to you?"

Willows nodded.

Parker said, "There's a rat in there the size of a Doberman."

"More than one," said Bradley. "Why don't we get a sanitation crew in here, let them do the heavy work."

Parker said, "I'll call it in." Willows nodded, and began to pick his way across the littered ground towards the viaduct. He hadn't been able to see it from the hotel window, but the men had pushed a big cardboard box over on its side and shoved it up against one of the viaduct's concrete supports. The box had probably held a refrigerator or large freezer. It was out of the rain, out of the wind. Given a choice between the box and a room in the Rialto, Willows would go for the box every time.

The men heard him coming, came out to meet him. There were two of them. They were both fairly young, tall and thin, unshaven, wearing dirty jeans and ski jackets, heavy boots. Unemployed loggers, maybe. Willows wondered how long

30

they'd been in the city. Long enough, by the look of them. He took a ten-dollar bill out of his wallet, told them what he wanted to know.

Both men nodded.

"Yeah, we saw him. There was a whole lot of yellin' goin' on. This was two, three days ago. In the morning. We're sittin' here drinkin' breakfast, eh."

"It's kinda cool out, but the window's open."

"You can see people in there, movin' back and forth."

"Hear 'em yellin'."

"All of a sudden this guy climbs out the window, his feet are kinda hanging out."

"Weird, man . . ."

"Next thing, he drops."

"Tucked himself into a ball, eh."

"Like when you jump into a river."

"Cannonball."

"Yeah, cannonball."

"He hits the garbage dead center."

"Perfect."

"Some stuff flies up, falls back. We're sittin' here with our eyes bugged out."

"He vanished, eh. Plain and simple."

"After a couple minutes it's like it never happened. The yellin's stopped."

Willows said, "Was there anyone else near the window when he went out?"

"You asking was he pushed? No way."

"Jumped of his own free will."

"Yeah, jumped. Got a smoke?"

Willows shook his head.

"We look up and the window's shut."

"Made us wonder if we saw what we saw, or just shared a dream."

The man who'd taken Willows' money snapped his index finger against the bill. "Now we know, eh."

"You gonna get him out?"

Willows nodded.

"Watch out for the rats, they're big as raccoons."

The city sent a dump truck and a backhoe, four men with shovels. The backhoe did most of the work. It began to rain. Bradley watched for a while and then went home. The men, once Willows had taken their names, disappeared into the gathering darkness. Parker stood beneath a black umbrella while Willows paced back and forth in the wet.

It was just past five when the backhoe uncovered Wendell. The operator carefully lowered his bucket and then swung it sideways, clearing a path to the body.

Parker shook the rain from her umbrella. Her face was pale.

Willows said, "Stay here, Claire. Back me up. If the rats get out of control, start shooting."

Parker gave him a wan smile. There were times Jack acted like a chauvinist, and she didn't mind at all.

Wendell was lying on his side. Willows slipped on a pair of clear plastic gloves, rolled Wendell over on his back. The clothes were right, but making a positive ID wasn't going to be easy. He stepped back, away from the body.

A uniformed cop standing next to the backhoe said, "Hey, listen to this!"

Willows turned, slightly alarmed.

The cop was cranking up the volume of his walkie. He caught Willows' eye. "We got a 'shots fired' at the Bank of Montreal at Kingsgate Mall." His radio crackled. His eyes widened. He said, "There's been a shoot-out. One down for sure, maybe more."

The Mall was on Broadway, a block off Main and no more than two or three minutes away. Parker folded her umbrella and ran towards the Caprice.

Willows tore off the rubber gloves as he picked his way through the garbage.

The backhoe operator lit a cigarette, leaned back in his seat. He had no idea where all the cops were going, and he didn't much care. He was making double overtime.

Wendell could wait, and so could he.

32

5

Greg blinked, got the world back in focus, and saw he was horizontal dancing with the bank manager and that the guy wasn't too happy about it. Greg caught a solid gold cufflink in the eye, yelped. Teeth snapped at him out of a face the color of a raw T-bone. The manager wriggled around on the floor as if he was having a seizure, but he was giving Greg the hug of his life, and he wouldn't let go.

Greg hadn't kept an accurate count of the number of times he'd pulled on the cop. Eleven, or maybe twelve. Somewhere in there. That left two or three rounds in the Browning, plus the clip in his back pocket. So, no problemo, he could burn one on the banker and still have plenty to spare. And since he'd done a cop and was looking at a mandatory quarter-century, zero chance of parole, he didn't exactly have a whole lot to lose.

He leaned over and buried the Browning's front sight in the banker's silvery hair and turned his head away, averting his gaze, knowing something messy was about to happen that he didn't want to have to remember to forget.

As he squeezed the trigger, Greg found himself being stared down by the twins, who'd been rendered mute by the adults' inappropriately childlike behavior but were nevertheless extremely interested in the proceedings.

My, what big eyes those babies had.

Greg brought his arm up, hammered the banker with the barrel of the gun. The banker went limp.

33

Greg climbed to his feet. He leered at the twins and said, "Big mans go nap-nap."

He glanced at his watch as he pushed through the door and stumbled on to the sidewalk. 5:06:47. The taxi in front of Bino's was just pulling away from the curb. Greg waved, but either the cabby didn't see him or was too pissed off to stop. A pair of blue and whites raced down Broadway, roof lights sparkling. No sirens. The cars were a full block away but Greg could hear the low moan of the motors.

The light was green. Greg trotted across the street. A Black Top pulled up right in front of him. The driver was an old fella, paunchy and bald. The windshield wipers slapped at the glass. Greg realized it had begun to rain.

Greg yanked open the rear door, climbed in. The driver's eyes filled the rearview mirror. "You the guy who called a cab?"

Greg said, "No, a Lear jet. But I learned a long time ago that the world we live in is full of second choices."

The driver pulled away from the curb, hit the meter. "Sorry to keep you waiting. The car was supposed to pick you up got rear-ended."

Greg said, "And that's something else I learned real early in life – watch your ass or somebody'll kick it."

The cabby cursed, stabbed at the brakes. Greg slid forward on his seat, reached out to brace himself. The driver'd stopped because he'd seen the pair of cop cars bearing down on them.

The lead car's turnsignal flashed as he turned into the Mall's parking lot, kept flashing as the car went up on its two offside wheels and then dropped, the screech of tortured rubber louder than any siren, all four tires smoking. The second car had pulled into the far lane, shot past.

The cabby said, "Jeez, he ain't gonna make it!"

The blue and white clipped a hydro pole, did a nose down three-sixty and drove straight into a silver BMW, vanished in a cloud of burnt rubber.

The cabby said, "Jeez, if only I had a camcorder."

34

Greg said, "If we don't get out of here pretty quick, you might as well kiss your shift goodbye."

"What'ya mean?"

"Witness reports – paperwork."

The second blue and white had screamed to a stop in the middle of the intersection at Broadway and Main. The siren wailed. The backup lights flashed.

The cabby said, "But . . . What if somebody's hurt?"

A humanitarian. What next. Greg shoved a fresh clip in the Browning, racked the slide. He said, "Even worse, what if that somebody happens to be you?"

The brown Taurus was exactly where it was supposed to be. Greg had the cabby drive up to the next level and made him park so he was blocking a blue Chevy Nova and a black Saab.

Greg said, "You're gonna have to spend some time in the trunk, okay?" He indicated the Nova and Saab with a sweep of his arm. "But sooner or later one of the people that owns these cars will want out. What's your name?"

"Max."

"They start kicking the tires, Max, that's your cue to yell 'help'."

Max stared at his hands gripping the steering wheel.

Greg said, "I'm gonna leave your headlights on, and the trunk key in the lock. Ten, fifteen minutes, that's all I need."

Max said, "Listen, I gotta take a leak, or I'm gonna explode."

"Okay, fine. Go ahead."

Max stared at him, unsure as to whether he was being told it was okay to relieve himself or perfectly all right to destroy his bladder.

Greg said, "Your choice, is what I'm saying."

Max had to suck in his belly to get out from behind the wheel. He went over to a concrete pillar and turned his back on Greg, unzipped. Greg popped open the trunk and waited, stood there by the taxi trying not to listen to the splash of urine on concrete.

35

Max zipped up, lit a cigarette and crawled awkwardly into the trunk.

Greg said, "Get rid of the cigarette, Max, or you're gonna asphyxiate yourself to death." He smiled. Good boxer talk.

Max took one last drag and butted the cigarette. It was pretty cramped in there. Greg said, "You wanna take out the spare tire, make some more room?"

"Somebody'd steal it, and I'd have to pay."

Greg said, "That reminds me . . ." He held out his hand, snapped his fingers. Max gave him a look he'd been practising all his life, a sour look of resignation and despair. He reached deep in his pants pocket and handed over his bankroll.

Greg slammed shut the trunk.

He had a list of rules that he'd worked out during the course of his career. One of the first rules he'd decided on was that he stayed away from his apartment for a day or two after every heist. If everything went the way it was supposed to, he'd stay with the victim of his latest robbery, consoling her.

Hilary lived in a pink and blue highrise topped off with what looked like a giant beanie. Greg dumped the Taurus three blocks away, in a no-parking zone in a lane.

He'd already lost the raincoat, cauliflower ears, broken nose and scar, the wig. The bulletproof Kevlar vest was too valuable and hard to come by to ditch, and he was still wearing it, under his shirt. The sidewalks were damp but it had stopped raining.

He checked his watch. Quarter to six. What time Hilary got out of there depended on how stupid the bank squad detectives were, but Greg doubted she'd make it home much before eight.

He wasn't hungry but maybe some food would settle his stomach and, anyway, he'd found that the best way to kill time was in restaurants. He walked down the street until he came to a Greek place he and Hilary'd eaten at two or three times, went inside and was given a two-seater by a window. The waitress remembered him, asked where his girlfriend was. Greg shrugged, smiled ambiguously, asked what was

36

good and lightly touched her several times as they went through the menu.

He ordered the rack of lamb, a beer, and a tossed green salad. He took his time eating. During the meal, the waitress dropped by the table several times, smiling and friendly. He had a *gellato* for dessert, coffee.

By the time he got out of there it was pushing seven-thirty.

By the time he walked to Hilary's apartment, it was quarter to eight.

The highrise had a security system. Greg pushed her buzzer, gave it a couple of quick jolts. No answer. He couldn't say he was surprised. The cops'd order Chinese or pizza, everybody'd sit around eating off paper plates. Depending on the number of witnesses, it could take all night to get the preliminary statements.

Greg'd known Hilary almost six months, but the last time he'd mentioned it she still hadn't quite been ready to give him a key. So he'd waited until her back was turned and then helped himself to the spare she kept in a little jar on top of the gas fireplace's *faux* marble mantle.

The key was to her apartment, though, not the front door. Greg pushed buttons until some unsuspecting fool buzzed him in, took the elevator up to the eighth floor, unlocked the door to Hilary's apartment, stepped inside and eased it shut. The apartment was tiny; a cramped one-bedroom unit with a kitchen the size of a small pork chop and a bathroom so compact every time Greg looked in the mirror he was amazed that the two of him had managed to squeeze in at once.

Hilary'd left every single light on – the apartment was ablaze with light but perfectly silent. Greg had a weird kind of dislocated *Twilight Zone* feeling that something was terribly wrong but he didn't know what. Then the fridge clicked on, and the reassuringly mundane sound brought him back to earth, wiped away the fear.

Nerves, that's all. Just nerves. He stripped off his jacket as he made his way into the kitchen and saw that the Browning, which he'd forgotten about, was jammed in the waistband of his pants. The weapon was cocked and ready to fire. He hadn't noticed and if he'd happened to bump up against the kitchen counter, he could've shot off his personality.

Greg slipped the Browning out of his pants, eased the hammer down. The pockets of his windbreaker were stuffed with bank and cabby cash. He rolled the jacket around the weapon and laid it down on the counter next to the sink.

He checked his watch. 7:53. He found vodka in the cabinet over the fridge. Ice in a blue plastic tray in the freezer.

He poured himself a stiff one, added a single ice cube and wandered into the living room and looked out the window at the stuff on the balcony – Hilary's mountain bike, the summer tires for her Toyota, a couple of webbed aluminum deck chairs and some potted plants that looked more or less dead. The balcony was on the north side of the building and was in perpetual and everlasting shade. About the only thing that would grow there was moss. Or maybe a crop of mushrooms.

Greg sat down in one of the chairs, lit a cigarette. The jet of flame from his disposable lighter carried him back to the bank. He saw the spurt of fire erupt from the Browning's muzzle, the *puta* cop take a round in the chest. Then another, and another.

Now Greg knew how many times he'd hit him, visualized the action more clearly as he sat there on the balcony than he had when it'd happened. Three pops. And the murder weapon was right there in the kitchen, waiting to tie him to a 25-year lease at a maximum-security prison. He had to get rid of the gun, for sure.

Greg took another hit of vodka. The cop was already on his way down when the Browning ejected the first spent cartridge. His body sagged, the disc of silver spun like a miniature frisbee, hit the terrazzo. The second round smacked into him.

The badge, the badge!

Greg yanked the black leather case out of his pants pocket, flipped it open. His fingernail scraped the tiny splash of blood away from the gold shield. There was a plasticized ID card in a slim compartment opposite the badge. Greg winkled it out. Garcia Lorca Mendez, in full face and left profile. *Policia*. *Cuidad de Colón*. The dude was packing heat, you could see the shiny brown leather of his shoulder strap under his sports jacket. Greg frowned. Colón – what was that, some kind of dumb joke. He noticed the accent and squinted as he took a closer look at the badge, turned it in his hand towards the splash of light from the apartment.

Detective was spelled wrong. Where did the badge come from, a cereal box?

Suddenly it all came into focus, and Greg felt an overwhelming surge of relief. The guy wasn't a cop after all. Or, if he was a cop, he was an export model, many thousands of miles out of his jurisdiction.

Greg tried to think of countries he knew where the language was Spanish. Mexico. What else. Costa Rica. Cuba. He flicked his cigarette butt over the balcony railing, took a hit of vodka and lit another cigarette. Bolivia – he remembered that from *Butch Cassidy and the Sundance Kid*. Peru. Colombia. Greg started thinking about drugs. He had to admit he liked to snort a little, now and then.

So exactly what was a cop from Colombia doing in the downtown branch of a very large Canadian bank?

Catering to a retirement party?

Greg swallowed some vodka. He'd registered the look in the man's eyes, seen the death grip he had on the briefcase. He'd acted on instinct, and he'd been right. A cop would make a perfect burro. But he hadn't carried a briefcase full of high-grade dope in for a deposit.

That left only one possibility – the dead cop was laundering money. *What a business*. One minute you were looking at a quarter-century of hard time, another beat of the clock and you were a fucking *millionaire*.

Or were you?

Greg glanced down, first to the left and then to the right. He must've left the briefcase by the door. No, wait a sec, that wasn't possible because he'd shut the door and walked straight into the apartment. So it was in the kitchen. The briefcase was in the kitchen. Or was it? Although he clearly remembered wrapping the gun in his jacket and laying the jacket down on the counter, he didn't remember the briefcase, where he'd put it.

Greg stood up, turned towards the sliding glass door. There was a guy, tall, with broad shoulders and a really good tan, striding across the carpet towards him. Greg almost put his hands up, then noticed that the guy wasn't wearing anything except a pair of light brown slacks, and that Hilary, naked, was leaning against the bedroom door.

Greg stood up, shoved the badge case in his pocket and snatched at the slider. The guy beat him by a nose, almost took Greg's hands off, he shut the door so hard.

Greg stared at the guy through the glass and the guy stared right back at him, waiting. Greg picked up the biggest of the potted plants and cocked his arm as if to toss it through the door. The guy backed up five or six feet, got set. Greg put the pot back where it belonged. He sat down. The cigarette dangling from his mouth had burned down to the filter. He dropped the butt in the lowball glass and lit up a new one, mimed offering the pack to Hilary's extra-curricular sweetheart. He was stunned, and he hoped it didn't show.

The stud gave him a suspicious look, turned and said something to Hilary that Greg couldn't hear. He peered through the glass at Greg and then turned and walked into the bedroom. Hilary turned her rump on Greg and followed the stud into the bedroom. What the hell was going on? Hilary was supposed to be in shock, all broken up by the day's trauma. She was supposed to fall into his arms, weeping and needy. The idea was that Greg was there when the chips were down. Strong, supportive. And then he'd dump her.

That's the way it had always worked before, the way it was *supposed* to work.

Otherwise, what was the point?

Greg made a snap decision that if either of them shut the bedroom door, he'd kick in the slider and go for the Browning.

40

Nobody shut the door, and the stud was only gone a minute or maybe two. When he came back out he was fully dressed, wearing shiny brown shoes, brown socks, the same brown slacks, a white shirt, maroon tie, and a brown vest over a double-breasted dark brown jacket with lots and lots of shiny brass buttons.

Greg watched him approach, stayed put.

The guy unlocked the door and cracked it open an inch or two. He said, "You going to make trouble?"

Greg said no, certainly not.

"I'm warning you, I've got a black belt in karate."

Greg said, "Yeah, and I got a pair of red suspenders from Sears, so little girls think I'm a fireman."

The stud hesitated, and then gave Greg a really nice smile. He pushed the slider all the way open and stepped aside. Greg walked into the living room, pushed the door shut behind him. The stud said, "How long have you known Hilary?"

"About six months."

"That long, huh. How'd you meet her?"

Greg, taking a chance, said, "Well, there was this lineup, see. And when I finally got to the end of it, there she was."

The guy laughed. Greg sat down on the sofa. Hilary came out of the bedroom. She was wearing a silk robe Greg'd given her, that clung in all the right places. She'd put on some lipstick, but hadn't bothered to comb her hair. That wild, untamed look. Delicious. Greg craned his neck but couldn't see the briefcase. It had to be behind the counter.

The stud introduced himself. His name was Randy Lucas. He told Greg to make himself at home, and went into the kitchen, to mix a pitcher of vodka martinis.

Hilary sat on the sofa on the far side of the room, about as far away from Greg as she could get. He gave her a warm smile, but she refused to meet his eye.

Greg watched Randy work around his balled-up jacket, not touching it but coming close.

Randy finished fooling around with the martinis and

brought the pitcher and drinks into the living room on a tray. He lowered the tray carefully down on a coffee table, poured three drinks, handed one to Hilary and one to Greg.

Greg slipped.

Randy said, "While you were out there on the balcony, Hilary gave me a very brief rundown of the situation. I want you to know that it comes as a complete surprise."

Greg said, "Yeah?"

Hilary said, "I've already explained to Randy about how we met at a mutual friend's and both had too much to drink and you insisted on driving me home and then maybe got a little bit aggressive. I've always wondered what happened to my key. Now I know."

Greg said, "The door was open. I phoned you at work but they said there was a robbery, told me you were busy and I couldn't talk to you." He gave her a nice, warm smile. "You okay?"

"I'm fine. Randy's been taking care of me."

The stud said, "She was a little shook up, but she's okay now."

Greg ignored him. He said, "We had a date, remember?"

Hilary glared at Greg. "Why do you keep *bothering* me? What's *wrong* with you?"

Greg glanced at the stud, to see if he was buying all those lies. The guy was buying, all right, and he was paying retail. Greg said, "We had a date."

"I called and cancelled this afternoon. I left a message on your machine. I'm sorry, but I shouldn't have agreed to go out with you in the first place. I just didn't want to hurt your feelings, that's all."

From Greg's point of view, Randy's wardrobe was a tad on the conservative side – it looked as if he'd found his clothes in a mound of cow dung. But he sure was a good martini mixer. Greg drained his glass and helped himself to a refill. He settled back, letting the cushions take his weight.

Randy said, "Just before I left town, Hilary and I became engaged."

Greg nodded, smiled.

"To be married," Randy explained.

Greg said, "Well, that's terrific. Congratulations all around."

Hilary said, "Randy and I have known each other for a very long time."

Greg said, "No kidding."

Randy said, "We work in the same building. I'm with McQuade and McQuade. Was assigned to the Toronto office about six months ago, a particularly difficult case." He smiled. "Just got back this morning."

Greg rubbed his jaw, mulling it over.

"Criminal law," said Randy, refreshing Greg's memory. He paused, letting it hang, and then said, "What line of work are you in, by the way?"

"Actor. I'm an actor."

"Really?" Randy leaned forward a little, interested. "Television, the movies . . . ?"

"This and that," said Greg. "Basically, whatever my agent thinks is good for my career. Might make him a few bucks, in other words."

"You working on anything now?"

"I got a callback on a series of Toyota commercials. Nationwide stuff. Should hear about it in a couple of days."

"Well," said Randy, "best of luck." He raised his glass in a kind of half-assed toast, drained the contents and put the empty glass down on the table. Greg'd been dismissed, and all three of them knew it.

He stood up. Jingled the change in his pants pocket, smiled. "I'll just get my jacket and briefcase, and be on my way."

Randy said, "Fine." He gave Hilary a wink.

Greg took a line towards the kitchen that should have forced Randy to move aside a little bit to avoid contact. Randy didn't even seem to notice Greg moving in on him, and Greg, shoulders hunched, was forced to alter course. He went into the kitchen and grabbed his jacket, held it firmly in his left hand so the gun wouldn't fall out. He'd thought the briefcase might be on the floor by the fridge, but it wasn't. He turned and looked behind him. Where'd the damn thing go?

Randy was watching him closely, as if suspecting he might pinch the silverware. "Lose something?"

"Can't seem to find my briefcase."

Randy glanced around the apartment, frowned.

Greg came back into the living room. He felt as if his body temperature had risen by at least ten degrees. The briefcase was out on the balcony. He took a quick step forward, and it metamorphosed into Hilary's goddamn summer tires. He turned on Randy. "Listen, I understand why you're upset. But I want my briefcase back, and I want it now."

Randy said, "I think you better leave, pal."

Greg squeezed the windbreaker. "Whose *pal* are you talking to? Not me, *buddy*."

Randy flushed.

Greg started towards the bedroom. Randy moved to block him. Greg stepped sideways, as if attempting an end run, then kicked Randy in the knee as hard as he could.

Randy lurched sideways, going down. A rib cracked as he hit the corner of the coffee table.

Hilary said, "Oh baby, are you all right?"

Greg reached down to pat her on the head. He said, "Don't worry about it, he never laid a finger on me."

"Not you, *asshole!*" Hilary was down on the carpet, cradling Randy's head on her restless thighs. The lawyer lay there, staring up at Greg. Hurt but still game, gathering strength.

Greg said, "Take my advice, *buddy*. Stay right where you are. Do the smart thing, not the right thing." He smiled fondly at Hilary for a moment, then turned back to Randy, letting his eyes go cold. "Otherwise, there's no telling who might get hurt."

Randy glared at him, not blinking.

Greg said, "See, I never took any night school lessons in the manly art of self-defense, but I got a black belt in *bad attitude.*" He caught the flicker of uncertainty in Randy's eyes, knew he had him.

There was a Polaroid camera and two empty glasses and a champagne bottle in a clear plastic ice bucket on the nightstand. A tangled heap of black and white striped sheets trailed from the bed to the floor. Shiny silver handcuffs dangled from the bedpost. A dozen photographs were spread out on the bed like a winning poker hand.

Greg checked out the champagne. Mumm's. He tilted the bottle against the barred light streaming in through the blinds. There was a mouthful left. Greg drank it down, tossed the empty bottle on the floor. He picked up the camera and took a shot of the bed and handcuffs, stuck the Polaroid and the rest of the photographs in his pants pocket.

The bedroom was small. The only furniture was the bed and the nightstand and a bureau with a mirror that was tilted just so. The closet was just big enough to hide a midget. It took Greg about ten seconds to decide that if he wanted to find his briefcase, he better look somewhere else. There was a pinstripe suit hanging in there, though, and in the pocket of the jacket, a black eelskin wallet. Greg helped himself to the cash and credit cards.

He tossed the Polaroid camera at the bureau mirror, smashing the glass.

In the living room, Randy had fainted or died, and Hilary was punching buttons on the phone.

Greg ripped the line out of the wall. He checked Randy's pulse, and said, "He's gonna be okay. If anybody asks, just tell them what happened – you had a couple too many, were goofing around. He tripped and fell on the table."

Hilary pointed a finger at him and yelled, "You're going to jail, Greg! You broke into my apartment and assaulted my boyfriend. I hope they put you away for life!"

Greg said, "You ought to talk it over with Randy, before you phone the cops. See, a thing like this could be bad for his career." He smiled. "How about you and me – I bet if we worked at it, we could patch things up just as good as new."

45

Hilary threw the phone at him, missed.

Greg said, "Okay, that does it – we're through!"

And he meant it, because he'd just that instant remembered where he'd left the briefcase full of drug money. It was in a towaway zone, on the front seat of the abandoned and unlocked Taurus.

6

Bradley introduced Martin Ross to Willows and Parker. Several hours had passed since the robbery and murder, but only now did Ross seem sufficiently recovered from his ordeal to be interviewed. During the interval, the crime scene had been sketched, measured and photographed. Every scrap of physical evidence had been gathered and marked for identification – the bank's walls deeply gouged where techs had recovered Greg's early wild shots.

The bank's staff had suffered through preliminary interviews and been sent home.

Body Removal Services – what the cops called the ghoul patrol – had bundled the anonymous victim's bullet-riddled corpse into a leakproof green plastic bag and transported it to the morgue.

Ross's injuries were painful but superficial. He'd accepted but so far hadn't ingested the painkillers and tranquilizers the medics had given him. He assured the two homicide detectives that he realized it was essential that he keep his mind clear.

Parker smiled, showing her appreciation. According to the paramedics, Ross had suffered a minor concussion. It had taken him a long time to get his act together, and although neither she nor Willows were very happy about it, they didn't let it show.

Martin Ross was in his late fifties, but he'd taken care of himself over the years, kept his weight down. He dressed well, had a rosy complexion and silver hair, perceptive but

47

kindly blue eyes. He was thinking that the female cop, Claire Parker, was probably young enough to be his daughter. But what the hell.

Ross looked her over, openly admiring her. She had a nice trim figure, jet black hair, huge brown eyes and a movie star's complexion. There were a few small lines around her eyes and the corners of her mouth. A homicide cop, she'd have seen a few things. He had a feeling he'd have to dig pretty deep to come up with a compliment she hadn't heard a dozen times before, and that she'd be well worth the effort.

Willows said, "I guess my first question, Mr Ross, is how well you knew the victim."

"I hardly knew him at all. He'd dropped by my office once or twice during the past year, but I'm not even sure he had an account with us."

"What was the nature of his business?"

"He sought general financial advice. My opinion on the trend in mortgage rates, that sort of thing. How's Hilary doing, by the way? She going to be okay?"

Parker said, "She went home quite some time ago. Her fiancé picked her up."

Ross massaged his forehead. "Greg, is that the young man's name? Very pleasant."

Willows said, "We haven't been able to identify the victim yet. It would be very helpful if you remembered *his* name, Mr Ross."

Martin Ross looked down, studied his wounded hand. He said, "Yes, I'm aware of that. I wish I could help, but I simply can't remember."

Bradley said, "How long have you been a bank manager, Mr Ross?"

Without a moment's hesitation, Ross said, "Seventeen years."

"And at this branch?"

"Five years."

Willows said, "What was in the briefcase?"

"I'm afraid I have no idea."

48

"Then why did you risk your life to retain possession of it?"

Ross shrugged. He said, "I was trying to detain the killer, not the briefcase. It wasn't a particularly intelligent thing to do, I suppose. Obviously I wasn't thinking straight, but the situation was completely out of control . . ."

Willows pressed a little harder. "Presumably – from the dead man's point of view – the briefcase contained something fairly valuable, something worth dying for."

Ross gingerly touched his head. He had a hell of a headache, but he wasn't ready to take any medication – not just yet. He said, "I have no idea what was in that briefcase, but as I'm sure my staff have already told you, the man who looked like a boxer shot first. Or rather, he drew his weapon first, and the dead man fired in self-defense. I may be wrong, but I was under the impression the boxer was completely focused on robbing my bank. In fact he didn't show any interest at all in the briefcase until the dead man tried to hide it from him."

Willows said, "Only one member of your staff happened to notice the victim before the shooting started. She's unclear as to whether the man was waiting in line to see a teller, or to see you."

"He hadn't requested an appointment, I can tell you that much."

"That's true, but your office door was partly open, and he was positioned so he could keep an eye on it. You were with another customer just prior to the robbery, is that correct?"

Ross nodded. The way his eyes glinted, Willows had a hunch the banker had called somebody on a demand loan.

Parker said, "The shooter – had you ever seen him before?"

"Absolutely not."

Willows said, "The reason we ask, he might've been a junkie wandered in off the street, but we have reason to believe otherwise. If we're right, he probably cased the bank for days or even weeks before he made his move."

Ross said, "A man like that – it wouldn't have taken long for someone to notice him."

49

Parker said, "I just can't understand why you took such an enormous risk."

Ross said, "I wish I knew. The circumstances were so *eccentric*. I suppose I felt responsible for the damn thing." He glared at Bradley. "I acted instinctively, without regard for my personal safety. That hardly seems cause for such a rigorous interrogation."

Bradley smiled. "Would you like to get in touch with your lawyer, Mr Ross?"

"Certainly not."

"Because that'd be just fine and dandy with us, if that's your preference."

Ross said, "Did I miss something?" He turned his bright blue eyes on Parker. "Am I a *suspect*, for God's sake?"

"No, of course not." Parker gave the banker a warm smile. It was her favorite lie.

Willows took out his spiral-bound notebook and a cheap ballpoint pen, turned the notebook to a blank page and wrote down the date and time. He said, "Let's start with the shooter. What can you remember about him, Mr Ross?"

Ross took his time, wanting to get it right. After a moment he said, "The thing I remember most clearly is the gun. It was an automatic. Old, and well-used."

Willows got it down, waited.

"The other thing," said Ross, "is that he had, what do you call them, that boxers get . . ." He held his hands up to the side of his head.

"Cauliflower ears," said Bradley, a fan.

"Yes, that's right. And his nose had obviously been broken, it was pushed over to the side of his face."

"Recently broken?"

"No, I don't think so; that isn't what I meant at all."

"What about the scar?" said Willows. "Where was the scar located?"

Ross brought his wounded hand to his chin, and then his thought processes caught up with the situation and he said,

"Since you already have this information, why are you wasting my time?"

Willows sensed Bradley frowning at him from across the room. Toying with witnesses wasn't usually a great idea, but he wanted to keep Ross off balance, wondering what was next. He shrugged, smiled politely and answered Ross's question. "You may turn out to be the best witness we've got. Naturally I'm interested in your observations and recollection of events."

Smooth, thought Parker.

Willows said, "Mind if I use your phone?"

The banker nodded. "Help yourself. Dial nine for an outside line."

Willows rested a hip on Ross's oversized oak-veneer desk, picked up the phone and rested it in his lap. He dialled a nine and then the number for the local weather forecast, picked up a ballpoint pen and drew a revolver on Ross's scratchpad.

The phone rang twice and then there was a click and the taped message began to play.

Parker resumed questioning Ross about the victim's identification. Ross was becoming agitated – why were they so interested in the dead man instead of the guy who shot him?

Parker paced the office as she grilled Ross. She dropped her notebook, knelt to pick it up. Her ballpoint pen slipped from her hand.

Ross stared at her, enjoying the view.

Ross's leatherbound appointment book lay open on his desk. Willows quickly hung up and put the phone back on the desk, turned the notebook towards him. Ross was a very busy man. His calendar was jammed, but only until 4:30.

From 4:30 on, the page was blank, his time clear and free.

Parker collected her notebook and pen. She stood up, straightened her skirt. Willows thanked Ross for the use of his phone. The banker swivelled in his chair, stared blankly at him. "You get through?"

Willows said, "Every time it rains, it pours."

Parker smiled at him.

Willows said, "Your secretary tells me you had a very busy day, Mr Ross."

"Nothing unusual."

"But that you specifically instructed her not to make any appointments from four-thirty right through to the end of the day."

Ross reacted to Willows' bluff by seeming to withdraw a little deeper into his pinstripes. When he'd collected himself he said, "Exactly what are you implying?"

Willows stared blankly at him.

Ross turned to Bradley. "If possible, I often leave a block of time open at the end of the day. It gives me an opportunity to tidy up any loose ends that might have developed, make a few last-minute phone calls, deal with emergencies. I'm sure you understand . . ."

Bradley said, "Yes, of course."

Willows checked his watch. He said, "Was any member of your staff absent today?"

The telephone on Ross's desk warbled. A red light blinked on and off. He said, "No, everyone was here." The phone continued to ring. He picked up, glanced at Willows and said, "Yes, just a moment," and passed the phone to Willows.

Willows listened for a moment, said, "Right away," and hung up.

Ross spread his arms wide and said, "Look, can I go home now? There was a piece on the six o'clock news. My daughter knows there was a shooting, and she's worried sick."

Willows glanced at Bradley, who looked away. Willows asked Ross for his home address, repeated it back to him as he wrote it down in his notebook.

Parker said, "Nice neighborhood."

Ross thought it over, reluctantly agreed.

Willows put away his pen, turned to Bradley. "Know how he got away?"

"Clean," said Bradley.

"That's right. The name Max Zimmerman mean anything to you?"

Bradley shook his head, no.

Willows said, "Max was his wheelman."

Parker listened to the staccato click of her heels on the blood-stained, bullet-scarred terrazzo as she walked towards the door. She broke stride and went into a brief tapdance routine she'd learned as a child, and had long forgotten that she still remembered. The acoustics were wonderful; the sound of her heel-and-toe work sharp and clear. Out on the sidewalk, the bank's janitorial crew waited patiently for her to finish her act.

The traffic squad sergeant had sent a pisskid rookie off to a nearby deli to buy Max a disposable foam cup of strawberry tea and a couple of poppy-seed bagels crammed with bean-sprouts and cream cheese. Max had eaten and now was sprawled out on the backseat of the pisskid's blue and white, watching the cops sniff his tires as he tried to figure out how he could sue the city for loss of income.

The taxi had been turned into a ghost by the dusting of white fingerprint powder that covered it from bumper to bumper. When he'd seen what they were up to, Max had gone over there and told them flat out that the guy with the busted nose had touched a rear doorhandle and nothing else. They'd ignored him. Naturally. He'd been driving almost his whole adult life, and had long since become resigned to being treated as if he was several rungs down the evolutionary ladder from a jellyfish.

But now he was shaking hands with a couple of cops who were treating him with a little respect; a gorgeous young woman named Claire and a guy, Jack, who had a nice smile and a solid but not overpowering grip. Max didn't say a word but to his eyes Jack looked a little underfed and overworked. The woman seemed to get along okay with her partner even though Max thought he wasn't quite right for her, was maybe a little too old around the eyes.

53

Max expected the cops to come on like gangbusters, beat on his ears about the guy who'd stuck a gun in his face and stiffed him for a three-dollar fare. Instead, they made a point of asking him if he was okay, was he offered medical attention, did he get enough to eat . . .

Nice.

And when they finally got down to nuts and bolts, Claire asking most of the questions and Jack slipping in one of his own now and then but mostly hanging back, they both listened carefully to his every word, treating him with respect.

He admitted he'd hardly even looked at the guy, until the gun came out. And after that, he'd been twice as careful to keep his eyes down. But he was able to give them a general description, height and weight, remembered that the guy's nose was smeared all over his face, that his ears were pretty banged up, lots of scar tissue.

Jack wrote it all down.

Parker said, "That's pretty good, Max. Anything else?"

"You mean about the way he looked?"

"Anything at all," said Parker, smiling.

"Well, he was pretty tense. But I got the impression that how things went was up to me. He wasn't like a lot of guys nowadays, that bust people up just for the fun of it."

Parker wrote her home phone number on a cream-colored card. "We'll be in touch, Max. But if you should happen to think of anything in the meantime . . ."

Max said, "He took my bankroll, plus I got stiffed for the fare. A hundred eighty, easy. Can you help me with that, talk to somebody at city hall?"

He saw that he'd been right about Jack. The guy was definitely looking a little old around the eyes.

One of the robbery squad team – "Windy" Windfelt, a tall, overweight guy with unfocused eyes and a heavily waxed wraparound moustache – had pulled a large metal key ring out of his pants pocket about ten minutes ago, and had kept himself amused rotating keys to the apex of the key ring, trying to balance them on end. As he let go of each key and it inevitably tumbled and slid down the ring, he'd utter a little grunt of frustration, and try again with the next key on the ring. The jangling was starting to grate on Willows' nerves.

Windy's partner, Sherman "Fireplug" O'Neill, had made the force when the mayor degraded the height requirement to tempt the ethnic vote. Fireplug was five feet eight inches tall and weighed a hundred eighty pounds. His explosive temper was legendary, his weakness for bright red shirts well-documented. Mel Dutton claimed to have taken a photograph of him being urinated on by a cockatoo outside the Hongkong Bank of Canada at Cambie and 42nd, but nobody had ever seen it.

Neither cop was very happy about turning the Bank of Montreal heist over to Willows and Parker. As they'd viewed the grainy black and white film from the bank's surviving security cameras, both detectives had become convinced that the guy they called "The Magician" had scored again.

And now that he'd actually used his gun, they wanted his ass *real* bad.

Parker said, "I still don't get it. You've got him pegged for what, twelve or thirteen heists?"

"Right," said Windy. "The guy's scored more times than Wayne Gretzky."

"Or even me," said Fireplug.

"But nobody's ID'd him, you don't have any physical evidence, the MO's never the same . . ."

Fireplug turned to Parker. "Ever get a hunch so strong it makes your hair stand up on end?" He grinned. "No, I guess not." He tried Willows. "Jack?"

Willows nodded without enthusiasm. It was late – a gallon of coffee and too many donuts past midnight. The unburnt adrenalin had left a sour taste in his mouth. He was tired and cranky.

Fireplug said, "What I'm talking about, me and Windy, we're both absolutely convinced that asshole up there on the screen is a one-man crime wave."

Cops were such macho, *hunch*-brained . . . Parker stared at the monitor.

They were getting to it now, the perp walking up to the teller's cage and the woman, Hilary Fletcher, smiling at him and then standing frozen for a moment before her mouth opened wide and she started screaming. Then he must have said something to her, something to make her shut her mouth, yank open the cash drawer and begin pushing money across the counter . . . There was nothing in the witness report about him speaking to her. Maybe it was just the initial reaction, fear, supplanted by shock. She'd forgotten to step on the silent alarm button or pass the wad of bills containing the dye bomb.

She'd done a great job of screaming, though. Too bad it was a silent movie.

Martin Ross had said it was the teller's scream that brought him out of his office.

There he was, on cue, coming into frame from bottom right.

The victim was waving something that looked like a badge. He had a gun, too. The ·32. Now the perp had *his* piece out. The 9mm semi-auto, the Browning. Parker clearly saw the perp shift his grip, his thumb come up on the hammer, the tendons of his wrist stand out as he cocked the weapon.

The perp and victim exchanged shots. The victim got off two quick rounds. The perp got off eleven. Parker'd counted the spent 9mm cartridges that were now bouncing off the terrazzo and out of frame. The victim raised his arms as if to ward off a blow. The badge – if that's what it was – fell out of his hand and skittered across the shiny waxed floor. The perp's last round caught him just above the right eye. Suddenly he looked as if he'd had all the sawdust let out of him.

Dead.

Deader than silent movies.

He dropped.

Camera two. Hilary screaming silently, pounding the counter with both hands. A ballpoint pen leapt out of its holder and rolled across the counter and disappeared out of frame.

The other teller's eyes were squeezed shut and she had her hands in the air.

Ross clutched at the perp's ankle, brought him down. The perp stuck the Browning's muzzle up against Ross's skull, then changed his mind and used the weapon as a club, mussed the banker's silvery hair.

Parker stared at the monitor.

Fireplug said, "The guy moves like a pug, don't he? Kind of a sideways shuffle, hunches his shoulders . . ."

Parker said, "You think he's the same guy, wearing different faces. Different personalities, even. Could he be an actor?"

"Or an actress," said Windfelt, "for all we know."

"If that's makeup he's wearing, he's wearing a lot of it. You check to see if he's in the film business, TV, or a related industry, modelling . . ."

Fireplug said, "You think the perp could be a makeup artist?"

Parker nodded.

Windfelt said, "No way."

"Why not?"

"'Cause we wore out a couple of pairs of shoes each, checking it out."

"*Expensive* shoes," said Fireplug.

Windfelt nodded his agreement. His eyes were sunk low in their sockets. He had all the charisma and spark of an elderly basset hound.

Ninety seconds later – the time recorded on the tape was 5:06:42 – the shooter hurried off camera. At 5:06:59 the bank was flooded with blue uniforms. A moment later, the videotape ended and the machine automatically began to rewind.

Parker stifled a yawn.

Fireplug said, "Bored? I got some terrific footage of that jewelry store robbery in Chinatown last month, the owner goes for his baseball bat and gets his ear shot off."

Willows said, "You catch those guys?"

"Nope. Recovered the ear, though."

Parker said, "That's the Asian Crimes Squad. What are you doing with the film?"

"We rented it."

"They got a better selection than Blockbuster Video," said Fireplug, "and they don't charge any tax. But don't forget to rewind, or they'll cut your nuts off." He gave Parker a slow wink. "Or whatever."

Parker said, "I'll bet you don't worry about that as much as most of the guys."

Fireplug leaned forward in his chair. "Why's that?"

"Less to lose," said Parker.

They rolled the film again. The perp walked up to Hilary. She cocked her head to one side, hair falling on her shoulder. Then started screaming.

Fireplug said, "Terrific body. Real nice hair. A natural blonde, too."

"Strawberry blonde," said Windy. "Twenty years old. I asked could I see her driver's licence. Twenty! Can you remember that far back?"

"If she helped me out a little, I bet I could."

The phone on the desk at the front of the room rang shrilly. Fireplug and Windy paid no attention at first, but after a moment, they turned on Parker. The look in their eyes was slightly puzzled, mildly disappointed.

Fireplug said, "They didn't teach you how to answer a phone at the Academy?"

"I must've missed it. Probably I was off somewhere learning how to wash dishes."

The phone fell silent, and then began ringing again. Willows pushed out of his chair and walked the length of the room and picked up. He listened for a moment, said, "Yeah, we'll be there," glanced at Fireplug, and hung up.

Windy said, "What was that all about?"

Willows walked back to his chair, but didn't sit down. He said, "Official police business."

"Don't gimme that shit. Why'd you look at Fireplug like that?"

58

"Like what?"

"You know what I'm talking about, Jack."

Willows grabbed his jacket. "Let's call it a night, Claire."

"Wait a minute," said Fireplug. "I was gonna suggest we go out for Chinese."

Windy gave Willows an evil grin, whispered, "Bet you got something even tastier in mind, right?"

"Right," said Willows, smiling back. The phone call had come from the morgue. Two spent ·38 calibre and nine spent 9mm rounds had been dug from the bank's ceiling and walls. The coroner had phoned to let Willows and Parker know he was ready to take up the hunt for the two missing rounds.

The City Morgue is located on Cordova, just around the corner from 312 Main. It's an old building, three floors high, with a façade of pale orange brick, white-painted mullioned windows, an antique cast-iron skylight on the top-floor ceiling.

The pathologist, Christy Kirkpatrick, was a large, heavily boned man in his mid-fifties. He glanced up from a tattered copy of *Mad* magazine when Willows and Parker entered the room, said, "About time you got here."

"Lonely?" asked Willows.

Kirkpatrick offered his freckled hand. "Nice to see you, Claire."

"And you, Christy."

Kirkpatrick held up the magazine. "Haven't read this stuff since I was a kid – I'd forgotten how good it is." He rolled up the magazine, shoved it into the back pocket of his crisp white lab coat. "Windy and Fireplug couldn't make it?"

"They weren't invited."

"Might as well get started, then." Kirkpatrick adjusted his facemask and tapped the microphone at the end of a metal stalk fixed to the ceiling above the autopsy table. He noted the time and date and gently pulled the pale blue sheet off the corpse. As he folded the sheet he said, "What we have here is a male of apparent South American descent, John Doe

59

number nine two dash four seven. All we can say for sure about him is that he isn't Elvis." Kirkpatrick smiled at Parker. "Know why I'm sure he isn't Elvis?"

"No. Why?"

"Because he's *dead*." When Kirkpatrick stopped chuckling, he noted the corpse's length in centimeters and weight in kilos. He made a minor adjustment to the angle of the microphone, cleared his throat, and said, "I'm now about to make the initial incision."

It was a warning, a formal declaration of intent. Christy Kirkpatrick's eyes above the cloth facemask were a cheerful, mischievous blue. The blade of the scalpel hung steady for a moment, a motionless sliver of light, and then descended, melted into melting flesh.

Parker's mouth was dry. The blood churned in her veins. She glanced at Willows, then Kirkpatrick, down at the body.

Star players in another silent movie.

7

The telephone was a see-through model with colorful bands of blue and pink neon that more or less matched the décor of Hilary's apartment. She'd bought the phone at a mall outside Bellingham, smuggled it across the border in the trunk of her car. The phone wasn't cheap – she'd paid forty-nine dollars and fifty cents for it in US funds. She hadn't bothered to save the receipt because the sales clerk told her that the moment she crossed the border the warranty was null and void.

The instant she lifted the receiver off its cradle it began sounding a busy signal. Hilary felt a sinking sensation in the pit of her stomach. She knew exactly what had happened – Greg'd thrown the phone at the wall and scrambled the instrument's electronic innards so badly that it was no longer able to digest information. What a jerk.

There was an identical forty-nine dollar and fifty cent phone in the bedroom, but she didn't want to go in there because she was afraid of what she might see. For example, what if Greg had fouled the bed in some awful way? She stamped her pretty foot, but the carpet easily absorbed the blow.

Randy's eyes blinked open. He clutched at the coffee table, sent an ashtray spinning.

Hilary said, "Poor baby." She sounded pissed.

Randy said, "If you're calling Domino's, forget it. I don't want a pizza anymore."

"Excuse me?"

Randy sat up a little straighter. Everything hurt but nothing was broken. He pointed at the phone. "Who're you calling?"

61

"The police, but I can't get through."

Randy said, "Good." He stood up, flexed his knee. It was a little stiff, but otherwise okay. He gingerly explored his skull. It felt as if someone'd slipped a walnut under his skin, but there was no blood. Lucky thing. He stained Hilary's bone-white *flokati*, there was no telling what she might do. Finish him off, maybe.

Randy said, "How long was I out?"

"You didn't miss anything, if that's what you're worried about."

Randy found that when he trusted his knee with his weight, the pain was pretty intense. He limped into the bedroom. His brand-new stainless steel handcuffs were gone. So were the Polaroids. The camera wasn't going to capture any more magic moments – it was in splinters. His new suit was still hanging in the closet, thank the Lord, but his wallet lay on the floor and his credit cards and the two hundred and fifty bucks he'd withdrawn from his checking account that morning were gone.

Sonofabitch!

Randy slammed shut the closet door hard enough to cause a shockwave of air to rattle the hangers.

Hilary, lounging hip-cocked against the bedroom door, said, "If you're going to indulge in a tantrum, I'd much prefer you went somewhere else and did it."

Randy said, "I'm gone six months, it's a long time, I don't expect you to hold your breath. But a guy like that . . ."

"He isn't that bad. Everything would've been just fine if you'd let him look for his briefcase."

"And you did have a date with him tonight, didn't you?"

"I was held up, remember? I had other things on my mind."

"Where'd you meet him?"

"What difference does it make – or are you the only one allowed to ask the questions?"

Randy said, "He took the pictures. What d'you think he's going to do with them?"

62

"Tear them up and flush the pieces down the toilet. He's a very nice guy, Randy."

"Or maybe sell them to a magazine," said Randy.

"I don't think he'd do that."

"Why not?"

"Because like I keep telling you, he happens to be a very nice person. Warm and gentle, loving. He wasn't nearly as twisted as you, that's for sure."

"You needed to spend a little more time together, that's all. Where does he work?"

"He's an actor, remember?"

Randy picked up a piece of the camera. He bent the sliver of plastic between his thumb and finger, let go. The plastic skittered across the room, disappeared behind the far side of the bed.

Randy said, "Right, an actor. Let me rephrase the question. Where does he *perform*?"

"He's in rehearsal."

"What's the name of the play?"

"I don't remember."

"Did he ever mention it?"

"I don't *remember*."

"Where does he live?"

"I don't know."

"Bullshit."

"It's true."

Randy'd paid five grand plus tax for the engagement ring. Bought it on time. Eighteen months, payments of three hundred and fifty bucks per month. He knew how it would go if he tried to return it.

He smiled at his sweetheart and said, "You always came here? To your apartment?"

"I only saw him once or twice. I don't know how he got in, he must've stolen a key. God, you make it sound like he was a big part of my life!"

"What's his phone number?"

"I'm not going to tell you, Randy. Just forget it, okay?"

Randy picked up another piece of camera. He bent it between his thumb and finger and let fly. The jagged chunk of plastic flew straight up and then veered away. Faulty aerodynamics. He said, "The camera and hand-cuffs, film, the cash he stole from my wallet, add it up, it comes to about five hundred bucks. And who knows what kind of damage he's gonna do to my credit cards. *Shit!*"

Randy used the phone in the bedroom to alert Visa, Master Card and American Express to the fact that he'd lost his credit cards. He told them he'd had his wallet boosted in a bar. Yes, of course he'd phoned the cops.

Hilary said, "Don't slam the phone down so hard. It isn't the phone's fault."

It would be three or four days minimum before his new cards arrived in the mail. What was he supposed to do in the meantime – spend cash?

Hilary said, "So what're you going to do, track him down and make him give it back? You better take a couple more judo lessons first, that's all I can say."

Randy brushed past her, limped into the kitchen and emptied a loaf of sliced white bread on to the counter.

'What *do* you think you're doing?"

Randy turned the plastic breadbag inside out and shook the crumbs into the sink, went out on to the balcony and scooped Greg's vodka glass into the bag. He held the bag up to the light. He couldn't see any fingerprints on the glass, but that didn't mean they weren't there.

Greg walked down the street as fast as he could and not risk bringing unwanted attention upon himself. The Ford Taurus was parked right where he'd left it, the rear end sticking out into the alley. The briefcase lay in plain view on the front seat. He saw he hadn't locked the door, shook his head. He strolled past the car and down the alley, made a circuit of the block. No cops.

The young guy with the spade beard and ears loaded down

with gold rings lounging in the doorway of a nearby bookstore wasn't the least bit interested in him.

Neither was the fat guy in the wraparound sunglasses busily plucking blueberries out of his icecream.

And he was willing to bet that the babe with the lacy black haltertop, nuclear lipstick and lemming haircut who looked as if she wished she was pushing her stroller towards a steep cliff wouldn't have noticed him if her life depended on it.

That left a couple of schoolkids, and an old guy idling at the far end of the block in a battery-powered wheelchair, and Greg sincerely doubted any of them was about to stick a gun in his face and read him his wrongs.

He yanked open the Taurus's door, snatched the briefcase off the seat, slammed the door shut and rubbed his hip against the metal, obliterating his fingerprints.

Still no cops.

He walked two blocks to a hotel, grabbed a window table with a nice view of the street, a better view of the bar. About the only thing that distinguished the bar from every other bar in the city was its size – it was small: a couple of four-seater booths along one wall and no more than a dozen tables. Otherwise, Greg could have been almost anywhere. The polished mahogany tables were plywood veneer, the leather chairs made of Naugahyde.

In the modern world, things were what they appeared to be either because the genuine article was cheapest, or because no artificial substitutes were available. Greg believed that was as it should be. Especially in bars, where it's pretty much taken for granted that appearances are meant to deceive.

The waitress arrived. She wore tight black pants and a crisp white shirt, a bow tie that was almost the same shade of red as her lipstick. Her auburn hair was short and spiky, and so was her attitude. Well, what the hell. If the haircut fits, wear it. Greg ordered a Kootenay Pale Ale, lit a cigarette and made himself comfortable in the fake leather chair.

As he drank his beer, his mind kept turning of its own

65

accord to the fact that he'd killed a guy – and then skittered away. He couldn't quite bring himself to look in the briefcase. What if it contained nothing of value? Had he killed for nothing? He told himself to settle down, reminded himself the cop had popped the first cap. He'd whacked the guy in self-defense, pure and simple. Anyway, it was too bad about the cop but what really tore at his heart was the way Hilary had deceived him. He robbed banks for the buzz, not the money. What made him glow the brightest was ministering to the wounded. He loved to rock those frightened women in his arms, love away the nightmares, be strong for them.

But somehow he never found the patience to see the trauma through. Inevitably, just as they were beginning to recover, he'd find fault with them. Let them know *exactly* where they were lacking.

Then take a walk. Start all over again. Man, it sounded so easy, but the time he burned getting it done. Women. He always had two or three or even four of them going at once. But this time, due to circumstances beyond his control – or maybe it was the cocaine – he'd put all his eggs in one basket. The days and weeks and months he'd wasted on Hilary, setting her up for what – so her dumbass blackbelt boyfriend could waltz in from Toronto and wipe away her tears?

Usually it was about at this point, right after he'd scored and as he was holding his traumatized baby's hand, that Greg, seeking comic relief from all those tears, selected his next victim from among the three or four he'd been courting. And now, just like that, he had nothing, nobody!

What a mess. *What a mess.*

Greg finished his first beer and then another, was starting to feel bloated and ordered a rye and ginger. The drink arrived. He lit a cigarette, saw in the tinted glass window the reflection of someone moving rapidly towards him. He glanced up, startled, as a woman in her mid-twenties slid into the booth, smiled warmly at him and said, "Hi, I'm Sylvia."

Greg nodded, held his tongue.

Sylvia said, "Look, I'm sorry I'm late, but . . ." Her eyes

widened. "Oh my God, you're not Walter Irving, are you?"

Greg said, "No, and I can prove it."

The woman glanced around the bar. Except for a trio of Japanese tourists, the bartender and the waitress, the place was empty.

Greg said, "You were supposed to meet a guy, you're a little late, and he didn't wait? Excuse me, don't think I'm handing you a line, but I find that hard to believe."

"You do?"

Greg introduced himself, made sure he'd heard her name right. He told her he'd never met a Sylvia before, it was a beautiful name, liquid-sounding, like falling water. He said he'd understand if she turned him down, but thought it would be really nice if she'd stay and have a drink.

Sylvia had curly blonde hair, big green eyes that laughed a lot. They made small talk about the bar and the weather and then Greg asked her what she did for a living, saw the eyes suddenly darken as she turned serious. He discovered she was an interior decorator, had taken a degree at Carleton and come out west to make her fortune.

Greg's ears perked up a little. He asked her how she was doing and she said it wasn't an easy profession to break into but she was getting by, making progress.

They had a couple more drinks. Time slipped by. The bar was completely empty now, except for the bartender and punk waitress.

Sylvia glanced at her watch, noticed that it was getting late.

Greg asked her if she'd like one last drink. After a moment's hesitation, she smiled and said yes. Somehow the conversation wandered back to the art of interior design. Greg said it sounded complicated.

Sylvia told him there was nothing to it, if you knew what you were doing. She'd completely remade her apartment, which was only a few blocks away. Would he like to take a look and see what she could do?

Greg said he thought that was a wonderful idea.

Sylvia's apartment was in a prewar three-story brick

building that might survive a point three on the Richter Scale but was doomed to collapse in a cloud of dust and crushed tenants, the day the big one hit.

Greg followed her up the stairs, waited while she unlocked the door, switched on the light.

Greg's first thought was that he'd been captured by an alien. The interior of the apartment was like a spaceship from a circa 1950 B-movie. The walls and ceiling were covered with shiny Mylar strips, Sylvia's furniture was stainless steel and glass and injection-molded plastic and the apparently riveted-in-place floor was fashioned of brushed aluminum panels. Droning electric motors powered miniature pastel search-lights no bigger than Greg's fists that roamed in fitful random patterns across the shiny walls. Squinting, Greg saw that the walls had been literally sprinkled with bits of macaroni spray-painted silver.

He brought his hand up, shielding his eyes.

Sylvia said, "Well – what d'you think?"

Greg said, "Fantastic."

"Really? You like it?"

One of the searchlights locked in on Greg's right eye, and a psycho with a torque wrench began playing with his skull. Greg gritted his teeth. "It's amazing," he said. "Very impressive." He'd tossed the killer Browning into a back-alley dumpster a block from Hilary's building. Huge mistake. He pictured himself burning a full clip, lights exploding.

He slipped his arm around Sylvia's waist, splayed his fingers across her hip. She asked him if he'd like to see the rest of the apartment.

Greg nodded happily, and was led down a corrugated sheet metal hallway to a door made of rainbow panels of plastic, then inside a giant soup tin lit by a pulsing red ball that looked like a harvest moon gone apoplectic that hovered over a king-size waterbed full of curdled milk.

Greg had an almost overpowering urge to start singing "Moon River", but fortunately couldn't remember the words.

At three o'clock in the morning a tiny unfamiliar sound

somewhere deep in the bowels of the apartment block pulled Greg out of a light sleep. As soon as Sylvia had finished with him, he'd pulled the plug on the red ball, so the only light in the room came through the curtained window from a distant streetlight.

Greg turned on his side, propped himself up on an elbow. His chest ached where the *puta* guy's round had smacked into him. The waterbed belched softly. Sylvia looked cute as a button in her Bart Simpson nightie. He swung his legs over the side of the bed, found his cigarettes and walked naked into the living room, lit up. Now that the pastel searchlights had been turned off, the apartment wasn't so bad, really. Almost peaceful, in a way. Like a nuthouse at bedtime, when everybody's been strapped in and had a sock stuffed in their mouth.

He wandered into the kitchen. No renovations here. He yanked open the fridge. Salad stuff. Too many flavors of yogurt to count. Two per cent milk. He tried the freezer and found it empty except for a tray of icecubes and a loaf of seaweed bread hard as a rock and probably not much tastier. He turned to the cupboards. Tins of minestrone soup and a package of Stone Wheat Thins. Yummy. There was a wall telephone. He dialled home and listened to Hilary's recorded message of doom and gloom, the bottom line being that she never wanted to see him again but he better get those pictures back real fast, or Randy was gonna call the cops, no kidding.

Chuckling, Greg hung up. He went into the living room and opened a window, ricocheted off the furniture until he found his jacket, squeezed pockets until he had a small plastic bottle of Bayer aspirins in his hand. He knelt on the floor, popped the childproof cap and shook five or six aspirins and about three lines worth of coke on to a fire-blackened glass table that looked like a recycled windshield from a doomed Boeing 747.

He picked the aspirins out of the coke, fashioned a straw out of the last page of a battered paperback copy of *Gone With The Wind*. He stuck the straw up his nose and leaned over the windshield and made happy snorting noises until the coke was gone.

The black leather briefcase seemed to weigh a ton. He unclasped the latches. Inside were numerous pockets of various shapes and sizes. Greg's fingers sized up the leather. He tried to imagine what the interior of an accordion must look like. Or bagpipes . . . It took him about ten minutes to riffle through the briefcase. It contained nothing of interest but a gold fountain pen, a pair of expensive sunglasses and a thick, unbound sheaf of computer paper covered with rows and rows of numbers.

Greg lit another cigarette. His brain had played a trick on him, tried to justify Garcia Lorca Mendez's death with a dreamscape of immense wealth.

Yeah, sure, *of course* the guy was a mule or courier, the briefcase was full of cash. And what was Greg full of, that smelled so sweet?

But what was an out-of-continent cop disguised as a cablevision repairman doing at Kingsgate Mall? And why was he packing a concealed weapon, and what gave him the right to try to blow Greg away?

Greg took a closer look at the spreadsheets, the orderly columns of dot-matrix figures that he gradually came to realize were all six-figure numbers.

Each column had a seven-digit number at the top left corner of the page. The top right corner of each of the sixteen pages had an identical six-digit number divided into three pairs separated by angled slashes: today's date; day, month and year. The top left numbers weren't sequential. The pages themselves weren't numbered. He scratched his head, wished upon a spray-painted length of pasta for more cocaine.

He smoked three cigarettes down to the filter and nibbled every last aspirin to death before he managed to work out that the seven-digit numbers were bank savings accounts, that the three columns on each page represented deposits and withdrawals and the current balance.

He went through the pages one by one. There were one

hundred and eighteen accounts. The smallest balance was eight hundred dollars and the largest was nine thousand, five hundred plus change. From what he could see, there was a fair amount of juggling going on, many small chunks of cash shifting from one account to the next.

He went into the bedroom and plugged in the light and gently awoke Sylvia. She said, "Wha . . ." and then her eyes popped open and she smiled, her teeth flashing red.

Greg said, "Have you got a calculator?"

She shook her head, no. Her hand listlessly stroked his thigh. She was really, really cute. Looking at her, you'd have no way of knowing what nightmare visions she was capable of realizing. Greg pulled the duvet up over her bare shoulders, kissed her lightly on the cheek and whispered, "It's late, go back to sleep." Sylvia closed her eyes. In a moment her breathing was deep and even.

Greg sat there on the edge of the bed full of curdled milk, in the bedroom of brushed aluminum and stainless steel that was stained the color of blood by the red light. He inhaled her perfume, admired the curve of her eyelashes, sniffed the musk of her perfume. Really, really cute.

What a shame.

He couldn't help giving her a last, lingering kiss.

She murmured, "Greg?"

He said, "Not really," and turned out the light.

8

Inspector Homer Bradley's office was located on the third floor of 312 Main, and over the flat tar-and-gravel roof of a neighboring building he had a terrific view of the mountains on the far side of the harbor. Grouse had a ski lift and gondolas strung up the slopes, and the top of the mountain had been clear-cut for the convenience of skiers who couldn't afford the time or expense to make the trip to Whistler. The other local ski hill, Seymour, had also been ruthlessly scalped.

But the night-lights at the top of the mountains were kind of pretty, especially when the slopes were covered with snow. And there was another reason Bradley liked to look out at the lights – it was because they so sharply and exactly defined the limits of civilization; the point at which the petty thefts, knife fights, assault & battery, muggings, rape and murder ended. There was nothing on the other side of those bright lights but hundreds and hundreds of square miles of peace and quiet.

A comforting thought, at times.

Bradley turned away from the window. "We ought to go fishing sometime, Jack. Outwit a few trout. Swap a few lies."

Willows had heard it all before. He leaned a little more heavily into a wall painted the same shade of green as a badly bruised granny smith apple.

Bradley said, "How'd Fireplug and Windy take it when you snatched their case?"

Willows shrugged.

Parker said, "About what you'd expect."

Bradley smiled at Willows and said, "If we paid you two by

the word, the city'd probably be able to balance its budget."

No response, naturally.

Bradley said, "They turn over the files?"

Willows nodded.

"Read 'em yet?"

Parker said, "We're working on it. We didn't get out of the morgue until almost three in the morning."

"Any surprises there?"

A copy of the report lay on top of the heap of papers in Bradley's IN tray, but *he* apparently hadn't had time to catch up on his reading either.

Willows said, "If somebody hadn't shot him, he'd have died anyway."

"Sooner than later?"

"Cancer of the prostate. The disease had progressed to the point where it was inoperable. Kirkpatrick gave him six months at the outside."

Bradley shrugged. "Even so, it looks like a second-degree murder rap to me."

Parker said, "You still want us to catch him, is that it?"

"If you can. What's next?"

"We're waiting for CPIC to run his prints. We'll show his picture around, see if anybody local knows him."

"You don't sound particularly optimistic."

"Kirkpatrick thinks he's from out of town," Parker explained.

"The dental work?"

Parker smiled, nodded. Bradley was old, but he was wise.

"You talk to the cablevision people?"

"We've already circulated photographs within the company. Nobody's recognized him yet. It'd be a lot easier if we had a positive identification."

Bradley drummed his fingers on his cherrywood desk, leaned far back in his ancient oak and leather swivel chair. He stretched his arms wide, spun the chair away from the desk and stared out the window. "What a beautiful day. Ain't nature grand?"

73

"Red in tooth and claw," said Parker. "Or maybe it depends what part of the woods you live in."

Bradley rotated the leather chair ninety degrees, rested his heels on his desk. His shoes were black and shiny. The laces hung loose. He said, "What about the shooter?"

Willows said, "Fireplug and Windy've been after him for over two years. They see him for eight banks, three credit unions and a trust company. They want him bad."

"Sure they do. But they've got a big problem – they don't have any way of tying him into the other stuff. Not that you can blame them for trying – it'd bump their batting average about fifty points, clear a lot of files. But they haven't got enough physical evidence to fill a thimble." Bradley kicked off a shoe, massaged his foot. "You want to know what they *do* have?"

Parker said, "What've they got, Inspector?"

"A hunch and a bellyache," said Bradley, "and that's about it."

"We're going to go over the security film from all twelve previous robberies," said Parker. "We might get lucky, catch something they missed."

"Got follow-ups scheduled for the witnesses?"

"This afternoon."

"The bank finish its audit?"

Willows said, "The shooter walked away with eleven hundred and sixty-eight dollars."

"And a black briefcase." Bradley's shoes came off the desk, hit the carpet with a dull thud. "The manager, Martin Ross. His name pop up anywhere?"

"He's clean, so far."

"So far?"

Willows said, "A couple of things are kind of nagging at us. The fact that he risked his life fighting for the briefcase when he claims he doesn't know what was in it. Also, nothing specific, but the way he handled himself when we questioned him struck us both as a little weird."

Bradley glanced at Parker for confirmation.

74

Willows said, "And another thing, he had no appointments after four-thirty."

Bradley said, "The reason he gave was plausible."

"Sure it was, but during that time frame the guy who got shot is hanging around, he's carrying the briefcase, packing an unregistered concealed weapon and a nice shiny badge, which he flashes before he pulls his piece and tries to blow the boxer away, gets popped."

Parker said, "He got popped, but he might've been a better shot than we first thought."

"Yeah?"

"We couldn't find the bullet, and in the film it looks as if the shooter flinches, a split second before he fires."

"He was hit?"

"It's possible, but we don't know. There was no trace of blood, body tissue . . ."

"He was probably wearing a full suit of body armour." Bradley leaned forward, flipped open the lid of a Haida-carved cedar cigar box. "I know *I* would, if I were in that line of work." He selected a cigar, shut the lid. "You mention Ross's name to Bernie and Pat?"

Willows nodded. "Fraud's never heard of him. If they had, he wouldn't be a bank manager, would he?"

Bradley kicked off a shoe, leaned down and massaged his foot. It was the rheumatism again – his toes ached and that meant the weather was going to turn ugly. "You going to take another look at Marty?"

Willows said, "We'll be talking to him."

"There's one thing that bothers me . . ."

Willows said, "Thirteen in a row, that's a pretty long string."

Bradley nodded, rolled the cigar lovingly between his thumb and index finger.

Continuing, Willows said, "But not much money. He's been coming away with fifteen hundred, maybe two grand a hit. The guy could make more money mugging paperboys. So I have to ask myself – if he's so smart, why does he rob banks?"

"Figure it out yet?"

"When we do, you'll be the first to know."

Bradley said, "That reminds me – Bob Conroy get in touch with you?"

"Nope."

"Claire?"

"Not recently."

Bradley said, "A bank robbery is a bank robbery is a bank robbery. But a shoot-out, a shiny black briefcase, and a dead Mexican – or whatever – is pretty hot stuff. Bob'd like something juicy to feed the blow-dried mob, a piece of meat they can regurgitate on the eleven o'clock news. Got anything for him?"

"How about a finger," suggested Willows.

"That's very helpful, Jack. Did you have a particular finger in mind?"

"He'll know the one," said Willows. He was halfway out the door – and then he was gone.

Farley Spears looked up from his desk as Willows and Parker came out of Bradley's office. He nodded to Parker and Parker nodded back. Spears looked awful. Three months ago, his doctor had told him quit smoking or die. Spears had cut his tar and nicotine intake to a pack a day and gained fifty pounds. He had an appointment with his quack at the end of the month and knew exactly what the guy was going to tell him – quit eating or die.

Spears said, "Bob Conroy was here a minute ago, said he needs something on yesterday's shoot-out, the vultures are pecking his eyes out. I told him I'd pass on the message, next time I saw you."

Willows said, "You do that, Farley." He and Parker made their way through the squadroom, past grey-painted metal filing cabinets sandwiched between rows of grey-painted metal desks. Willows unlocked the squadroom's door. One of the civilian secretaries at the front desk smiled at him, but he didn't seem to notice. He pushed the door open, strode towards the elevator, punched a button.

76

Parker said, "What about Conroy?"

Willows said, "You want to talk to him, go ahead. I haven't got the time."

Martin Ross seemed to have fully recovered from his ordeal. The carefully brushed silver hair, imported tan and confident smile, his sparkling white shirt, heavy gold cufflinks and the immaculately tailored suit that had cost two thousand dollars if it had cost a dime; everything about him looked brand spanking new and eager to do business.

Willows unbuttoned his three-year-old sports jacket, which had been ticketed at two hundred but discounted at an end-of-lease sale to half price.

Ross said, "I talked to Inspector Bradley. He gave me his personal assurance that you would not require more than a few minutes of my time."

My precious time, thought Parker. She glanced at Willows and saw that he'd been thinking along the same lines.

Willows said, "Your current address is 1980 Ogden, is that right?"

"I've been living there since the house was built, Detective."

"When was that?"

"Eight years ago this spring."

Willows nodded. "Tell me. How long does it take you to get to work?"

"Half an hour, give or take a few minutes."

"You're still driving a dark blue Chrysler Imperial, tagged NST four-nine-nine?"

Ross nodded.

Willows said, "You bought the vehicle quite recently, is that correct?"

Ross's eyes dropped for a split second to Willows' clamshell holster, the blued steel of his ·38 Special.

Willows said, "A bank manager, I guess you have to drive a car like that, don't have any choice, really."

"You don't like Chryslers?"

77

"No," said Willows. "What I meant is I suppose you always have to consider your image, what your customers expect from you." He smiled. "We're all in the same situation, really. You lease, or buy?"

"I'd never recommend a lease. I just don't see any advantage. The monthly's far too high and the buy out's ridiculous." Ross toyed with a desk drawer. Willows wondered if he had a bottle tucked away in there, along with a shotglass and lifetime supply of breathmints.

Ross said, "Tell me, what kind of car do *you* drive, Detective?"

"Whatever's available from the car pool." Willows adjusted the weight of the pistol on his belt. "Now that you've had some time to think it over, can you tell us anything else about the man who was killed?"

In a fraction of a second, Ross was transformed from unjustly aggrieved banker to sympathetic, grieving fellow human being. He said, "I understand the victim was an officer of the law."

"Not *our* law," said Willows. "But we're looking into the possibility."

Ross nodded solemnly. He said, "I wish I could be of more help. But I've given it a great deal of thought and I'm afraid I can't add to what I told you yesterday. The man dropped by my office once or twice in the past year or so. I can't remember what we discussed, but it wasn't anything out of the ordinary."

"Nothing memorable?"

"Exactly."

Parker, trying to keep Ross off balance, said, "What's a car like that cost, if you don't mind me asking?"

Ross removed his glasses, held them up to the light, obviously didn't much care for what he saw. He plucked a silk handkerchief from the breast pocket of his suit, scrubbed at a lens, tossed the handkerchief on his desk and put his glasses back on. "You want to know how much I paid for my *car?*"

Smiling, Parker said, "Just curious."

"I believe the exact figure was thirty-two thousand five hundred and eighty dollars and sixty-seven cents."

Parker said, "They wouldn't round it off for you?"

"I didn't ask."

"You paid cash?"

"If memory serves, I wrote a check."

Willows said, "There's a park across the street from your house, and then the beach?"

"You know the neighborhood, Detective?"

"Happened to drive by last night," said Willows. He shut his notebook. "How's your wife taking this, she holding up okay?"

"My wife passed away some time ago."

"I'm sorry to hear that." Willows glanced at Parker. "Did you have any more questions, Claire?"

"Not at the moment," said Parker.

Pale October light slanted down through the bank's plate glass windows. A tiny red light blinked on each of the bank's four security cameras. The fluorescents high up on the ceiling glowed with a faint tinge of pale blue. Light flashed on the dial of a watch, a pair of glasses, a teller's gold chain.

The plate glass window didn't have any bullet holes in it any more – the location of the holes had been measured and the angles of impact gauged, and then the window had been photographed from all angles, inside and out, while the glaziers smoked cigarettes and watched and made small jokes. The thick white chalk a detective had used to draw the dead man's sprawled outline on the black granite floor had been wiped clean by a janitorial team working double overtime. The blood had been mopped, squeezed into a grey plastic bucket and poured down a drain. The grout had been scrubbed clean. The bright yellow plastic crime scene tape was now crisscrossed across the bedroom door of a patrolman's thirteen-year-old son. The heavy black extension cords were gone and the lights were down. The revolver, spent brass and other physical evidence was locked away in a vault at 312 Main.

Money was still money, it seemed.

Thick grey velveteen ropes on brass stands formed a maze-like corridor to help keep the customers in line. According to the testimony of Hilary, the teller who'd been held up, the shooter had stood exactly where Willows was standing now.

Willows tried to see the bank through the killer's eyes. If Fireplug and Windy were right, and the guy *had* burned a baker's dozen worth of banks – he was either very lucky or very smart.

Or maybe a whole lot of both.

Willows turned to Parker. "You keep track of the number of questions we asked Ross about his car?"

"I think it was seven. I kept waiting for him to blow his stack."

Willows smiled. "Me and you both."

"Makes you wonder, doesn't it."

Willows said, "Want to get something to eat?"

"Not particularly."

Willows kept backing the unmarked beige Chevrolet into the parking spot until the rear bumper nudged the tall, green-painted wooden fence at the rear of the parking lot.

A carhop balancing five four-foot-long green plastic trays on his shoulder hurried past. A napkin fluttered in his wake.

Parker said, "The carhop won't take your order unless you signal him with your lights, Jack."

Willows hit a switch and the red light hidden behind the car's grill whirled and flashed. The carhop grinned at Parker, kept going.

"Headlights," said Parker, "but I think he got the message."

Willows studied the menu painted on huge sheets of ply-wood attached to the side of the restaurant. "What're you going to have?"

"Diet Coke, half a Caesar."

The carhop came towards them, order pad at the ready.

His blond hair was cut in the style of a new-mowed lawn, and he had too many freckles to count. He crouched and peered into the car, smiled at Parker and asked her if she was ready to order.

Parker ordered her soft drink and salad, Willows a cheeseburger platter and coffee.

The carhop said, "Was that a large Coke, ma'am?"

"Small," said Parker.

The kid nodded, wrote it down, snuck another look at Parker. "Be right back."

Parker smiled, looked out the window.

Willows held his fire until the carhop was out of earshot and then said, "Another broken heart."

"That probably depends on the tip."

Willows checked his watch. He said, "I've got a bad feeling about this one."

"How d'you mean?"

"The guy's pulled thirteen armed robberies and we've got absolutely nothing to go on. You've been over the files. It's like, when the guy isn't out there working, he ceases to exist."

"He keeps busy," said Parker. "Sooner or later, we'll nail him."

"He's in and out and gone in less than two minutes, on average. That isn't much of a window. Fireplug and Windy did good work – flogged their snitches to death, asked their witnesses all the right questions . . ."

"Okay," said Parker, "let's look at it this way – what can we learn about the guy from what we can't find out about him?"

Willows was still thinking it over when she said, "In the past two years the guy's hit thirteen banks and left more than a hundred witnesses in his wake. But so far, none of those witnesses has been able to pick him out of a photo lineup. We don't even have a *tentative* ID. No picture, no prints . . . If the guy was local, you'd think somebody'd have rolled him over by now. The thing is, we've got all that film but no idea what he really looks like. We probably know what he *doesn't* look like, but how does that help?" She unbuckled her safety

81

belt and reached behind her to massage her lower back. "I'm starting to ramble, aren't I?"

Willows said, "He might be from out of town – it's possible. Or maybe he's a loner, knows how to keep his mouth shut . . ." Or maybe Windfelt and Fireplug's snitches travelled in the wrong circles. Now that he and Parker had the files, *their* snitches had a chance to show what they could do. Willows would put out the word – anyone who dropped a dime on their shooter could expect to walk on anything this side of child abuse.

A green plastic tray slid past Willows' nose. The carhop had blind-sided him. The bill was pinned to the tray by his coffee cup. Eleven dollars and forty-three cents. Willows paid with a twenty, watched as his change was counted out on to the tray.

The carhop, smiling at Parker, said, "If you need anything, just flash your smile."

Willows scooped up his change, every last nickel of it, and dropped it in his pocket.

Parker said, "Ruth Urquhart, did I mention she said that after the shooter'd blasted Mendez and cold-cocked Ross, he made a joke about it to her kids on his way out?"

"So?" Willows took another bite of his cheeseburger. A perky brown sparrow scrabbled across the slippery slope of the Chevrolet's hood.

"So the guy stayed pretty cool – maybe it wasn't his first shoot-out. Maybe we should alter the profile, toss in the shooting and run him through the computer again."

Willows said, "It's worth a shot, if we can get the time." He added cream to his coffee. The sparrow pogo-sticked across the hood. Willows tore a small piece of meat from his hamburger.

Parker said, "It isn't going to eat that."

Willows tossed the meat out the window, on to the hood.

The sparrow pounced, wolfed the meat down.

Willows said, "He's hit banks and trust companies and

82

credit unions all over town, east side and west. What's he do, toss a dart at the yellow pages?"

Parker toyed with her salad. The sparrow made a sound like Michael Jackson clearing his throat.

Answering his own question, Willows said, "I don't think so. He had a reason for hitting those particular banks. He picks his spots. Those banks don't *appear* to have anything in common, but they do – they've all got something in common, something that appeals to him. We just haven't found out what it is yet."

Willows tossed another piece of meat out the window, and the bright-eyed sparrow gobbled it up.

Bait. What they were looking for was the right bait. If they found the right bait, the shooter would pounce, and then it would be their turn.

9

The night of the shooting, Greg spent several hours poring over the spreadsheets – taking a break now and then to raid his date's liquor cabinet. The sun came up at a few minutes past seven. Now that he could see where he was, Greg had to get out of there. He used a phone that looked like a miniature rocketship to summon a cab.

In the bedroom, Sylvia called his name and the sheets made a wet, slithery sound.

By the time Greg hotfooted it down to the street his cab was right there, gliding up to the curb.

Fifteen minutes later he was standing in the lobby of a downtown motorhotel, scrawling somebody else's name on the registration card, paying sixty-eight dollars plus tax for a room with a sixty-eight cent view.

The motel was a three-story cinderblock walk-up, the kind of place that didn't count on a whole lot of repeat business. Parking was at the rear. On the registration card Greg wrote that he was driving a brown Ford Taurus, vanity plate HOT. He asked for a room overlooking the parking lot, said he was a lingerie salesman, his samples were in the vehicle, he liked to be able to keep an eye on it. No problem.

Was the clerk interested in anything? Greg thumped the briefcase down on the counter. He was about a size fourteen, right? Hey, just kidding.

Now he was lying on the bed in his room, the window open just wide enough to take a header through, should such drastic action be required.

The badge in its leather case lay heavy on his chest, scrawled thin, silvery lines of reflected light across the ceiling as he breathed, his chest rising and falling.

He lit a cigarette, rolled over on his side. He'd spent a pound of change at the motel's newspaper vending machines, bought all the local papers. There was nothing in the *Globe & Mail*. *The Sun* had a sidebar, maybe fifty words. No mention of Hilary.

The Province, a tabloid-format daily, had a blurry front page color shot of Garcia Lorca Mendez lying right where he'd dropped. He looked like he was taking a nap, except for all the blood, the bullet hole, and the fact that his eyes were wide open.

Greg hadn't noticed the sunglasses tucked into the breast pocket of Mendez's coveralls, or the white shirt and gaudy tie he was wearing under the coveralls, or the bushy eyebrows, expensive haircut . . .

There were a lot of things about Garcia Lorca Mendez that Greg hadn't noticed – not that he was an unobservant fellow. It was just that it had all gone down so fast. There'd been time enough to pull the trigger and that was about it.

Greg had always liked the Browning, the go-to-hell look of it, and the lovely shape and weight and balance of it as he held it in his hand. The magazine, packed with fourteen rounds, was a thing of beauty. He liked to turn it in his hand and watch the play of light and shadow on the rounded snouts, staggered brass cartridges. He took sweet pleasure in the strength required to rack the slide, and the crisp metallic click when he manually cocked the hammer was a musical note so pure it was like the song of some sweet bird.

Sure made a racket when you popped a cap, though.

The silvery line of light skittered faster and faster across the ceiling as Greg remembered the shoot-out, silk ripping in his ear as Garcia Lorca Mendez wasted a round, the Browning doing a happy little jig in Greg's hand as he returned fire, missed repeatedly without understanding why, frustration and terror building in him, Mendez's second shot thumping

85

into his chest. For a split second there, he'd forgotten he was wearing the Kevlar.

Man, that had been a bad piece of time. He'd felt the bullet *rip* through him.

But he'd kept shooting and missing and shooting and missing and shooting and missing until suddenly an enormously complicated look came into Mendez's eyes and his arm was swinging wide in a sloppy, half-assed salute.

The twins were bathed in blood. Mendez, his dark eyes full of regret, began to fall. The fight leaking out of him . . .

And Greg, the Browning the only part of him that was under control now, couldn't stop himself until he'd fired once more; Garcia Lorca Mendez shrugging massively as the 9mm round drilled into him, smacked him down.

Underneath the photograph in *The Province* it said – story on page 32A.

Greg turned the pages, found himself in one of those "no news is good news" situations. Nobody knew who the victim was. Nobody knew what he was doing in the bank. Nobody knew anything about him.

There was a short, uninformative interview with the bank's manager, Martin Ross.

Now you know his name, thought Greg. He skimmed through the rest of the article – lots of guesswork but not much in the way of hard news. No mention at all of the shiny black briefcase, but that didn't mean anything.

Greg smoked and watched TV and dozed through the morning. At a little past one he went through the brochures he found in the top drawer of the motel's blond oak-veneer credenza, settled on a nearby pizza joint and used the phone to order a small anchovies and green pepper and mushrooms, a six-pack of Diet Coke.

He ate the food standing by the window, looking down at the empty parking lot, melted cheese dribbling on to the mud-brown carpet.

He guzzled three Cokes, washing down several slices of pizza. The anchovies made him thirsty. Or maybe it was all that heavy brain work. Thinking, maintaining concentration, was hard labor. He'd rather dig ditches.

He went back to the credenza, pulled out a battered copy of the Metro Vancouver White Pages, AKA phone book. He found the name Ross on pages 1298 through 1300. There were 43 listings for M Ross, a Maria and a Melville, but no Martin squeezed in between.

The motel charged fifty cents per for local calls. A string of bad luck, he could blow twenty-five bucks. He picked up the phone, put it back down again.

What was he going to do, say, "Hi, this is Greg, you might've caught my act yesterday, I'm the guy who . . ."

Before he made the call, he had to decide who he was. Or rather, who he was going to be.

The name Tod Erickstad came to him. He thought about it for a minute, and then remembered that Tod was a Ford salesman Greg had met while cruising a lot on Southeast Marine, about nine months ago. Greg wanted to test-drive the five-liter Mustang and see if it was a useful getaway vehicle. He had a hunch the rear-end was too light, and he was right; had ended up stealing a LeBaron.

Anyway, Erickstad. It'd been mid-February, one of those days when it might rain and it might snow, and in the mean-time there's a wind off the sea and the air is grey and clammy, miserably cold. So Erickstad spots him kicking tires, probably the only living customer in the hemisphere, and he comes roaring out of the showroom with his afterburners on full power and his tie flapping in the wind. He's wearing a cheap suit that's about the same shade of brown as the motel carpet, his hair is cut shorter than a graveyard lawn and his baby blue eyes are bright with a lifetime accumulation of stupidity. He's got a great smile but his breath smells of diesel fumes. His name is Tod. But much worse than all of that is his relentless, unfocused optimism. It cuts through Greg like a dull knife.

So Greg tells Tod he's been thinking about a new five-liter Mustang and notices there's a nice moss green cabriolet on the lot, how much?

Tod avoids numbers. He walks Greg around the car, shows him the interior, stereo system and intermittent wipers, all that chrome and glove leather.

Want to take her for a spin?

Sure, says Greg.

Tod trots back to the showroom for the keys.

Greg slips on a pair of black pigskin gloves. Turns his back on the showroom windows to check the load in his ·357 stainless.

Yo, six rounds.

Tod's back, winded from jogging across at least fifty feet of asphalt. He unlocks and opens the door, reaches inside and hits a button that unlocks the passenger door.

Greg gets behind the wheel. Tod reminds Greg to fasten his safety belt.

They turn on to Marine Drive. Tod asks Greg is there anywhere in particular he'd like to go.

Costa Rica, says Greg. Tod loves it, cracks up. He actually slaps his thigh. Greg, staring at him, says he just wants to cruise around. He lights a cigarette. Tod powers down his window. The wind is Arctic. Greg turns the heater on full blast. He fiddles with the radio, finds some rap and cranks it.

Tod asks him does he like rap music. He has to yell, to make himself heard above the blast of noise.

Greg ignores him.

After a couple of blocks they turn up a side street. Greg accelerates, brakes hard. By now Tod's a little worried. Greg powers into a blind corner, the Mustang's tires smoking as the car slides nicely into a four-wheel drift.

Tod says, "Okay, that's enough." Not so jolly, all of a sudden.

Greg nods and power-shifts from fourth gear straight into first. The Mustang's nose dips and the engine howls but hangs together. Greg swerves sharply up to the curb. They're in a working-class neighborhood dating from the fifties. Picture windows and single car garages, stucco. Greg hits the trunk release. The lid pops open. He turns off the ignition and tosses Tod the keys, says, "Get in the trunk, stupid."

Tod's jaw drops, but the rest of him doesn't move an inch.

Greg points the ·357.

After more than a quarter-century, Tod has finally learned something worth knowing. His eyes are a little darker now – the baby's leaking out of his blue.

Smiling, Greg dialled the first number in the phone book. He introduced himself to the woman who answered as Detective Tod Erickstad of the Vancouver Police, asked to speak to Martin Ross.

Told that he had a wrong number, Greg disconnected without a word.

And dialled the next number. And then the next.

Now it was his turn to have what you might call a learning experience. The third number he dialled, there was a fight going on in the background, he could hear glass breaking, people screaming. The fourth number he was treated to a very abusive X-rated answering-machine message. Next up was a guy who worked night shift. No bank manager, he. Then an elderly woman who claimed she was hard of hearing but was actually deaf as an India-rubber plant.

Greg lit a cigarette. He dialled eleven more wrong numbers. It was surprising how many people were home in the middle of a working day. Unemployment. A hysterical woman who'd backed her car over her daughter's pet rabbit assumed he was the veterinarian, returning her call.

"Never mind the fucking bunny," yelled Greg, losing patience. "Is your husband a fucking bank manager – yes or no?"

The woman assumed he doubted her credit rating, and matched him oath for oath.

Greg waited until the snuffling died down and said, "I heard from the woman lives across the street, owns the little black poodle, that you got a little behind, Sears had to repossess your fridge."

"What?"

Greg said, "I said I heard you had a little behind, lady. But even if it isn't true, I'll tell you this much for free – if the bunny dies, your daughter's pregnant."

And hung up. It had taken him most of the afternoon to make, let's see now, eighteen calls. He counted the M Rosses that he hadn't used his ballpoint pen to draw thin black lines through. Twenty-seven calls to go.

Greg lit another cigarette, popped the tab on a lukewarm Coke. He went over to the window and looked out at the parking lot.

There was a black stretch Lincoln down there, late-afternoon sunlight splintering off glass and chrome. As Greg stared idly down at the car, the rear door swung violently open and an anorexic blonde clutching a huge champagne bottle staggered out of the car. She tossed back her head and drank, holding the bottle with both hands, sparkling rivulets streaming over her breasts.

Greg sipped his Coke, leaned into the windowsill for a better view. A soft and careless breeze played with the blue smoke from his cigarette.

The woman lowered the bottle, lost her balance and fell against the gleaming black flank of the stretch, finally noticed Greg looking down at her. She smiled and blew him a kiss, then lost her nerve and scuttled back inside the limo. He heard laughter. The door slammed shut.

Greg went back to making cold calls, his mind full of back-seat sex and radically flattened rabbits, the sharp and salty smell of anchovies and the watery look in Tod's eyes as Greg slammed shut the lid.

The next three numbers he dialled, all he came up with was a busy signal. He flexed his dialling finger, saw that he was out of smokes.

Greg went down to the lobby and got change for the machine. He noticed that most of the brands available were American, and asked the clerk why.

The clerk shrugged. Greg said, "Maybe to avoid the taxes,

somebody makes a midnight run across the border every once in a while, huh?"

The clerk got busy with his paperwork.

Greg punched up a softpack of Camels and went back to his room. He ate a slice of cold pizza and dialled the next M Ross in the book.

A woman picked up on the third ring and Greg identified himself as Detective Tod Erickstad and said he wanted to speak to the wife of Martin Ross, the bank manager.

The woman said, "Mrs Ross died quite some time ago. I'm his daughter, Samantha. Can I help?"

Her voice was soft as a feather pillow, sticky-sweet as the world's biggest lollipop. Greg neglected to dwell on the fact that she'd offered to help, instead of merely take a message.

He asked would it be okay if he dropped by for a few minutes, he just had one or two questions he needed to ask about yesterday's hold-up. Half an hour later, the front door opened and there she was, a slim blonde with waffle-iron hair, the kind of body you usually only got to see by ripping shrink-wrap plastic off a five-dollar magazine, eyes the same deep, steady green as offshore water, a smile that'd dazzle a blind man's dog.

Greg, loping up the walk, smiled back.

She said, "Detective Erickstad?" He nodded, and she smiled again and moved away from the door to let him in.

Greg said something about appreciating her seeing him on such short notice. Then flashed his new badge at her, taking sudden unexpected pleasure in her reaction, the way those deep-water eyes widened in a kind of low-level shock. He caught a whiff of her perfume as she shut the door behind him.

The house was even larger than it had looked from the street, the spacious entrance hall dominated by twin stairs on either side that curved up to the second floor.

Greg glanced around. "Nice."

"Paul Tabler designed it for us." She saw the name didn't mean anything to him, added, "When it was built, Paul was

91

the hottest thing in residential architecture. You pretty much had to let him have a free hand, and hope you could live with whatever he built for you."

"Seems to have worked out," ventured Greg.

She gave him another one of those killer smiles and led him into the living room, which was situated to take advantage of the view of the park. It wasn't much of a park, as parks go. More like an oversized boulevard – lots of green grass and a few maple trees. Beyond the park there was an unseen drop to the beach, the Burrard Street Bridge and Coast Guard wharf; private mooring for a few hundred sailboats. Across the harbour was Sunset Beach and then the West End's picket fence of highrises.

Before parking in front of the house, Greg had driven around the block, down the lane at the back. The house was red brick, surrounded by a low red-brick wall topped with black-painted wrought-iron spikes. The building had lots of arches that led nowhere, fake turrets, a steeply pitched slate roof and a front door made of thick slabs of varnished wood. The door had a wrought-iron peephole and massive wrought-iron hinges. The security system was state-of-the-art, though, high-tech electronics and fiber optics, twenty-four digits, green and red lights, a nine-number code that offered a thirty-second response window and a direct line to a top-notch security company.

Greg made himself comfy on the sofa. Coffee for two was laid out on a silver tray. He admitted he wouldn't mind a cup, watched her closely as she bent to pour. She carried her own cup to an upholstered chair on the far side of the room, about fifteen feet away. Greg watched her hips move under her skirt.

There were cookies, too, crumbly thin wafers with white chocolate linings. He helped himself, chewed and swallowed, saw she was openly staring at him and almost wiped his fingers clean on his pants leg, remembered his napkin just in time.

She said, "I've never met a policeman before. Not a detective, I mean . . ."

"Uniforms," said Greg. "You snag a lot of traffic tickets, I bet."

"What's that, a lucky guess?"

Greg said, in a mock-official voice, "I happened to observe the shiny white Samurai in the driveway, ma'am."

She cocked her head to one side, smiled, ran her finger through that ripply hair. Her ring winked hard blue fire at him. She wore a suede skirt that was a delicate shade of green, a stone-wash black silk blouse, matched diamond earrings and a thin gold ankle chain. No shoes, or nylons or pantyhose, either. Greg's mouth suddenly felt as if it had been sponged dry.

He drank some coffee.

Samantha Ross said, "I know what you're thinking – how can a bank manager possibly afford a house like this? Am I right?"

Greg nodded, even though that hadn't been what he'd been thinking at all.

"Daddy's extremely good at handling his own money as well as everybody else's," she said. "You should see him play with a calculator. It's almost erotic."

Greg nodded solemnly.

Samantha said, "Plus my mother died in a boating accident when I was eleven years old, and there was a *lot* of insurance money." She gave him a brief, oddly twisted smile. "I was an only child. Daddy never remarried. He said he didn't see the point."

Greg said, "I'm sorry . . ."

"Me too." She looked out the window at the park for a long moment and then said, "Are you married, Detective Erickstad?"

"Call me Tod . . ."

"Are you married, Tod?"

He shook his head.

"Divorced? Separated?"

"My wife was killed by a drunk driver," Greg said. "It was a lovely spring evening, and she felt like going for a walk. She was on her way to the corner store to buy a quart of milk."

She gave him a helpless look, and said, "How awful for you, I had no idea . . ."

Greg shrugged. "It was just one of those things. We weren't getting along all that well, to tell the whole truth and nothing but."

Samantha made a soft mewing sound, of sympathy and perhaps even comradeship.

Greg hesitated. He said, "I probably shouldn't be telling you this . . ."

"No, please."

"The fact is, she was on her way to the liquor store when it happened, had gone out for a quart of vodka, not milk. And she wasn't on foot. She was in her Mustang, ran a red light. The poor bastard she hit was sober as a judge. She died instantly but he's still strapped into a wheelchair, paralyzed from the waist down."

"My God . . ."

Greg said, "It's not that I'm ashamed of her. I've come to terms with the kind of person she turned out to be. It's just that I got tired of people being sorry for me for the wrong reasons. Know what I mean?"

Samantha nodded. Her eyes were moist.

Greg shifted his weight on the sofa. "This is kind of an odd question, but my weapon's digging into my ribs – do you mind if I remove it?"

"No, please, go right ahead."

Greg slipped his hand under his jacket and came up with the stainless, laid it down on the coffee table so the barrel wasn't quite pointing at her.

She stared at the gun.

Greg said, "Look, this is kind of awkward for me, asking you questions about your father . . ."

"It's okay, go ahead."

"Well, have you noticed any change in his behavior recently?"

Samantha hesitated and then said, "How do you mean?"

94

Greg shrugged, waited. He'd been on the other side of the Q&A sheet, knew how intimidating silence could be, how the pressure built and built until that silence *had* to be broken, no matter what the risk.

She said, "He's been a bit short-tempered lately. But then . . ."

And let it sit there, the unspoken confession that her daddy was a nasty sonofabitch at the best of times.

Greg said, "Has he received any unusual phone calls recently? Especially late at night?"

Her eyes widened. "How did you know?"

"Foreign accents?" said Greg, smiling, openly having a little fun with her, showing off.

She leaned forward. Her cup rattled against the saucer. "Is my father involved in something he shouldn't be, Tod?"

The question took Greg by surprise. He was aware of the rising and falling of the silk as she breathed, the way the fragile material absorbed and deflected light. Those dark green eyes of hers were so calm, almost icily detached. As if she were ready, or even eager, to hear the worst.

How would a real cop handle a toughie like this? Greg scooped up his ·357 stainless, thoughtfully rotated the cylinder.

Click, click, click.

Her perfume swirled through his brain. Lust raked him head to toe. Then the room snapped back into focus and he was aware of her sitting next to him, only inches away, pouring him a refill, silk rustling and her fine blonde hair clean and pure as sunlight, suede sliding off a golden thigh. She returned Greg's cup to him. Their fingers briefly touched. Electricity wriggled through him like an eel.

She said, "The man with the accent, do you know what he wanted?"

Greg cleared his throat. "Beats me. A point shaved off the mortgage, maybe. It doesn't necessarily have anything to do with the robbery. I mean, I wouldn't make any assumptions."

He risked a quick look into the green depths of those

depthless eyes. There was a delicate scattering of tiny freckles across that cute little nose of hers, too, dammit. He said, "The man with the accent, how often did he call?"

"I don't know. Usually, I don't answer the phone if it rings late at night."

"Why not?"

"Daddy prefers it that way?"

"Don't you have boyfriends?"

Samantha's cheeks were pink as cherry blossoms. Had she blushed? Greg couldn't believe his eyes.

He said, "Do you have a job, or . . . what?"

"I'm a student."

Greg nodded. Was she gay? But there'd been a spark, as he'd come up the walk and they'd first locked eyes.

Samantha said, "Daddy always gets a late-night call on the first day of the month. Usually between midnight and one o'clock in the morning. He'll answer on the first ring and he hardly says a word except hello and goodbye."

Greg said, "I'm not sure I understand what you mean."

"Sometimes the calls will last half an hour or even longer, and all he'll do is listen, and take notes."

"What kind of notes?"

"Numbers."

"Numbers?"

"Rows and rows of numbers."

Greg had a sudden image of Martin Ross squirming around on the floor of the bank, his silvery hair a mess, his face bright shiny red and all puckered up like the south end of a baboon.

Samantha moved a little away from him. "What are you thinking about, Tod? Why do I get the feeling that you know a lot more than you're telling me?"

There were flecks of gold caught somewhere in the depths of green. Her eyelashes and eyebrows were thick and black. She couldn't be more than, what, twenty-one or two? Now she was staring at something that wasn't there for Greg to see, her slim, pale fingers twisting and pulling at the hem of her skirt.

After a moment Greg said, "Just between you and me, your daddy's future doesn't look too bright right now. This thing that happened at the bank, the midnight phone calls . . ."

She turned to face him more squarely. Her knee pressed up against his, and then she shifted and moved away. "What should I do?"

"Talk to him, I guess. See if you can convince him to do the right thing."

She smiled.

Greg said, "If he decides to co-operate, I'll do what I can to minimize the damage . . ."

"But if he's involved in fraud or something, he'll have to go to jail, won't he?"

Whatever she'd paid for her perfume, it was worth at least twice as much. And he was right, there'd been a spark and she'd felt it too, there was something going on in those lively, gold-flecked eyes – she was close enough to kiss and knew it. Her mouth waited for him. Or was he imagining things?

Greg shifted on the cushions and now their knees were touching again, ever so lightly. A flock of lightning bugs swirled and danced across his body. He was sweating heavily, shorting out at every pore.

He abruptly grabbed the stainless, stood up, brushed a few cookie crumbs into the palm of his hand and dumped them into his empty coffee cup.

Samantha's eyes snapped back into focus. She looked a little disoriented, surprised. She said, "You have to leave?"

Greg ducked his head. "Gotta get back to the office."

She gave him a very direct look. Straight on and holding nothing back. "Will I be hearing from you again?"

Greg said, "It's possible."

"Do you have a card . . ."

Greg flipped open Garcia Lorca Mendez's badge case, took a quick peek and snapped it shut. "Sorry, I must've run out . . ."

She brushed away a strand of hair.

Greg said, "I'm hardly ever in the office anyway . . ."

97

Now she was looking at him in a way that he'd seen many times before. A bubbling stew of pain, sadness and betrayal, stir in a pinch of anger. He recognized the look for what it was, and decided to take a chance, trust his judgement.

He said, "It's against department policy, I really shouldn't do this, but how about if I give you my home number, would that help?"

"Fuck department policy." They were both a little shocked. She gave him a crooked smile.

Greg didn't have a notebook on him, or even a pen. She disappeared into another part of the house and he heard drawers opening and closing and then she was back, a brightness in her eyes, offering him a scented writing pad decorated with lambs jumping over a split rail fence, and a heavy gold fountain pen. Greg had taught himself to write in generous, gently looping letters, rather than the cramped and impoverished style that came naturally to him. He wrote his number on the pad in green ink, added "Tod" at the bottom.

He screwed the cap back on the solid gold pen and returned the pad, at the same time slipping the pen into his shirt pocket. An automatic gesture. He couldn't say if he'd done it on purpose, or not. She folded the sheet of notepaper over and over again until it was small enough to hide in the palm of her hand.

As if it was a sudden afterthought, Greg said, "Oh yeah, one more thing?"

She waited, looking up at him, ready for anything.

Greg said, "Several departments are involved in this thing – fraud, robbery, homicide. Right now, there's a certain amount of internal squabbling going on. I don't want to step on anybody's toes . . ."

"You'd rather I didn't mention that you dropped by, is that it?"

Greg rubbed his jaw. "Well, for the time being, at least. Yeah, that'd be appreciated."

"What about Daddy?"

Greg said, "That's up to you, I guess."

She touched his arm. "Daddy's always got all kinds of secrets, and I never have any." She gave his arm a quick, conspiratorial squeeze, let go.

Greg said, "Oops!" and gave her back the pen.

She saw him to the door, didn't shut it until he was at the gate. In the car, as he was reaching behind him for the seat-belt, he glanced across the street and caught a glimpse of her standing at the window, well back from the glass, in her father's house of red brick and black iron, that looked so much like a jail.

10

Willows worked until a few minutes past midnight, drove home under the light of a full moon. The mail had been pushed through the door slot with such enthusiasm that it was spread out all over the hall. There was nothing of interest except an unexpected letter from his daughter, Annie. He tore open the envelope. There was a drawing of the view from her bedroom window and three crumpled pages scrawled in her childish hand. Willows draped his coat over the newel post. The house was cold.

He turned up the thermostat and went into the kitchen and poured himself a good three pages' worth of Cutty on the rocks, took his drink and letter into the dining room and settled down at the table to read all about Annie's new teacher, classmates, the weather in Toronto, and how terribly much she missed him.

He finished the letter, read it through a second time, refolded it, slipped it back in the envelope. It had been a long day. He hadn't eaten since lunch, but his appetite had come and gone. He made himself another drink, went into the den and turned on the television. The latest news on the deterioration of the ozone layer was not good. He turned the sound down until it was barely audible, stretched out on the couch, and soon drifted into a deep, dreamless sleep.

When the telephone in the kitchen woke him, the first thing he did was check the time – realizing as he did so that there was light enough to see by.

It was eleven minutes past seven. Willows stood up,

stretched his arms wide. His knees ached. The phone was still ringing. He hurried into the kitchen, snatched up the receiver.

"Jack?"

It was Parker. She sounded as if she'd been up for hours. Willows mumbled his reply.

Parker said, "The Sedgewick, can you find it?"

"Depends."

"Suite eighteen seventy-four," said Parker. "It's on the top floor, costs five hundred a night."

Willows, waking up fast, said, "I'm touched, but how can you afford something that expensive?"

"I can't," said Parker, "not unless they rent it by the hour. But Garcia Lorca Mendez could, and I bet he paid with cash. That's probably why he kept a machete under the bed, to protect himself from thieves."

Willows had to think about it, but not for long. The guy in the bank – he'd looked like a Garcia Lorca Mendez from head to toe.

Parker said, "You still there, Jack?"

"Give me half an hour."

Parker's voice was a low, husky whisper. "I'll leave the door off the latch, sweetie." Laughing, she hung up.

Willows shaved under the shower, towel-dried his hair and dressed in dark grey slacks, a black cableknit V-neck sweater, button-down white shirt, black leather jacket and sturdy black shoes.

His ·38 Special and speedloader were on top of the Sony. He shoved the revolver and spare rounds into his jacket pocket. Now, if only he could remember where he'd left his keys . . .

As Willows stepped on to his front porch, a fat grey squirrel bounced lightly across the lawn. As he walked towards his car, the squirrel swiftly dug a hole in the lawn and buried an acorn. Willows unlocked the Celebrity, climbed in and started the engine.

The car's windshield was smeared with dew. He turned on

the wipers and heater. The glass began to clear. He switched on the police radio, adjusted the volume.

When he put the car in gear, the squirrel spun around to face him, gave him a look that was partly inquisitive, but mostly suspicious and defiant. Willows had seen that look before. He pulled away from the curb and drove down the quiet street. The road was concrete, the huge slabs bound together with wavy black lines of tar. The early morning sun tilted at him through the gaps between the neatly tended houses. The maple trees, always the first to turn, were already shedding their leaves. Soon the gutters would be clogged with leaves and the autumn rain would overflow the sidewalks, flood basements . . .

Willows turned off the wipers. At the end of the block he braked for a *Vancouver Sun* carrier dragging a bright orange two-wheeled cart across the street. The city's three dailies were all morning papers now, each of them full of yesterday's news. The kid glanced at him, waved hello.

Willows cruised down Tenth Avenue, made a left and drove five blocks and made a right on to Fourth Avenue. Traffic thickened and slowed with each block as he headed towards the downtown core. Even the bus stops were more crowded, despite the notoriously inadequate service.

The city's downtown core is serviced by four main bridges and a number of smaller viaducts. Willows had a choice of two bridges: Burrard or Granville. The latter offered a more direct route but the Motorola was telling him there was a radar trap at the apex of the bridge, and the shiny mix of speeding Volvos, BMWs, Saabs and Jaguars had already clogged two of the three northbound lanes at the far end of the bridge.

Willows was the last car into the green at Burrard and Fourth. Three cars behind him slipped through the yellow; another ran the red.

On the Granville Street Bridge, traffic was zipping along at twice the speed limit. Willows used his siren and light to force his way into the flow. Not for the first time, it occurred to

102

him that driving in the city was like playing a video game – an unrelenting flow of unexpected and dangerous encounters. The object of the game was simple – to pass as many cars as possible while at the same time preventing anyone from passing you. Since the game was pointless, only fools liked to play. Even so, there was never a shortage of participants.

Willows took the Seymour Street exit, made a right and then a quick left. Now he was on Pacific Boulevard, a twisty section of road that, during the Labor Day weekend at the end of August, was part of the Vancouver Indy race car circuit. During the other three hundred and sixty-two days of the year, the road fed into acres of parking lots surrounding the domed stadium and Expo '86 site – the joyrides and exhibits long gone now, the grounds a drab and barren wasteland surrounded by a high chainlink fence topped with barbed wire.

But at least the grotesquely ugly McDonald's barge had finally vanished, sent kicking and screaming out to sea by an irate city council.

The stadium, with its sixty-odd thousand empty seats, was directly in front of Willows now, Coal Harbour and the last of Granville Island to his right, three- and four-story red-brick warehouses to his left. He moved into the curb lane, took the Cambie Street exit and cruised past a couple of empty parking lots and made a right on Beatty.

The hotel was built of red brick with green-painted ornamental metal trim, and had clearly been designed to fit in with the renovated strata-titled and condo-ized, earthquake-proofed warehouses that surrounded it.

Close, but no cigar.

The scale was too vast, the bricks a little too red, all the edges just a little too sharp.

Willows pulled the beige Celebrity off the street, parked under a domed roof of polished aluminum and naked lightbulbs. A two-handed man dressed like Captain Hook asked him if he could park his car. Willows flipped the sun visor so the man could read the POLICE VEHICLE plate. He

103

unzipped his leather jacket, put his hands in his pockets, and strode into the hotel.

The grey-uniformed clerks at the front desk clocked him before he was halfway to the elevators. The taller one reached for a phone. Who was up there, Jimmy Cagney?

Willows had his pick of three elevators. He chose the nearest, stepped inside and thumbed eighteen. The doors slid shut. His weight flowed towards his ankles. A few seconds later, the doors opened on a wide hallway decorated in tasteful grey and blue pastels and trimmed with the product of several acres of rain forest.

Eighteen seventy-four was off to his left, at the far end of the corridor. The door was wide open and there was a sweeping view of Coal Harbour – or would've been, if not for the broad shoulders of the uniform guarding the door.

Willows offered a quick glimpse of his badge as he brushed past him.

The suite had two bathrooms. He found Claire Parker sitting on the edge of the tub in the ensuite, searching Mendez's toiletry kit.

Parker glanced up at him, smiled. "Morning, Jack."

"Morning, Claire."

"*Pasta de dientes*, what's that sound like to you?"

Willows shrugged. Parker held up a green and white striped tube of toothpaste.

"How about this, *hoja de afeitar*?" She gave him a nice smile. "Razor-blades. The techs are in the master bedroom, hunting for prints. Mendez's passport was hidden – if that's the right word – under the mattress. Along with a couple of thousand in cash, a loaded Beretta and spare magazine, a few lines of coke and the machete."

Willows said, "Even if it was none of my business, I couldn't help wondering how Mendez managed to get to sleep at night."

"There are worse things to share your bed with."

"I'll take your word for it."

Parker dumped the razor-blades and toothpaste back in the

kitbag. She said, "There was a quart of chocolate milk and a dozen mixed donuts on the table in the dining alcove. Also a pocket calculator. The milk had soured and the donuts were stale, but the calculator's batteries were just as good as new, despite the fact that whoever'd last used it hadn't bothered to turn it off."

"And?"

"And the numbers on the screen were a five and five zeros, followed by a decimal point."

"Five hundred thousand."

"Right."

"Dollars?"

"Or calories," said Parker. "By the way, there's fresh coffee in the machine in the kitchen."

"All the comforts of home. More, in fact."

Parker stood up, moved towards him. Willows backed out of the doorway. Parker walked slowly past him, into the bedroom.

Willows said, "We call them, or did they call us?"

"The maid found the stuff under the mattress when she was changing the sheets. She called a bellhop, he called security. Security called management and you can guess the rest."

"The panic bone's connected to the cop bone."

Parker gave him an odd look. "Maybe you better have a coffee before we get rolling on this."

"I thought you'd never ask."

"Or if you're hungry, breakfast is on the house."

Willows stared at her. "You're serious, aren't you?"

Parker said, "Always."

"True enough," said Willows, smiling. He phoned room service, ordered breakfast and began to prowl around the luxurious hotel suite. There was a Panamanian passport with Mendez's photograph but somebody else's name hidden in the kitchen, taped to the back of the fridge. Under "occupation" he'd written *Policia*. Parker discovered a small quantity of cocaine hidden in a spare toilet paper roll in the bathroom.

She said, "That's a new one. Smart, too. Even if Mendez's prints were all over the roll, there's no way you could take him to court."

"We couldn't take him to court if we found a couple of kilos of Peruvian flake in his hip pocket," Willows said. "He's dead, remember?"

Parker said, "Why would he keep a machete under his bed?"

"Chopping the coke?"

"Or maybe he was taking a correspondence course – learning to be a barber."

The man who delivered Willows' scrambled eggs and toast was in his mid-fifties, wore a grey three-piece silk suit, pale blue shirt and a splashy tie. He peered at Willows through tinted glasses as he placed the tray on the table at the foot of the bed, offered his hand.

"Edward Mullholland, the hotel manager. Security informs me that Mr Mendez had a perfectly valid reason for failing to keep his account up to date."

Willows introduced himself, Parker. He said, "Had Mendez stayed at the hotel before this, Mr Mullholland?"

The manager nodded. "He was a regular, for the past three years he phoned from Panama and made a reservation every three months. Always for this suite. He usually stayed with us for one or two nights, never more than three."

"What can you tell us about him?"

"Not much, really. In this business, it doesn't pay to be too inquisitive." Mullholland's eyes strayed to Parker, back to Willows. "I believe Mr Mendez mentioned that he was in the business of purchasing farm machinery. Let me see, what else can I tell you . . . He dressed well, his English was more than adequate. Oh yes, one other thing – he always arrived in a limo."

Willows drained his glass of fresh-squeezed orange juice, poured himself a cup of coffee, sprinkled a little pepper on his eggs, dug in.

"Everything all right?"

106

Willows nodded, his mouth full. The manager seemed genuinely concerned.

Parker said, "Did Mr Mendez ever meet anyone here, at the hotel?"

Mullholland hesitated. "How do you mean?"

Willows swallowed and said, "What she means is – did Mendez ever meet anyone at the hotel."

"No, he didn't."

"Did anyone *accompany* him to the hotel?"

"This is a very large hotel, Detective Willows. As you can well imagine, people come and go. It would be impossible for us to keep track of all our guests, even if we wanted to."

Willows glanced at Parker. They waited.

Mullholland said, "However, there was a young woman who usually stayed with him whenever he was in town . . ."

"What's her name?"

"I'm afraid I don't know."

Parker said, "What did she look like?"

"Well, let me think. She was young, in her early twenties. A blonde, very attractive . . ."

Parker wrote it all down, and by the time Mullholland ran out of steam she had, although she wasn't aware of it, a fairly accurate description of Samantha Ross.

Willows said, "But you don't know her name, never heard Mendez speak to her . . ."

"No, I'm afraid not. Mr Mendez wasn't the type who loitered in the lobby, or cared to make small talk with the staff."

"You'd have records, wouldn't you, of outgoing phone calls he made during the past few days?"

"He never used the telephones provided in the suite. He may have used one of the pay phones in the lobby, but I never saw him do so."

Parker said, "How many times has Mendez stayed at the hotel, altogether?"

"Eleven."

"And your records indicate that he never once used the telephone?"

"That's correct."

"What about incoming calls?"

"I'm afraid we don't keep a record of calls directed *to* the hotel, unless the caller leaves a message with the switchboard."

Parker nodded. She said, "Jack, can you think of anything else?"

Willows shook his head, dug a card out of his wallet, handed it to Mullholland.

Parker said, "If you happen to think of anything, no matter how insignificant it may seem, please call us right away, all right?"

"Yes, certainly."

Parker helped herself to a triangle of whole wheat toast from Willows' tray. "If you don't mind, we'll just poke around a little while longer and then be on our way."

"Fine, certainly."

Parker waited until the uniform at the door had let Mullholland out, and then turned to Willows and said, "What d'you think?"

Willows said, "No question, it's the best blackberry jam I've had in my life. No preservatives. Better try some, before it goes off."

"I mean about Mullholland."

"By the time you'd finished with him he looked like he got an eye transplant from a cocker spaniel."

Parker gave Willows an exasperated look. "I mean, what do you think of him as a source of information?"

"As a source of information, he's the very soul of discretion. Does a pretty fair bellhop, though."

Parker nodded in agreement, but her mind was on the bed. She'd thought king-size was as big as they got; the one Mendez had hidden his guns and drugs and money under was half again as wide. What kind of person always used limos instead of taxis, and slept with a machete under the mattress? The suite's refrigerator had been stuffed full of liter bottles of champagne. A dozen identical off-white linen suits, all of

108

them brand new, hung in the closet. There was also a shopping bag full of unopened gift boxes of women's silk underwear in the closet, with receipts totalling over a thousand dollars.

Parker glanced through the bedroom doorway, saw that the cop at the door had his nose between the covers of one of the suite's complimentary magazines – *Vanity Fair*. She kicked off her shoes and stretched out on the bed, spread her arms wide and couldn't reach the sides.

Willows wiped his mouth with a linen napkin.

Parker gave him a saucy smile. "What do you think?" Before Willows could respond, she said, "I mean about Mendez."

Willows held the used napkin aloft, as if to perform a magic trick. He said, "Looks as if he might've been in the laundry business."

"Funnelling drug money through Martin Ross."

Willows balled up the napkin and tossing it on the serving tray, nodded.

Parker said, "Mendez flies into town, gets rid of the cash. He and his girlfriend spend a couple of days celebrating – drinking champagne, shopping, drinking some more champagne." She slipped a goose-down pillow under her head. "It's a rotten job, but I guess somebody has to do it."

Willows said, "The thing is, where's his return ticket?"

"Somewhere else," said Parker, "I can tell you that much because I know it isn't here."

Willows said, "Maybe he didn't have a return ticket. Maybe this time he didn't plan on going back."

Parker closed her eyes. With every step you took, the perspective changed, the situation was altered. If Mendez had planned a cash withdrawal of half a million dollars, Martin Ross would certainly have known about it, if he was involved. Maybe Ross didn't want Mendez to empty the accounts – or maybe Ross had abused his powers of office and spent the money. So he had Mendez killed. No, that wasn't possible. The shooting in the bank was just bad luck.

But it was time they had another talk with Ross. Do it at 312 Main this time, maybe.

The bed was very comfortable, the mattress not too soft and not too firm. Parker opened her eyes.

Willows quickly looked away.

11

Martin Ross hit the remote and the iron gates to his driveway swung wide. A hinge creaked ominously but Ross couldn't hear anything over the sound of the radio and the steady *whoosh* of the Imperial's climate control system, which had turned the car into a refrigerator on wheels but had failed to lower his sweat production by so much as a single drop. His handkerchief was drenched. When he wiped his forehead it felt slushy.

The gates swung shut behind him. The garage door gaped open. He eased the big car inside, past Samantha's white four-wheel drive Samurai, her motorcycle – thank God that phase was over – her skis, her snowboard, the thousand-dollar mountain bike that she rode around the block the day she bought it, but hadn't used since. It felt like he was parking in somebody's sporting goods department, rather than his own garage.

He got out of the car, triggered the alarm, checked the door to make sure it was locked.

Music from somewhere deep inside the house thumped against him, seemed to push him back. Then the sound died and a silence fell upon him. She must have seen the car turn in off the street, he supposed. He became aware of an irregular ticking sound coming from under the hood, a sound like the last few seconds in the life of a bomb. He knew it was only the engine cooling down, metal contracting. But even so, he had to lean against the Chrysler's fender for a moment, while he struggled to get himself under control.

He made his way around the car, climbed the short flight of stairs to the door that led to the laundry room and then the kitchen.

Samantha was there to greet him, help him off with his jacket, loosen his tie. A little more than twenty-four hours had passed since the hold-up, but it was clear to her that he was still suffering the after-effects of the shock and strain.

Was he all right? He nodded, gave her a reassuring smile. She gave him a doubting look, then reached up and dragged a fingertip across his forehead. Did he have a temperature? He told her he was just fine and dandy. She told him supper was ready, hesitated, and then asked him if he wanted to take a shower before he ate.

She was wearing black again, a tight black sleeveless T-shirt, tight black jeans and a wide black leather belt, black running shoes with the laces removed. He hated it when she wore black. Worse, he'd once made the mistake of telling her how he felt.

He said, "Do I *need* a shower?"

"You certainly do. Want me to run the water for you?"

"No, honey, I don't."

Samantha followed her father out of the kitchen and up the stairs to the second floor, along the hall as far as the bedroom door. It was the first time she'd had a chance to talk to him since the robbery, and she pelted him with questions. The radio had said an innocent bystander had been shot dead, but on television they said there'd actually been a shoot-out between the bank robber and the victim. What was the truth? Ross said he didn't want to talk about it. He told her she knew as much as he did, maybe more.

When he came downstairs, supper was waiting for him. Samantha had opened a bottle of red wine. She filled his glass to the brim, but barely wet the bottom of her own glass.

Ross chewed, swallowed, chewed, swallowed.

Samantha said, "Like it?"

"Excellent."

"It's boeuf bourgignon."

112

"So I noticed."

"I cooked it myself. In the microwave."

"Very impressive."

"Wait'll you see dessert."

"I can hardly wait."

Samantha toyed with her food. If she ever actually ate anything, it wasn't in his presence. She said, "I had a visitor this afternoon."

Ross stared at her. She sipped at her wine, licked her lips. Finally he said, "Anyone I know?"

"Possibly."

Something liquid and glittering fell into his plate. He glanced up, at the crystal chandelier suspended above the table.

Samantha said, "You're sweating again. Are you sure you're okay?"

"I told you, I'm fine."

"Do you want me to get a thermometer?"

Ross pushed the food away. He said, "Who was it? Who was here?"

She smiled. "I think it's about time you told me about the robbery."

"Samantha . . ."

She cocked her head. "Yes, Daddy?"

Samantha had been in bed, asleep, by the time he'd gotten home the night of the robbery, and she'd still been sleeping when he'd gone back to work that morning. She'd phoned him at the office after watching a report about the hold-up on television, but he'd told her he didn't have time to talk and quickly disconnected. Now he said, "I don't have much I can tell you, I'm afraid. By the time I realized something was going on, it was all over." He leaned back in his chair. The boeuf bourgignon had a glazed look, as if it had been sprayed with liquid plastic.

"You didn't see *anything*?"

"A lot of unhappy people, but that's about it."

"Did you see the robber?"

113

"The police think he was wearing a disguise, some sort of mask, or theatrical makeup."

"Is it true that a man was killed?"

"Yes."

Samantha picked at her food, moving it about on her plate. Her next question caught Ross by surprise. "Do you know any police detectives?"

Ross smiled. "I met quite a few yesterday, let me tell you."

"This one was fairly tall, medium build, dark wavy hair combed straight back . . ."

Ross shook his head. "Doesn't ring any bells."

"He said his name was Erickstad. He had a badge, but I didn't get a very good look at it. I don't know what it was about him, but somehow he didn't seem . . ." Samantha hesitated, then said, "*authentic*."

Ross pushed his plate a little further away, leaned forward. "I don't understand. What do you mean?"

"After he left, I phoned the police department and asked to speak to him and they told me there was nobody by that name on the force."

Ross saw that his wine glass was empty, managed to pour himself a refill.

Samantha said, "On TV today they said the victim's identity is still unknown."

Ross got most of the wine down, but his hands were unsteady, and he spilled a little.

She said, "But we know who he is, don't we?"

Ross's stomach felt as if he'd swallowed a ferris wheel. The wheel spun faster and faster, spun him back to the first time he'd met Garcia Lorca Mendez in person, the ride Mendez had given him across town in a borrowed stretch limo to a steam vent tucked away in the shadows of an eastside viaduct. The wheel kept spinning and he saw the Panamanian reach down and haul a derelict out of his cocoon of scrap foam and bits of cardboard, drag him moaning and crying down a concrete slope into an open area below the viaduct, shove the man's arm up against a concrete pillar, the machete glide up

114

into the light and the derelict's mouth open in a toothless scream . . .

Steel striking sparks off concrete.

"*Muy bonita*," said Mendez. "One chop, eh? Off she comes." He studied the machete's blade, rubbed the ball of his thumb across a nick in the polished steel. High above them, traffic thundered across the viaduct. Mendez cocked his head, listening, then glanced at the derelict, who had either fainted or died, and now lay on his side on the filthy concrete. "He's only a bum, but you gotta admit he handle the situation pretty good, huh?"

Mendez slapped the banker with the flat of the blade, left a smear of blood on his cheek. "Look at him!"

Ross stole a quick peek, turned away and lost his supper.

Mendez's eyes glittered, his teeth shone bright. He said, "You wanna congratulate him, shake his hand?"

Ross spat, used the sleeve of his jacket to wipe clean his mouth. Mendez flicked the machete clattering into the night. "No? Well, maybe you change your mind, wanna do it later. *So here, take it with you.*"

Laughing maniacally, Mendez stuffed the amputated hand into the breast pocket of the banker's suit.

The ferris wheel shattered, and flew apart. Chunks of hot metal rose up in Martin Ross's throat. In those days it had just been him and Mendez. Ten per cent and ninety. Then Samantha had found out what was going on, volunteered for a piece of the action.

The banker knocked over his chair as he pushed to his feet. Thrusting his napkin between his teeth, he ran for the bathroom at the far end of the hall.

115

12

Greg owned – although the car was registered in a dead man's name – a late model dark blue Pontiac, a four-door model with a V-8 engine and blackwall tires, tiny no-nonsense hub-caps. The Pontiac vaguely resembled an unmarked police vehicle and so yielded him a measure of respect on the road.

Driving was about the only thing, except for robbing banks and breaking hearts, that Greg did with any degree of caution or sense of restraint. The rest of his life was pretty spon-taneous. He had been subject to whimsical behavior ever since grade school. His mother once told him that he was like a human microscope – in and out of focus in the blink of an eye. Now that he was an adult, opportunities to indulge him-self came thick and fast. For example he'd seen a picture in a magazine of a beat-up boxer, a man who'd been a punching bag all his life, and was instantly *inspired*.

In his time, as well as being a failed boxer, he'd stepped into the role of busted-up rodeo rider, postman. Once he'd spent an entire day making himself up to look exactly like the famous author Norman Mailer, but since nobody'd ID'd him, the effort was wasted. He'd also been a one-armed man and a blind man, a beggar man and a man all covered in warts big as marbles. He had even dabbled in cross-dressing once or twice.

But one thing he'd never done, he'd never walked a mile in the size thirteen shoes of a cop. So it was kind of interesting, a major power surge, when he'd discovered how easy it was to flash the badge and a smile and pass himself off as a detective. The way Samantha Ross's eyes had lit up when he identified himself was amazing. Cops were always getting into woman trouble. No wonder.

There was something about Samantha Ross's behavior that scratched at him, though. In retrospect, it seemed as if she'd told him an awful lot about herself and her daddy that he hadn't quite gotten around to asking. And not all of it was good. It was almost as if she had it in for her father.

Slouched behind the Pontiac's wheel, Greg cruised the neighborhood, let his high beams rake the shrubbery and interiors of parked cars while he peered through the windshield looking for ERT guys all dolled up in black balaclavas, stun grenades and automatic weapons. After a while he decided that if they were out there, they were buried too deep to crawl out in time to catch him, should he make an appearance. He pulled up to the curb opposite his apartment, and used his cellular to phone home. The machine invited him to leave a message. He said, "I know you're listening, Greg. Quit fooling around and pick up, or I'm gonna come over there and beat you senseless!"

No response, but what did he expect? He hung up and drove around until he lucked out and found a parking spot big enough to wedge the Pontiac into, locked the car and walked back to his apartment, cutting through the park across the street to save time.

There were no cops lurking in the park, or on the boulevard.

There were no cops in the lobby. Or loitering in the elevator or in the hall.

Greg put his ear against his apartment door. What a kick it must be, to pull your gun and tin shield and kick in, having no idea what was on the other side. Or maybe it was just plain scary. He was tempted to trash his own door, just to see what it felt like. But if he was going to kick in someone's door, it made more sense to save his boots for Hilary. He'd invested a lot of time in that girl's cheating heart.

He turned the key, pushed open the door. Marilyn chirped

twice, to draw his attention, and then turned her cute little feathered rump towards him. If she was a little put out, he didn't blame her. It couldn't be all that much fun, trying to get a good night's sleep with her cage uncovered and the streetlight coming in through the window. No wonder she was pissed off. He shut the door and shot the bolt, went into the kitchen nook and opened a pack of salt crackers. Marilyn saw what he was up to and trilled excitedly, forgiving all.

Greg leaned against the kitchen counter and watched the canary burn off tension hopping from the low perch up to the high perch and back to the low perch again, and so on. As a pet, she was a long way from perfect. But he had to admit she had an impressively short attention span. He went over to the cage, ate most of the cracker while she stared at him, beady-eyed and ravenous, then stuck the last piece between his teeth, steadied the cage with both hands and pressed his face against the chrome bars.

Marilyn immediately hopped up on the bridge of his nose, snatched at the cracker with her beak. Greg bared his teeth, snarled like a pit bull and held on tight. The bird's tiny claws scrabbled across his nose, dug into the flesh. Her beak closed on the cracker again.

Greg growled low in his throat, then let go.

He checked his answering machine. Hilary wanted him to know that unless Randy got his handcuffs back he was going to break . . .

There was a sudden silence, dead air broken only by the hiss of the tape, as if someone had clamped a hand over the phone. Break *what*, wondered Greg, *wind*? Then Randy was speaking to him, assuring Greg that their little tussle was water under the bridge but he wanted the Polaroids back, since they were kind of personal.

Greg moved on to the next message. It was the pet food store, they were having a sale on wild bird seed and thought he might be interested.

Next message.

Samantha. Checking to make sure he'd really given her his home phone number. Click.

Greg lit a cigarette, went into the kitchen and got himself a beer out of the fridge. He sipped at the beer while he peeled and sliced two large potatoes, dropped them in a stainless steel pot of lightly salted water and cranked up the heat. He watched the water until it boiled, then trimmed every last scrap of fat from a six-ounce T-bone, heated a frying pan until his spit bounced, and slapped down the meat. In the crisper there was a head of Romaine, a fat red tomato and most of a green pepper. He washed and dried the lettuce, quartered the tomato, paused to turn the steak and then cut the green pepper into ribbons, diced half an onion and chucked everything into a clear glass bowl, added a spoonful of Paul Newman salad dressing.

By now the potatoes needed mashing. He lowered the heat under the frying pan, drained the pot and pounded the spuds into fluff, then cracked another beer and set the table for one, lining up the stolen hotel cutlery just so.

While he ate, Greg tried to figure out how to deal with Martin Ross. If Ross was laundering drug money for Mendez, or people Mendez was working for, it wouldn't take the cops too long to bust his ass. Then the money would be gone forever, seized and swallowed whole by government gluttons.

He also had Mendez's employers to consider, unless it turned out he was a one-man show. How long would it take for the bad news to make it to head office, and then what? He imagined that drug lords must be a fairly pragmatic bunch of guys. They'd shrug off their losses, personnel and financial-wise, and move on to something else. What else could they do – take a quickie Berlitz immersion course in English followed by a midnight parachute drop into the city?

Greg ate some potatoes, carefully cut the steak away from the bone. His molars exploded a radish.

What about going over to the house, holding Samantha hostage while Ross made some heavy cash withdrawals?

He cut the chunk of meat into squares and triangles, pushed

119

the odd-shaped fragments to one side of his plate and stabbed down with his fork. The tines pierced the meat and rang against the plate.

Marilyn thought he was being musical and tried to form a duet.

Greg yelled, "Shadup!"

Playing the hostage game with Samantha could be lots of fun. She'd had a certain look in her eyes – Randy's handcuffs might be a popular item . . .

On the other hand, giving her his telephone number had been an amazingly dimwit thing to do, a real bonehead play. But as long as she believed he was a cop, he'd be okay.

Until she told some other cop about him.

But there were more than a thousand cops on the VPD – no way they'd all know each other.

Greg knocked back his T-bone, his jaws single-minded and relentless, rising and falling in a savage, graceful rhythm that soon emptied his plate. As he ate, Marilyn fluttered restlessly in her cage, watched him with dark and glittery, unintelligent eyes.

Snatching Samantha and using her as a hostage wasn't such a great idea because – Greg kept thinking about it as he stole another beer from the fridge – if her banker daddy decided *his* bottom line was more important than *her* bottom line, all he had to do was dial 911 and it'd be game over. Cops, tear gas and tears. Judgement.

But what if he made a date with her, treated her to a romantic weekend at a surprise destination, some sleazy out-of-town motel, and she had no idea what he was up to? Once he'd spirited her away, all he had to do was phone daddy and make it clear that if he didn't cough up Garcia Lorca Mendez's dough, he'd never see his daughter again.

Kind of a vague plan, Greg.

How much money, for example? Greg had studied the briefcase full of spreadsheets until his head was stuffed with every number you could think of, and all he'd had to show for his labours was double vision and a powerful thirst. Also, whatever amount he demanded, ten grand or a cool million, how would he arrange safe delivery?

What he liked about banks, it was nice and simple, a steak-and-potatoes kind of thing. You walked in, grabbed the cash and turned around and walked out.

Greg washed and dried the dishes, snatched another beer out of the fridge. He went into the living room and turned on the television, tuned in the channel that told you what time it was.

It was 9:17:32, and moving right along, one second at a time. Greg flipped through to TSN, the sports network. He stretched out on the sofa and watched race cars that looked like toys drive around and around and around. The cars were painted in bright primary colors and plastered with advertising decals. Flame shot from their exhaust pipes. The tires were fat and the cockpits were tiny. Every so often there was a closeup of a helmet and a pair of goggles, but there might have been poodles tucked in there behind those windshields, and he'd never have been able to tell the difference. There was very little sense of speed. Once in a while a driver would miscalculate and smash into another car or a concrete wall, but other than that, it was kind of boring.

Greg's eyes began to glaze over. He fetched himself another beer and a clean ashtray. The cars droned around the circuit, white noise. There was no chance he'd fall asleep in his chair and set himself on fire, however, since he couldn't get all that money out of his mind. Buckets of cash that were gathering dust in a vault somewhere and didn't belong to anybody, really.

He had a vision of himself strolling out of the house of red bricks and wrought iron, the shiny black briefcase stuffed with hundred dollar bills, Samantha running after him, wanting to be with him . . .

The television cried out. Greg's eyes snapped open in time to watch the instant replay as a glossy blue car suddenly became airborne, touched down hard and rolled. A wheel broke loose. Chunks of shiny blue metal danced across the asphalt, and then the car suddenly vanished in a huge orange fireball laced with black . . .

Greg said, "Holy shit!"

And found himself staring at a smiling babe who looked an awful lot like Hilary, and was crazy about her boyfriend because of his choice of aftershave.

He turned off the TV and went hunting for another beer, discovered he'd killed them all and broke open a bottle of rye whiskey, ice from the freezer.

Driving formula one race cars and robbing banks were both risky businesses. But the glossy blue car wouldn't have turned into a fireball if the driver hadn't been in such a hurry.

Greg leaned against the sink. Maybe he was better off sticking to bank robbery. Maybe he ought to forget all about his ambition to get rich quick. Maybe the smart thing to do was forget about robbing and stealing altogether, take early retirement. He drank some rye, found himself remembering his first bank. The teller's name was Lesley. She had soft brown eyes and mouse-brown hair with a wide streak of white in it, that she could not explain. He learned on their first date that she had a weakness for witchcraft, black magic. He was just starting out, and lacked confidence, so he put up with her weirdness, the incense and pentagrams, candle wax on his best pair of pants.

The original idea had been to seduce her, sweet-talk her into committing major bank fraud. Then grab the money and abandon the honey. It hadn't worked out that way, though. That first heist had been an accident, pure and simple. He was supposed to meet Lesley for lunch. Just for laughs, he'd showed up wearing a false mustache and a cheap wig. Walked up to her wicket and said, *This is a stick-up* in a low, growly voice. Her face had gone white as that witchy streak of hair. Without a word, she'd emptied her cash drawer on the counter. He stood there, struck dumb, waiting for her to look at him, but the best she could manage was to look right through him.

It struck him then how frightened she must be. And that

he was being filmed, that she might have activated the silent alarm and that he better get the hell out of there.

Ten minutes later, the wig and mustache stuffed down a sewer grate and the cash locked away in the trunk of his car, he'd driven back to the bank with an apologetic look on his face, late for lunch and sorry about it. A uniformed cop at the door had held him back but promised to deliver the message. That first heist, he'd grossed over two thousand dollars. Not bad, when all he'd hoped to get for his trouble was a look of shock, and a laugh.

But it was a real kick, listening to Lesley, between sudden gusts of tears, describe to him in great detail how the robbery went down and how terrified she'd been. For a week or two, the hold-up was all she wanted to talk about. He was an avid listener. She started seeing a therapist, and told him about that, too.

Fascinating stuff.

But then he happened to meet a woman named Bobbi who had sparky green eyes and bleached-blonde hair, lived to ski and smoke dope and supported her vices by working at a seven-wicket credit union.

Greg chewed on an ice cube, realized the only reason he was doing it was because he'd drained his glass. He reached for the bottle, almost knocked it over, unscrewed the metal cap and poured himself a really stiff one.

Bobbi had been a lot of fun, full of vim and vinegar. He walked into her bank wearing a latex skull cap, bushy false eyebrows, bags under his eyes, used glasses bought for a couple of dollars from the Salvation Army, a brand-new nose and a slab of foam that he'd stuffed between his shoulder-blades, a pair of elevator shoes that added three inches to his height and made him walk with a two-legged limp. If he'd been a donkey they'd have shot him. Might do it anyway. He grinned, wiped rye from his chin. He'd hobbled into the bank looking, he hoped, like Peter Lorre after a growth spurt.

Bobbi listened to his sales pitch, blinked twice and slid

123

open her cash drawer, pulled a twenty and told him to scram or she'd call the cops. No, really.

Then, when he'd dropped by her apartment that night, looked him straight in the eye and said exactly the same thing, in exactly the same tone of voice.

Scram, or I'll call the cops.

Greg touched up his drink and went into the bedroom, put his glass down on the bureau and yanked open the top drawer. He had a picture of Bobbi tucked away in there, a silver-framed shot he'd taken down by the beach, at English Bay. Bobbi with her wet hair combed back and off to the side, squinting good-naturedly into the sunlight, hands on her hips. She was wearing a pink two-piece that still made him want to look everywhere at once.

Searching for the picture, Greg pushed aside a pair of grey socks that felt particularly heavy. He gave them a shake and a ·22 calibre Bumblebee Pocket Partner fell into his open palm.

He nipped at the rye, tried to remember where the little gun had come from. A bar in Yakima, Washington. He'd gone down there with some woman . . .

And then he was off and running again, remembering another bank, another whirlwind romance, another heist and another betrayal. What was *wrong* with him, anyway? He sank a mouthful of rye, peered hazily at the level of liquid in the glass, then slammed it down on the bureau and pulled the Bumblebee's slide back half an inch, until he could see the tarnished wink of brass verifying that there was a round up the pipe.

He shoved the gun in his pants pocket and resumed rooting around in the drawer. His clumsy fingers bumped up against cold glass. There she was, he had her now. He tilted the frame to minimize the glare of light from the ceiling fixture. Bobbi smiled up at him as if she didn't have a care in the world, no regrets.

Greg said, "Hey, quit *looking* at me like that!"

Bobbi's smile didn't falter. When he'd asked her to pose

124

for the snap she'd pushed her sunglasses high up on her head, into her hair. The lenses, pointing almost straight up, reflected two perfect burning yellow suns.

Greg lost his balance and lurched sideways, rattled the mini-blinds as he fought to regain his balance. He studied her eyes and her hair and the curve of her lips, the tanned skin and blue sky and tight pink bikini, how all the pastel colors and curving lines came gracefully together and slipped away.

He felt the hot, salty tears rise up in his eyes and spill down his cheeks. He'd completely forgotten about the sunglasses and probably a lot of other stuff as well, meaningful details, unbearably sweet moments.

The worst part, of course, was that there was no way of knowing what he'd lost.

The phone rang, a soft and melodic warbling that he liked to believe drove Marilyn half-crazy with jealousy.

He stumbled over to the unmade bed, let himself fall across it, a spring creaking under his weight. Snatched at the phone.

Someone said, "Is that you?"

It was as if he'd been lying face-up far below the dark surface of a still-water pond, and a sudden gust of wind had unexpectedly swept aside all the small green things that grew upon the surface. Despite the booze, his mind was clear. He could see forever, even beyond the horizon.

He said, "Bobbi?"

But it was too late – whoever he was talking to had already hung up.

13

Eddy Orwell extended his muscular arm, locked his elbow, aimed carefully and squeezed the trigger. A fine spray of Windex pebbled the rectangle of glass, frosted the anodized aluminum frame. He put the plastic bottle down on his desk and wiped the glass clean with a paper towel stolen from the washroom.

Eddy Jr beamed up at him. The kid didn't have any teeth and he was a little out of focus, but he sure had a nice smile.

Farley Spears, peering over Orwell's brawny shoulder, said, "His eyes are set even closer together than yours, Eddy. You must be proud, huh?"

"Piss off," said Orwell, not looking up. His desk was cluttered with five framed snapshots of his newborn son, two more of his wife and child together. Every morning, Eddy fouled the air with the vinegary smell of window-cleaner as he sprayed and wiped clean each of the photographs in turn. The daily ritual ate up at least fifteen minutes of his time. The other detectives had found his antics amusing, at first. After a few weeks, though, Orwell's mindlessly cheerful routine started to get to them. When Spears suggested that someone fill the Windex bottle with urine stained blue with vegetable dye, nobody volunteered. But nobody vetoed the idea either.

Eddy picked up another picture. Gazing fondly down at it, he reached for the Windex bottle.

Parker said, "Eddy, would you mind pointing that in another direction?"

126

"It bothers you?"

"Just a little."

Orwell said, "You oughta be ashamed of yourself."

Willows abandoned his paperwork, leaned back in his chair, smiled at Parker. Dan Oikawa stopped sharpening his pencil. Spears said, "Why is that, Eddy?"

"Ask yourself a simple question – what's wrong with a father having a little pride in his family?"

Parker said, "That isn't the issue."

"Yeah?" Orwell's blue eyes focused on Willows' desk, the dusty school photographs of Sean and Annie squeezed together in a single frame.

Oikawa said, "Air pollution's what we're concerned about, Eddy. Not filial love."

"That's your story, huh? Well then, you'd better stick with it, hadn't you?"

Smiling moodily, Oikawa finished grinding his pencil to a needle-sharp point.

Linda, one of two civilian secretaries who worked the squadroom, walked briskly up to Willows and handed him a sheaf of flimsies. A lengthy fax. He thanked her, glanced at the top page. Parker was watching him. He said, "Colón finally got back to us. In English, too."

According to the fax, Garcia Lorca Mendez was born 18-11-48. He'd been with the Colón police department since 1970, served the past five years as a sergeant in the drug squad. During his career as a police officer, he'd been promoted regularly and received three citations for meritorious conduct. He had been shot once, during a drug raid. He had been on an official leave of absence at the time of his death. His reason for travelling to Vancouver was to attend the funeral of a younger sister. He was survived by a wife and five children.

Parker, indicating the printout, said, "Did they give us the sister's name and address?"

"Sure did."

Orwell said, "Five kids. Jeez."

127

"It must've taken him half his shift to Windex all those pictures," said Spears.

Nodding, Oikawa said, "Hard to imagine how he found time to get any work done, isn't it?"

Orwell gave him a sour look.

Willows said, "She lives on Fraser, the six hundred block. Her married name is Springway."

"Is there a phone number?"

Willows shook his head, no.

"Kind of an unusual name. Can't be that many in the book."

"Probably not."

Parker had spent most of that morning since getting back to the squadroom on the phone, laboriously working her way through the more than fifty limousine services listed in the yellow pages. Her ear needed a break. She said, "Your turn, Jack."

Willows bent to yank open the bottom drawer of his desk, pulled out the Metro phone book.

There were only three listings for Springway, none of them on Fraser Street. The deceased sister's first name was Maria. Willows started dialling. No one answered his first call; the second and third were wrong numbers. He shoved the phone book back in his desk drawer. "Let's drive out there, see if anybody's home."

"Or if they're all at the funeral. Any instructions from Panama regarding the disposal of Mendez's body?"

"The family wants it shipped home."

"Who's paying the freight?"

"Not me, I'll tell you that much."

Parker said, "I'm going to sign out a car. I'll meet you out front in about ten minutes."

Willows, concentrating on his paperwork, nodded but didn't look up. It appeared that the prosecutor's office was prepared to accept Karen "Honey" Wallace's defense of reasonable force in the stabbing to death of her pimp, Chet Russell. The autopsy had determined that the night clerk, Wendell Sharp, had died of asphyxiation, and that the various injuries he'd sustained were consistent with the circumstances of his death. An inquest determined that he'd leapt from the Rialto's window of his own accord. Honey was going to walk.

Parker signed a pale green Ford out of the car pool, drove around to the front of the building. Willows was waiting for her, climbed into the car. Parker headed up Main to King Edward and made a left.

Willows glanced at her, back out the window. "Where are you going?"

"Six thirty-five Fraser, right?"

"Should've stayed on Main."

Parker said, "This way I can make a left on Fraser and we can park right in front of the house, don't have to cross the street."

Willows nodded thoughtfully. "That's important to you, is it?"

"That's a busy street, Jack. Four lanes, it's a miniature freeway, and you can walk a mile before you find a marked crosswalk."

Willows said, "Why is that?"

Parker said, "Because of the graveyard. It's fenced all the way around, the only way in is via four or five access roads . . ." She gripped the steering wheel so hard her knuckles showed white. "Dead sister's funeral, my ass."

Willows narrowed his eyes against the sun as they turned a corner. They drove past a gap in the cypress hedge that surrounded the graveyard, open black iron gates that framed a view of a narrow asphalt road and close-cut lawns that gently rose and fell, slabs of stone and rare bright splashes of wreathed flowers.

Parker scanned the house addresses on the far side of the street. "How're we doing – we must be getting close . . ."

Willows said, "Pull in behind that blue pickup."

Parker eased her foot off the gas, pulled up against the curb. The pickup's tailgate was down, and the bed was hidden in soft drifts of fine grey sand. She turned off the ignition, dropped the keys in her purse, checked the side mirror for traffic, and pushed open her door.

635 Fraser was a squat cinderblock building with a flat tar-and-gravel roof, iron-barred dusty plate-glass windows and a rusting sheet-metal door. A small sign, faded black letters on a grey background, hanging over the door said, *Terminal City Memorials Ltd Est 1943*.

Willows said, "Is this what's called getting the last laugh?" He tried the door. It wasn't locked.

Inside, the air was cool and dim, and the film of dust on the window bled all the color out of the long, narrow room.

A heavy workbench ran the length of the far wall. On the bench there was a heavy-duty upright drill press and a number of smaller power tools whose purpose Willows was unfamiliar with and could not easily divine. A thin layer of fine grey dust covered everything except the man slouched in a wooden captain's chair near the rear door.

The man was short, muscular, balding. He wore a grey sweatshirt, faded black pants, heavy black boots, glasses with black plastic frames. His pants were smeared with dust. His worn boot heels rested upon a slab of polished granite. A hand-rolled cigarette dangled limply from a corner of his mouth, and a twisted worm of smoke crawled slowly up the side of his face and was swallowed in the greyness of the air.

Willows said, "Mr Springway?"

The man's head tilted towards them. He coughed. Ash fell from the cigarette, exploded on his chest. Willows realized he'd been caught napping. The man's eyes were a soft, milky blue.

"Mr Springway?"

The man stretched, yawned, lifted a booted foot and scratched his leg. He picked up a power drill, squeezed the trigger. The drill's motor whined shrilly and the sharply pointed bit spun so fast it was a blur. "Who's asking?"

Willows showed Springway his badge.

Parker saw that the slab of polished granite was a blank

130

headstone, realized that the drifts of grey dust were powdered stone carved from monuments to the dead.

Willows said, "Are you married, Mr Springway?"

The milky-blue eyes were calm, but the cigarette-end glowed brightly. Springway exhaled a stream of smoke, coughed. "Yeah, I'm married. Kind of." His voice was soft, barely audible, as if his lungs and throat were clogged with the grey dust that lay everywhere, covered everything.

Willows said, "Is your wife's maiden name Mendez?"

Springway nodded. He removed his glasses and wiped the lenses on the grey sweatshirt, put the glasses back on and took another look at Parker. "You're a cop too, right?"

Parker admitted it.

Springway said, "You want to know about her brother, is that it?"

"Garcia Lorca Mendez."

"Nice guy. I saw on TV what happened to him, that he was killed in that bank hold-up. What a rotten break."

Parker said, "Why didn't you get in touch with us, Mr Springway?"

"Too damn busy."

Willows, indicating the workbench and machinery with a sweep of his arm, said, "Carving headstones, is that what you do for a living?"

Springway laughed harshly, fumbled the cigarette out of his mouth, coughed, spat into the dust. "There's no hand-work done anymore. Used to be, but not any more. I got an office over on Commercial – a sample book like if you were looking for wallpaper. All I do is take the order, farm it out to a company in Burnaby. They got standard-size slabs, machines you wouldn't believe, can carve a stone in minutes. Computerized. Anything you want, they can do it. Hearts and flowers, gorillas and goldfish . . ." He smiled at Parker. "Custom work, too. You'd be surprised, the weird stuff people want written on their stones. Like the name of a favorite pet, for example. Once in a while you'll run into someone, always a woman, who's after revenge. But the nasty stuff, you got to

131

say no, because they won't let you stick it in the graveyard anyway . . ."

Willows said, "Have you been drinking, Mr Springway?"

"Yeah, a little. Why?"

"Could we speak to your wife?"

Springway dropped his cigarette butt on the floor, stomped on it with the heel of his boot. "No way."

Parker waited until Springway had finished rolling another cigarette, then said, "Is she in the house?"

Springway laughed harshly. He wiped his face. The milky eyes were wet, glistening. His pale flesh was smeared with grey. He said, "Cops! You got a strange sense of humor, lemme tell you!"

Willows said, "What'd you mean?"

"What d'you *think* I mean? Of course she's in the house. Where *else* would I keep her, in the trunk of my fucking car?"

"Good point," said Parker. "We'd like to talk to her."

"Tough."

"With or without your co-operation," said Willows.

Springway stood up, kicked the chair out of his way and unbolted a door at the back of the shop, led them up a flight of crumbling stone steps and across an unmowed, weed-freckled lawn and into the house.

Maria Springway was in the living room, perched on the mantle over a dead fireplace, in a brass urn shaped like a rocketship. Springway picked up the urn, handed it to Willows. He turned and looked out the window at the soft green landscape of the graveyard.

A match flared. Willows smelled the fire, smelled the brimstone.

Springway, his back still to them, said, "Go ahead. Ask her anything you want."

Parker gave Willows a look.

Willows hefted the brass rocketship and said, "Was your brother on the take – a crooked cop? What was he doing in the bank?" Willows raised his voice a little. "Tell me something,

132

Maria. Was your brother laundering Panamanian drug money?"

There was a small silence.

Willows said, "I don't think she can hear me." He gave the rocket a quick shake. "I think we better let her out. How do you get this open – unscrew it?"

Springway spun on his heel, reached out and yanked the urn out of Willows' hands. He said, "Garcia visited us once, about two years ago. Arrived in a stretch limo with a couple of bottles of champagne, flowers. The big reunion. He stayed long enough to tell us what a hero he was, about all the bad guys he'd put away, show us a scar on his leg where he'd been shot, get drunk and throw up all over the sofa. I was helping Maria clean up, didn't even notice him leave. Like I said, that was almost two years ago. I never heard from him since."

Willows said, "He told his superiors in Panama that he was flying out here to attend the funeral."

"Well, he didn't."

"How did he know Maria had died?"

"I called him on the phone."

"You talked to him?"

"No, I left a message." Springway was staring out the window again. A fractured halo of cigarette smoke hung in the air above his head.

Parker said, "How did Maria die, Mr Springway?"

"On a marked crosswalk. Some kid in a stolen car hit her. She was killed instantly."

Parker made small, muted sounds of sympathy.

Willows said, "They get the kid?"

"He hit a bus. Totalled the car and waltzed away without a scratch. He wasn't even wearing a seatbelt – the fucking airbag saved his worthless life."

The rocketship had extra wide fins for stability. Springway put it back on the mantle. "Sometimes I think she's up there somewhere, drifting among the stars."

Parker couldn't think of anything to say.

Springway said, "Garcia was probably up to something, but

133

I don't know what it was. If I did, I'd tell you." He flicked his cigarette into the fireplace, and started to cry.

Willows left his card on the mantlepiece, well away from the urn.

"Now what?" said Parker as they walked back to the car.

"More of the same, and then we die."

Parker said, "Sooner than later, if you don't cheer up."

Willows smiled. "I'm a little less fatalistic, on a full stomach."

"Then you must be awfully hungry, most of the time."

Willows watched Parker fumble in her purse for the keys to the unmarked car. After a moment he said, "Want me to drive back?"

Parker said, "I wouldn't trust you behind the wheel of my hearse, Jack."

14

Greg's eyes felt as if Mr Sandman had taken the night off, and his good buddy Mr Glueman had worked his shift for him. And their pal Mr Sledgehammerman had joined in, put in a solid eight hours on Greg's head. He forced his eyes open a little wider. He had no idea why, but he felt an overwhelming sense of *dampness*. Bright round beads of sunlight glinted on the shiny chromed links of a chain. Pink tiles glistened. Greg blinked twice, and everything suddenly came into focus. He was in the bathroom, curled up in the tub. The tap leaked. He had a wet towel for a pillow.

He struggled to a sitting position. His knees ached. His head throbbed mightily. He stood up, promptly lost his balance, snatched at the plastic shower curtain and tore it to shreds, sat down hard on the edge of the tub.

One of his suede penny loafers lay half-submerged in the toilet. He suspected its mate had flown out the bathroom window, which had a shoe-sized hole in it.

He rested for a little, collecting his thoughts, then climbed weakly to his feet and made for the medicine cabinet above the sink. He gobbled a near-lethal dose of aspirin, splashed the cobwebs from his face. His head felt as if it had spent the entire night being repeatedly dropped upon an unyielding surface from a great height.

He retrieved his shoe from the toilet, urinated and flushed, turned on the shower. A spray of water pebbled the linoleum floor. He swore, but without much energy or conviction. The ruined shower curtain was heavy-gauge blue plastic decorated

135

with a repeated pattern of groups of naked women huddled under red umbrellas. It was one of the few things he owned, and it hadn't come cheap. On the bright side, though, it was so ruthlessly tasteless that he was confident that when it wore out he wouldn't have any trouble finding a replacement.

Taking his time, making no sudden movements or loud noises, Greg showered and shaved, slipped into a shirt fresh from the dry cleaner's, faded Levis. By the time he finished his third cup of coffee he was starting to feel human again, and the world had become brighter and more vulnerable.

Good thing, too, because before he'd set out on the previous night's journey into drunkenness, he'd added up the wad of crumpled bills hidden in the fridge in a box of frozen waffles. He was worth less than three grand. Twenty-eight hundred and fifty bucks to be exact. Add in the cash in his wallet, he had enough money to last about a week, if he stayed home nights and watched TV.

Unlikely.

He poured a fresh cup of coffee, sat down on the sofa and began to page through his little black book, spiral bound with a leather cover, what he liked to think of as his *Encyclopedia of Possibilities*. He studied the names of all the women he'd conspired to meet during the past eighteen months, studied their descriptions and the names and addresses of the trust companies, banks and credit unions where they worked.

Greg had a large-scale map of the city. Every time he started dating a woman he drove a pink stick pin into the map where she lived. Another pin, a black one, went into the map at the scene of his crime. He was careful that the pins never formed a straight line or followed a predictable direction. Patterns, he knew, were death on criminals in general and bank robbers in particular. He always worked alone, had no friends and stayed sober in the company of strangers.

He had a theory – as long as the cops had to *react*, they'd always be so many moves behind they might as well be playing on a different board. If he avoided the trap of predictability, the only way they'd ever catch him was because he'd made a seriously stupid mistake. Hilary had been a blonde, the one before her, a redhead. He noted the names of the first half-dozen brunettes listed in his black book, used green pins to fix their work and home addresses on the map.

One of the green pins landed on the same block as a pink pin.

Greg checked his cross index. February, last year, he'd gone out with a woman named Janet Sutton, who worked at a credit union on West Pender. She was the pink pin. The green pin, a woman named Tammy Liebow, was employed by a bank halfway across town. The two women didn't know each other but had three things in common: their jobs, where they lived, and Greg. He plucked Tammy Liebow's pin from the map, obliterated her from his past, present and future with a single stroke of his black felt pen.

The next brunette on the list, Barbara Robinson, was a teller at a downtown branch of the Bank of Montreal. Greg tried to place her, failed. Or was she the tall one with the ponytail, liked to spend her time at the track? Greg's mind fogged over. It was frustrating, he couldn't pin her down. Had the mole under her chin, smoked skinny menthol cigarettes . . .

Greg dialled the bank's number, asked to speak to Ms Robinson. The voice at the other end was so detached it was barely human. Greg was put on hold, treated to a Muzak serenade.

He leaned back against the sofa, cracked the mini-blinds and peered warily out. The world had a bleached, faded look. In the park across the street a couple of guys in jeans and sweatshirts were throwing a football around, taking turns being the quarterback and the ham-fisted receiver. As Greg watched, the receiver ran a complicated pass route, turned to catch the ball and crashed headlong into a tree, hit it hard enough to shake loose a storm of yellow leaves that almost buried him as he lay on the grass, unmoving and apparently unconscious.

Interested, Greg cracked the blinds a little further apart.

137

The quarterback trotted over to his pal, knelt down beside him, jumped suddenly to his feet and looked wildly around.

The Muzak was abruptly cut off – right in the middle of the theme from *Robin Hood*, too. Barbara said, "Sorry to keep you waiting, hello?"

Greg pitched his voice a little higher and said, "You probably don't remember me, it was quite a while ago, but we bumped into each other in the mall. I was carrying the bowl . . ."

"Neil! How are you?"

Greg heaved a sigh of relief. He hadn't made a note of the name he'd given her. Con man's block. But it was a lot better than a cell block, you betcha. "I'm fine," he said, "I've been meaning to get in touch with you, but I've been out of town . . ."

"Where?"

"The Yukon," said Greg. Now where in hell had *that* come from? He said, "Did I mention I'm an artist? I was up there painting the moose and caribou, leopards . . ."

Barbara knew three moose jokes. Pretty good ones, too. Greg could hardly stop laughing. They traded small talk for a few minutes and then Barbara said she had to take a call on another line. Would he mind holding? It was a game they all loved to play, making Greg wait. He tossed the phone on the sofa and lit a smoke, remembered the guy who'd run into the tree. He was still there, but there was no sign of his pal. Greg exhaled into the thin shafts of light coming through the mini-blinds.

Barbara said, "You still there, Neil?"

"I'd have waited forever," said Greg.

"If it meant you'd eventually get what you wanted."

"I was thinking along the lines of a little bit of candlelight and a whole lot of wine," said Greg.

Barbara giggled. He was starting to remember the details now, the rhythms of Neil's speech, the way Neil carried himself, how Neil tossed his head when his hair fell into his eyes, Neil's shy, corner-of-the-mouth smile, the jaunty way Neil flicked his cigarette butts into the gutter as he was walking down the street. His fondness for foreign films, interest in sports. Greg liked the idea of being an artist. It gave him all the reason he needed to have an artistic temperament. Fly off the handle, in other words.

"And a good steak," he said to Barbara. "You like venison? There's a place I know about where they keep the animals down in the basement in a big cage. You can choose one and shoot it, no extra charge."

Barbara said, "Neil, are you on drugs?"

Greg denied it.

Barbara said, "Me, neither, but I wish I was. This place is so *boring*."

"How can money be boring?" Greg asked her.

"When all you do with it all day long is count it out and smile and hand it over to strangers, *that's* when it's *boring*."

"Sounds like you need a night out on the town, Barb."

"Pick me up at seven?"

Greg said, "Okay." But too late; she'd already hung up.

There was an ambulance up on the boulevard by the park, and a couple of burly-looking guys in whites were loading the football star on to a stretcher. Greg was a little surprised. He hadn't heard a siren. He went into the bedroom, checked out the closet. If he was an artist, he'd better wear black.

Was it Neil who wore the chip diamond in his ear? He was going to have to crank up the computer, check it out . . .

Greg stripped, letting his clothes fall where they may. He went into the bathroom and stared at his body in the mirror.

No doubt about it, he was starting to look a little chunky. Time to cut back on the pizza. Was it Robert De Niro who starred in the fight movie *Raging Bull*, and deliberately put on fifty pounds so he'd look and feel right for the role? Greg admired the actor's dedication to his craft. He brought up his hands, hunched his shoulders and danced around a little, feinted with a left hook and then drove a hard right into the mirror, jagged lines suddenly leaping across the glass. Greg glared at De Niro's reflected image. He said, "Want another one, fat boy?" and lashed out at the mirror again, the blow shattering the glass, fragments of Greg's face exploding, pieces of his face crashing into the sink, gone.

Greg picked a sliver of glass out of his fist, sucked away the blood. He needed a shower. He needed to find a new way to comb his hair. Comb it straight back. Was it long enough to go for the pony tail look? He whinnied softly, ran his fingers through his hair, pulled it away from his forehead, jockeyed to find a piece of mirror he could look into. Yeah, very nice. With his hair swept back, his eyes looked larger, and darker. He looked a bit like the famous actor Michael Douglas in *Wall Street*. What about a mustache? Greg tried to remember when he'd first met Barbara. Months ago, he'd had plenty of time to grow any kind of mustache he liked. But what style would a bank clerk find attractive?

Greg went into the bedroom, turned on his Macintosh and summoned up Neil's electronic image on the computer's big color screen. Neil had a bandit's mustache, wide and droopy. His hair was dyed black, cut short. No part. Neil had really bushy eyelashes, so bushy they dominated his face. His eyes were amazingly blue. Greg smiled. He had a weakness for blue eyes – it was ridiculous, but they made him feel special.

He used the computer's mouse to trim the mustache, accidently cut away too much on one side, so it looked lopsided. Now he resembled Adolf Hitler on a bad day. He worked the mouse, gave himself a cowlick. Fired up a cigarette, added sideburns and a pirate's eyepatch, blacked out a front tooth.

Ash from his cigarette exploded on the keyboard. He tilted his head and blew the ash away.

Enough goofing around. He wiped the changes. Neil's original image filled the screen. He turned on the printer and punched up a dot-matrix color printout, then cleared the screen and called up Barbara's file.

He'd met her on a Friday, four months ago to the day. The bank had an escalator at one end that gave access to a mini-mall. Greg had loitered on a bench outside the Sky Train station across the street, sipping a warm Coke and smoking, watching the world go by. It was a bright, sunny day in late June. He'd figured that she'd want to eat her lunch outside, catch a few early-summer rays. But no. She took the escalator down to the mall and Greg was forced to play catchup, was almost whacked by a taxi as he crossed the street against the light. By the time he made it to the escalator, she was gone.

Sitting there in front of the computer, he remembered frantically patrolling the mall, checking out the shops and restaurants, working hard to avoid making eye contact with the sales clerks as he hung out by the door to the public washroom. He couldn't find her anywhere. It was as if she'd jumped inside her purse, vanished. He ran around the mall for three-quarters of an hour, then gave up the hunt and loitered near the escalator until he saw her strolling towards him, idling along as if she didn't much care whether she made it back to work on time, or not.

He cut in front of her as she turned to look at a frantic MTV video showing on a television in the window of a record store. She walked right over him, her spike heel coming down hard. Greg grunted in genuine pain, staggered and dropped the cheap punchbowl he'd bought at a discount glassware store and been carrying around for what seemed like his entire life.

Greg smiled, remembering. The woman who'd sold him the punchbowl asked him if it was a gift and Greg said no and she asked him if he was hosting a party, maybe even a wedding. He told her he was buying the bowl because he wanted something that would break when he dropped it. He remembered the way the light faded from her eyes, as she realized he wasn't kidding.

And suddenly Greg was remembering the way the light leaked out of Garcia Lorca Mendez's eyes, how the huge black pupils swallowed the irises as Mendez fought the gathering darkness, and lost.

Greg shuddered, dragged his mind back to the mall. The punchbowl was in a plastic carry bag, but even so, there was lots of glass to be picked up.

Barbara, apologizing like mad, hiked up her skirt and

pitched right in. Greg had cut himself on that day, as well, been nicked by a chunk of punchbowl as he'd picked it up off the mall floor. He still couldn't say if he'd injured himself by accident or design. Luckily, Barbara always kept a bandaid in her purse in case she tore a nail. By now they were sitting on a bench, Greg watching her as she wound the bandaid around his finger. As she ministered to him she asked him if it hurt. He gave her a spicy grin and said to tell the truth it felt pretty good. She smiled back, holding her own, and offered to pay for a replacement punchbowl. He said no, it was his fault, introduced himself, told her he was an artist, a painter. Had she heard of him? She wasn't sure. Maybe. It was possible. She said she had to get back to work. She didn't sound too happy about it. He asked her what she did and she told him what he already knew.

He watched her walk away, didn't avert his eyes when she reached the escalator, turned and waved.

He waited until a week had gone by and then dropped by the bank, asked her to lunch as she changed a ten for him. She'd told him she'd love to, but couldn't make it. Greg told her he wanted to paint her. She blushed and he thought he had her, but all she said was maybe some other time . . .

Greg *never* pushed. Like the man said,

> *Wanna be your sweetheart baby*
> *yes I do yes I do yes I do*
> *but if you don't feel the same*
> *as me, babe*
> *well then you and me are through*

So Greg wrote off the punchbowl and moved on, concentrated on Hilary, the most promising of several women he'd met and seduced earlier in the year. Worked his ass off to make her fall in love with him. Stole her heart and then emptied her cash drawer, knew from the look of fear in her eyes how badly she needed him for support, how much she'd miss him when he was gone. His big moment, and the trigger-happy cop blew it for both of them.

On the other hand, by the time he made it to Hilary's apartment, he'd calmed down enough to realize that she'd *really* be traumatized, desperately in need of what he had to offer.

But the way it worked out, Greg did all the work of setting her up and it was Randy who'd waltzed in to take advantage.

This thing with Barbara was nothing but smoke. He was running scared, had instinctively turned and headed for familiar ground – the business of setting women up and knocking them down, and getting paid to do it.

He'd played out the shooting over and over again. Initially he'd been sure that Mendez had fired first – the guy yelled something and Greg had turned towards him and the crazy fool fired without warning. Or had they both pulled at the same time, Mendez popping him in his two hundred and fifty dollars plus postage and handling charges mail-order Kevlar vest as Greg shot up the bank? Or did Mendez react in self-defense, shoot only after Greg'd started burning rounds? One thing for sure, he remembered the heavy, wet sound as the first bullet had slammed into the man.

And he remembered Mendez's face going blank and then looking betrayed, remembered him falling, dying as he dropped.

Where was the truth? Greg wasn't sure. But he knew that his heart had been filled with terror. He'd made a snap decision not to fall down easy. He wasn't even sure any longer that he'd noticed if Mendez was armed.

Either way, if the cops nabbed him, he was looking at armed robbery, assault with a deadly weapon, a possible count of first degree murder. And snatching the cabby, what was that? Kidnapping, unlawful confinement? He'd go down forever, minimum.

His best bet was to get rid of the spreadsheets and badge, throw everything he owned into his car and get out of the city. But if he left town, he'd be turning his back on maybe the only chance in his life to make a major score.

What was the point of whacking Mendez, if he didn't

take advantage? The poor guy would've died in vain. A waste.

Greg stared at his computer screen. He lit a fresh cigarette and took the mouse for a stroll, using it as an eraser to wipe his electronic image from the screen.

15

The sun was low on the horizon, dropping fast.

Parker turned on the heater, rubbed her hands briskly together.

Willows stared out the windshield. The graveyard had brought back a wealth of memories. He was thinking about the partner Claire Parker had replaced. Norm Burroughs had died after a long and painful battle with cancer more than five years ago. A lot had changed, since then. Willows' wife had left him, taken Sean and Annie with her. He and Parker had become a little too close.

His thoughts turned to Parker. She'd graduated first in her class at the Academy, immediately gone undercover. Narcotics exploited her freshness, her vulnerability. Trial by fire. Her job was to buy soft drugs at street level, dime bags of marijuana, a gram or two of coke. Spend two or three months hanging out with the lowlife dealer trash cluttering the Granville Street strip. By the time she'd finished, narcotics had a millionaire wholesaler on the rack, as well as a truckload of smaller dealers. Parker was good in court, too, remained poised and articulate under pressure.

Impressive credentials and good timing. Bradley had snatched Parker out of the Oakridge sub-station, dropped her in Willows' lap while Norm was still fighting it out in the cancer ward at Royal Columbian. Naturally Willows resented the way Bradley had trampled all over his fierce loyalty to Burroughs, the circumstances of Parker's promotion. It wasn't her fault things had happened the way they did, but who else was there to blame? He hadn't made it easy for her, those first few weeks.

Then they'd got into a situation, and Parker had come through, saved his cop bacon. They'd had a few drinks, celebrating. A week or so later Norm had died, and of course they'd had a few more drinks, commiserating, and become a little too close, skittered away.

Then Sheila finally lost patience with the constant uncertainty, fear, and bullshit, lost patience with being married to a guy who was married to his job. Took the kids, took a walk.

Cops. When you chose a partner, it was like being married but taking an oath of celibacy. You shared every damn thing but sex. When your partner was a female, not even that rule applied. Jack and Claire had been off and on lovers for a long time. More often than not the relationship didn't seem to be going anywhere. Sometimes it seemed they were on a fast track to disaster. Willows was unsure as to which situation he preferred.

A couple of months ago, at summer's end, he and Parker and his two kids had spent a lazy week together at Long Beach, on the west coast of Vancouver Island. Sean and Annie had met Parker several times before their parents split up. Neither of them indicated that they thought there was anything odd about the situation, had adjusted to Parker's presence in the adjoining cabin with an ease and simplicity that Willows found somewhat unsettling. He'd wondered if the children had previously experienced a similar situation while with their mother in Toronto. But hadn't asked. At the end of the vacation, Willows had reluctantly put his children on a plane back to Toronto.

He wasn't sure he understood why, but during the past two months his relationship with Parker had deteriorated. Maybe it was being thrown together with the children, the sudden *domestication* and unacknowledged tensions of such a temporary reality.

Before the summer, he and Parker had spent most of their nights together, usually at his house, less often at her apartment. But more and more, recently, Parker had preferred to spend her time alone.

Parker nudged his arm. "Enjoy your nap?"

Willows said, "I don't know – I slept through most of it." They were at the corner of King Edward and Main, waiting for the light to change. He said, "Wasn't it Will Rogers who said, 'I've never met a nap I didn't like'?"

Parker nodded. "Want to drop in on Alain Bernard?"

"Yeah, sure."

When she hit the yellow pages, Parker discovered to her surprise that there were fifty limousine services in the city. White Shadow had been very close to the bottom of the list. It was a one-man outfit. When she questioned him, Alain Bernard had admitted, with just a hint of regret, that he'd worked for the dead Panamanian.

Willows hadn't sounded very enthusiastic. Parker said, "You got a better idea?"

The light changed from red to green. Parker waited for strays. Her patience wasn't wasted. A delivery van sped through the intersection against the light. On the far side of King Edward, a pale blue Honda disappeared in a cloud of burnt rubber as the driver hit the brakes. She thumped the steering wheel. "What a *jerk!*" Turning to Willows, she said, "Remember when it used to be *safe* to drive in the city?"

"Not really."

Parker said, "You used to get red hot about guys like that, cowboys."

"Yeah, but it didn't change anybody's driving habits. So I quit."

Parker made her left, drove down Main. "You don't seem too enthusiastic about talking to Bernard."

"You think Mendez confided in his chauffeur? A guy like him, he probably wouldn't give his lawyer the time of day."

Parker braked for another red. Willows watched a kid in raggedy jeans and a black leather jacket sidle up to a glossy black 5-series BMW worth seventy grand. The kid pointed something at the car. The alarm chirped as it was deactivated.

147

The kid unlocked the door, climbed in. Sensing that he was being observed, he turned and glanced behind him, saw the unmarked four-door with its blackwall tires and cheapo hub-caps. He grinned at Willows, waggled his keys.

Parker said, "When I started out in this business, I used to put guys like him away. Now that he's made his bundle, he's gone straight and we can't touch him."

Willows nodded. It was as if she'd been reading his mind. Again. He said, "The light's green."

Parker checked the intersection, left and right. It was clear. She hit the gas.

Willows said, "The limo guy, what's he like?"

The limo guy had a dead cigar in his mouth and dead-smelling feet up on his desk. He wasn't wearing any shoes, but then, neither was he wearing any socks. A crumpled newspaper rested in his lap, but it was only a prop – unless he'd learned to read through his eyelids.

The office door was open. Parker followed Willows inside, saw Alain Bernard flinch as Willows reached out and flicked his big toe.

Bernard opened his eyes one at a time, seemed more inter-ested in Parker than Willows.

Willows said, "I don't know which one of these little piggies went to market, but I'm pretty sure he didn't buy any soap while he was there."

Bernard smiled. "You're callous and abusive, but you ain't family. So it must be cops, right?"

"Right."

"Here about Garcia Lorca Mendez, right?"

Parker nodded.

"Well, if I seem a little nervous, it's because I am. And I got plenty of reason, believe me. I mean, aside from being questioned about a guy I worked for got shot to death."

"For instance," said Parker.

"Drinking in the limos. Sex in the limos. Too many passen-gers in the limos. Sex in the limos. Drinking in the limos . . .

148

Am I repeating myself? No wonder, since it keeps happening over and over again. And it's going to keep on happening. There's nothing I or anyone else can do about it. Know why?"

"Human nature," said Willows.

Bernard pointed the cigar at him. "Ask an expert. An expert's always got the answer." He leaned forward, pulled open the top drawer of his desk. His socks were long and black. Parker looked out the window as he put them on.

After a moment Willows said, "It's okay, you can turn around, he's decent."

"When I'm dead and buried," said Bernard. He used a disposable lighter to fire up his cigar, blew smoke at the world. "And maybe not even then."

Willows said, "You and Mendez got along pretty well, didn't you?"

Bernard squinted up at him. Was it the smoke that narrowed his eyes? "What makes you say that, copper?"

"Your sense of humor. Mendez was a real prankster, from what I hear."

"Well, my friend, you heard it wrong."

Willows said, "What *was* he like?"

Bernard smiled at Parker. "A mouse with an accent. Very *quiet*."

"No sex in the limo?" said Parker.

"No sex, no drugs, no sticking his nude behind out the window. Didn't smoke, either. But then, nobody's perfect."

Willows said, "You drove him from the airport to his hotel. Where else?"

"Wherever. If it was on a road and Garcia wanted to get there, that's all I had to know."

"Garcia?" said Parker.

"He was an informal kind of guy. Liked people to call him by his first name." Bernard studied the sludge at the end of his cigar. "See, he'd gimme a call from Colón about a week before he was due in, tell me what flight he was on and how long he was gonna be in town. I'd pick him up at

149

the airport, he'd pay me in advance, cash, for the duration."

"You're telling us you worked a twenty-four-hour day?" said Willows.

"I ate in the limo, slept in the limo, read the paper in the limo, burped in the limo and dreamed sweet dreams in the limo. When you come right down to it, there were only two or three things I didn't do in the limo."

"Where else did you drive Mendez, other than to his hotel?"

"I got a list here . . ." Bernard shuffled the papers on his desk. "Had it a minute ago . . ."

The cigar was making Parker nauseous. She said, "Has the limo been in use since Mendez's last trip?"

"Nope."

Willows said, "You drove him to the bank, didn't you?"

Bernard held out his hands as if he expected to be cuffed. "You got me fair and square, copper. Color me guilty, guilty, guilty."

"What happened, you were waiting in the parking lot, heard the shots and hit the gas?"

"No way. Garcia told me he wouldn't need me for an hour, said to pick him up at six. I figure, about the time he got blasted I was into my third beer, easy."

"You went off somewhere for a drink?"

"The Waldorf."

"Anybody likely to remember you?"

"Yeah, my brother. He's a waiter, served me the beer."

Willows said, "Did you get a look at the guy who did the shooting?"

"The boxer."

"Yeah, the boxer."

"How could I, when I was knocking back the suds at the Waldorf?"

Bernard glanced at Parker, rolled his eyes. Parker said, "Has the car been cleaned since Mendez used it?"

"I don't know. I got some people come in and clean the cars on a regular basis, except they're not all that reliable. So

150

it could go either way. Why, you think he might've left a *clue*?"

"Evidence," said Parker.

Bernard dug deep in his pants pocket, tossed Parker a key ring. "The oval gold-colored one gets you inside, the square-ended gold one fits the ignition. The blue one's my house on East twenty-ninth, I'm in the book." He winked at Willows, "You find any money fell between the seats, we'll split it down the middle."

Twirling the key ring around her finger, Parker left the room.

Bernard turned to Willows, saw the look in his eyes, swallowed his *bon mot*, busied himself riffling through the untidy mess of paperwork on his desk. "That list, I got it somewhere, here we go . . ."

Willows rested a hip on Bernard's desk as he studied the limo's worksheet. He pointed at a column of figures on the righthand side of the sheet. "This represents distance travelled?"

"Roundtrip, in kilometers."

"Is it accurate?"

"Yeah, sure. Fairly. I got a trip odometer. Once in a while I forget to reset it, but not often. If the numbers don't add up, I just don't bother to write 'em down."

If the limo's log was to be trusted, Springway had told the truth when he'd said that Mendez had not visited him in the recent past. Glancing down through the list Bernard had prepared, Willows saw nothing of particular interest. Mendez had a weakness for shopping malls and restaurants. The only location he'd made a repeat visit to was the White Spot restaurant on Robson Street – he'd been there on three separate occasions, twice during his first full day in the city.

Willows said, "He meet anybody at the White Spot on Robson?"

"Not a soul."

"You're sure about that?"

"I went in with him. That wasn't routine, usually I waited

151

outside, in the car. But this, as you can see by the times, was for breakfast and lunch. Both times we were there, he ordered a hamburger platter. He was nuts about that special sauce they put on the burgers."

Willows said, "Did you make up your own mind, or did somebody tell you I was an idiot?"

"Excuse me?"

"Mendez was crazy about White Spot hamburgers; that's why you went there twice in one day and again the morning he was shot."

"Yeah, right." Bernard was having too much fun to be lying. He spat a chunk of cigar at the wastebasket, and missed.

Willows said, "Did you talk to anybody while you were there?"

"The waitress. Waitresses. They was different, each time."

"Anybody else?"

"Yeah, one of the cooks. The last two times we was there, we went into the kitchen. The first time, Mendez and the cook had a long talk. I couldn't hear what about because I was standing next to the deep-fryer. But they shook hands when we left, so I know everything was okay. Also, the next morning, after breakfast we went back in the kitchen again, and Mendez bought a big plastic bucket of special sauce. Ten gallons. Paid the cook a thousand bucks, I saw the money change hands. We went right back to the hotel, put it in a fridge in the kitchen so it wouldn't go bad."

Bernard saw the look on Willows' face. He said, "No, really, it's the truth. Mendez had two hamburgers for breakfast, three more for lunch. Five in one day, and he had extra sauce on all of them. Triple-O, they call it. The stuff was all over the place, gooping out of the bun when he bit down on it, splattering all over his hands, the plate. You think you've been around. Lemme tell you something. You ain't seen nothing until you see Mendez lick his fingers. Totally disgusting. Totally."

Outside, a car door slammed shut.

Bernard said, "That's the limo. Left rear. I drove him to

152

every White Spot in town. There's ten locations, plus three more out in Burnaby. He offered the managers five grand for the secret sauce recipe, and every single one of them turned him down. That ten gallons we bought? I had to stick it in the trunk, drive Garcia back to the hotel, haul the stuff into the kitchen and stand there like a dummy, holding it in my arms like I was in love, while he paid a chef to make room in the fridge so it wouldn't go bad."

The way Bernard wielded his cigar reminded Willows of Bradley – the cigar was both a sceptre and a weapon.

"You see where we're going with this, Detective? We are going absolutely nowhere. I mean, this was the way Mendez liked to spend his time, eating hamburgers. Take a look at his social life. Boring. The only people he met were waiters and bellboys and sales clerks. He liked to eat things and he liked to buy things, and that was about it. The perfect consumer."

"What kind of things did he like to buy, Alain?"

"Clothes, lots of clothes. This suit – you like it?"

"Very nice," said Willows. And it was. Or might have been.

"Garcia bought it for me. A thousand bucks, and it don't even come with an extra pair of pants. But what he most loved to buy was ties. That was his favorite thing, buying ties. I'd limo him to one of the malls, Oakridge or Metrotown or whatever. Know where he felt relaxed, at home? The upscale menswear shops. Harry Rosen's, places like that. Ever shop at Harry's?"

Willows shook his head, no.

Bernard said, "Garcia, he'd wander over and pick up a tie, ask me what I thought. Places he shopped, you got maybe ten seconds and bingo! there's a salesman in your lap. Mendez'd tell the guy to hold out his arm, hang as many as fifteen, twenty ties on him, using the arm for a tie rack. The salesman's standing there, sweating from muscle fatigue, trembling all over, smiling away, buried in miles of silk at eighty, even a hundred bucks a yard."

Bernard grinned at Willows. "That's another thing, he always bought silk, nothing but silk. And the colors were real noisy. Let's say you were staying at a hotel and the guy in the next room had a tie Garcia'd bought? You wouldn't get a minute's sleep, believe me. *Loud*."

Bernard's cigar had gone out again. He said, "The salesman's arm feels like it's going to fall off, you can see it in his eyes. But so what? He's on commission, getting rich!" He re-lit the cigar, puffed hard.

Willows said, "What happened if Mendez chose a tie and you didn't like it?"

Bernard tilted his head as if there was something in his ear that was bothering him and he hoped would fall out. He said, "How's that again?"

"You said Mendez would pick out a tie and ask you what you thought. What I'm asking you is – what happened if it was an ugly tie and you said so, advised him to take a pass?"

"I tried that twice. The first time, he ignored me."

"And the second time?"

"He went around behind me, wrapped the tie around my neck, stuck a knee in the middle of my back. I was down on the floor, I couldn't breath. We're standing behind a rack of cashmere winter coats. Nobody can see a thing."

"What'd the salesman do?"

"Garcia tells him don't worry about it, him and me got an understanding. He starts telling him a joke about a farmgirl and an octopus. They're laughing their heads off. By the time the punchline rolls around, I'm barely conscious, ready to black out."

"Why'd you keep working for him?"

"Because now we understood each other. The nature of our relationship. And also because of the money."

"And the coke," said Willows.

Bernard's eyes widened in horror. His cigar glowed red. "Whoa, wait a minute. Coke? No way. Garcia was a hamburger freak. He might've had a cholesterol problem, but that's it."

Willows said, "Want to read the coroner's report?"

"I don't think so."

154

"Mendez'd snorted a snowstorm, the day he went down. C'mon, Al. You really expect me to believe he kept his nose clean while he was in the limo?"

Bernard shrugged, looked away. "He might've done a few lines. It ain't part of my job to spy on people. I'm a pro – I mind my own business. Whoever's in the back is the guy who's paying the bills. Okay?"

"Where'd Mendez score his product?"

"I couldn't say."

"What side of the counter was he on, Al? The buying side or the selling side?"

"I wish I could help. But really, I got no idea."

"He give the tie salesman a taste, just to calm him down?"

"Like you say, calm him down."

"And you never took him anywhere except to malls and restaurants."

"Plus his sister's place just that one time, and back and forth from the hotel, airport."

"What about his girlfriend – what's her name again?"

"He never got around to making introductions."

"How many times you pick her up?"

"Lots." Bernard showed his teeth. "Must've had a special sauce of her own, I guess."

"Where did you pick her up?"

"Always at one of the town's more decent watering holes. The Ramada, Bayshore, places like that. He'd go in, be gone a couple of minutes."

"Then what, she'd spend the night with him?"

"Never happened. Usually he saw her during the day. Sometimes she was with him at night, but not very often. And she was always out of there by eleven-thirty, and in a hurry. Like if she didn't get home by midnight she'd turn into a pumpkin."

Willows said, "Tell me what she looked like."

Bernard had a good eye. He described the woman in such detail that Willows knew he'd recognize Mendez's girlfriend

155

the moment he saw her. He asked Bernard a few last questions and then said, "If I find out you're lying or holding back . . ."

Bernard lifted his pudgy white hands to the ceiling. "You got the whole truth and nothing but the truth, I swear it on my soul!"

Smiling, Willows said, "Don't think for a minute I'd let you off that cheaply."

Outside, Claire Parker was sitting behind the wheel of a black stretch Rolls-Royce, toying with the stereo's controls. She powered down a deep-tinted window. Alain Bernard was standing at his office window, so motionless he might've been a cardboard cutout; the *before* picture in a weight-loss program.

Willows said, "Find any *clues*?"

"Not a chance. The damn car's been vacuumed to death from stem to stern, and you can still smell the cleaning agents."

Parker left Bernard's keys in the ignition. She and Willows walked across a span of oil-stained asphalt to their unmarked police car. Parker tossed Willows the keys. "You mind driving?"

"Yeah, sure. You okay?"

The windshield had fogged up. They sat quietly, waiting for the heater to clear the glass. Willows told Parker about Mendez's penchant for White Spot hamburgers.

Parker said, "It's starting to slip away from us, Jack. Special sauce. You want to write that down in the report, that Garcia Lorca Mendez flew all the way from Colón to pick up ten gallons of *special sauce*? No wonder the Panamanian cops won't tell us what he was doing here – they're too embarrassed."

"Or don't know. If they were involved in a money-laundering operation, you'd think they'd send somebody out here to clean up the mess. The way I see it, Martin Ross is the only person who knows anything about Mendez's business in Vancouver. And Ross isn't talking."

156

Parker said, "He'd talk if we squeezed hard enough. You can see it in his eyes. No guts."

Willows smiled at her.

Parker said, "Something funny?"

"No, absolutely not."

"What?"

Willows said, "You ought to hear yourself – you sound tougher than a three-dollar steak."

"Don't try to sweet-talk me, Jack. It might work, and then what would you do?"

Willows gave her a fleeting, crooked smile. He had no business putting in unauthorized overtime or working a stake-out without telling Parker what he was up to, but he'd made detailed plans to spend the night huddled in his car, parked in the deep shadows of the Maritime Museum lot across the street from Martin Ross's house. He'd while away the hours drinking lukewarm coffee out of a stainless steel thermos and listening to Coleman Hawkins and Sonny Rollins tapes, waiting for the man who'd killed Garcia Lorca Mendez to make his move on Martin Ross.

Part of his problem with Claire was that after Sheila left him, he adjusted to living alone with a speed that surprised him. He relished the lack of routine, freedom from responsibility. But what he valued most was being able to roll out of bed in the middle of the night, grab his badge and gun and prowl the streets, come and go as he pleased.

The sweet sound of sirens and saxophones wailing in his ears.

16

Greg inhaled deeply, lovingly pulled the last fat white worm of coke past the bushy filter of his false mustache and up into his nose. He dug his jewelry box out of the bureau and poked around in it until he found his favorite earring, a chip diamond a black slide guitar player named Jeremy had given him. He stuck the gold post through the little hole in his left earlobe, glared into the mirror like that singer whose name he couldn't think of – dyed his hair blond and always needed a shave, wore black leather.

Greg fumbled around in the closet, found *his* black leather, the superbutch model with the floppy lapels and too many zippers to count. He slipped the jacket on his otherwise naked body, shivered at the heavy touch of the cold leather on his skin. Was the coke all gone? Yeah, the coke was all gone.

Greg pranced around the apartment, snarled viciously at his shadow, fell over laughing, jumped up and lashed out, bounced his knuckles off the wall.

"Hey, Randy, that hurt, didn't it?"

Greg took another shot at his shadow. His knuckles were bloody. He left a smear of blood on the wall. The shadow crumpled. Greg kicked out, stubbed his toe.

"Damn!"

As he fought and played, he slyly checked himself out in the mirrors that were everywhere, admired his form. Eventually, he ran out of energy, tired of the game. He snatched a cold beer from the fridge, drank it down and then went back to the bedroom. He finished the beer and then ditched the leather jacket, slipped into a pair of black silk boxer shorts decorated with little red devils wielding tiny pitchforks, plain black silk socks, a black silk shirt embellished with leaping red and blue-striped largemouth bass, a single-breasted light-weight black wool suit with a split vent and onyx buttons. The suit had an Italian designer sweatshop label and cost him almost five million lira. Or about two thousand bucks, in domestic currency. He'd made a joke while the clerk was chalking him, asked how much for just the label. *So funny*. Greg tried to look down her neckline as she adjusted the drape of his pants, but she was wearing one of those tricky little numbers that clung tight in all the wrong places.

He picked up the shaving mirror he'd used to chop the coke. Yup, it was all gone. No visible traces, anyway. He licked the mirror clean. His mustache fell on to the glass. Was he coming unglued? No way. Now what? He needed a tie, chose a dark green number patterned with wide open shark jaws – just the jawbones and teeth.

Finally, he slipped into a pair of glossy black shoes with pointy toes and custom-built heels that raised his required clearance well above the six-foot mark.

It was a few minutes past seven when, all dressed up and ready to go, he dialled Black Top. While he waited for the cab, he went into the kitchen and poured himself a large vodka on the rocks. He felt restless and edgy, full of anxious, high-impact energy. The park across the street, illuminated by sodium-vapor streetlights, was a verminous yellow along the perimeter, black where the vegetation was thickest.

Greg drank most of his vodka. A taxi cruised slowly up the street, stopped in front of his apartment block. Greg saw the guy's face in the cab's window as he peered up at the rows and rows of windows. Greg stepped closer to the glass. He waved at the cabby as he finished his drink, then grabbed his Ralph Lauren trenchcoat, slammed the door shut behind him.

Barbara lived in one of those big old houses that had been gutted and ruthlessly stripped of all its original charm, then

159

internally subdivided, turned into fourplexes and rented out to the kind of people who were willing to pay a premium to live in a big old house that had been stripped of all its original charm. Barbara's unit was number G-4. Greg found her ground-level apartment tucked into a corner at the rear of the house. He stabbed at the doorbell but heard nothing. He knocked. Listened to a little more nothing. He knocked a little harder, and heard a faint cry from within.

He tried the door, walked inside. The combination kitchen-dining room was on his left, the combo living room-bedroom on his right. What you might call an open floor plan. A glass door offered an unobstructed view of the off-street parking. Greg walked down a short hallway and poked his head in the bathroom door.

Barbara, leaning into the mirror, gave a little yelp of surprise, covered her breasts with her arms and told him she was almost ready, all she had to do was finish dressing. Obviously. What was he *doing* there, by the way? Had she left the door unlocked again? Greg smiled. Barbara asked him would he please stop staring at her like that? Greg said okay but didn't even blink. She told him to go mix himself a drink, waved him away with little flips of her hand. He helped himself to another long, lingering look and then went into the kitchen to do as he'd been told.

There was an unopened bottle of Black Label in the cupboard, squeezed in next to a family-size box of prefab croutons and a couple of tins of tomato soup.

Greg dug a reasonably clean glass out of the built-in dishwasher, poured himself a fat slug of Scotch, filled a Winnie-the-Pooh soupbowl with croutons and went into the living room and stretched out on the sofa that you could turn into a bed whenever the time was right.

He could hear Barbara tinkering away in the bathroom. She sounded pleased with herself, and why shouldn't she be, with a body like that? Greg glanced idly around the apartment. He toyed with the idea of tossing the joint. There was no quicker way of getting to know a girl than pawing through

160

her drawers. But what was there about Barbara that he needed to know?

Greg gobbled a handful of croutons, washed them down with a mouthful of Scotch. He felt himself beginning to relax, slip into character. That was the way Neil dealt with life – gulped it down in handfuls and mouthfuls.

He was looking at a picture of Cher in an old copy of *People* magazine with the name of a downtown dentist on the address label when he smelled perfume. He dropped the magazine and stood up. Barbara was wearing an ankle-length black dress and high-neck black sweater in a soft, fuzzy material that looked like cashmere. It was the kind of outfit you might wear to a job interview if you were trying to find work as a nun. Greg searched hard but could find nothing in the least bit provocative about the way she was dressed or her demeanour. The perfume had a strange effect on him, though. His nose seemed to have relocated in his groin.

Smiling shyly, Barbara said, "How's your drink – have we got time for another?"

Greg checked his watch. "Yeah, sure."

She moved a little closer, took his glass. He tried for some touchy touchy finger touchy, but she was too quick for him. She said, "What happened to your mustache?"

"It fell off."

She smiled, a little confused but being good-natured about it. "Are you really an artist, Neil?"

"Don't I *look* like an artist?"

"Sure, but so does everybody else."

Trying out the artistic temperament thing, Greg made his face go all surly and said, "I don't see why that has to be one of my goddamn problems!"

"You make any money?"

"More than I can bother to spend," Greg said. He was starting to get the feel of Neil, slip under Neil's skin. He said, "I'm famous and in demand because I'm real good at painting animals hanging around in the tundra, life-size stuff, big, the kind of art that looks best in carved oak frames that cost

161

three hundred bucks a lineal inch. Everything I do is on commission. Corporations that specialize in the destruction of natural habitat hire me to cover their boardroom walls in the kind of art that soothes their greedy little consciences. And yeah, you're right, I'm a cynic. But I'm a *rich* cynic, and I'm what I always wanted to be – an artist."

Barbara blinked twice and nodded and then went over to the kitchen counter, pulled another glass out of the dishwasher and poured them both a fat shot. Directly above Greg, the ceiling suddenly creaked as if under great stress. Barbara came towards him. She seemed to be avoiding eye contact and her hips might've been connected to a gyroscope – they hardly moved at all. She sat down next to him on the couch that was a bed. Close, but not too close.

The perfume had something in it of every woman Greg had ever known. How was that possible? He buried his nose in his drink.

Barbara said, "So tell me, what do you think of my apartment? Small, isn't it?"

Greg said, "What I've seen of it."

"How do you mean?"

Greg said, "Well, you haven't given me the tour yet. I mean, I haven't seen the bedroom . . ."

Barbara patted the sofa. "You're sitting in it."

"Really?" Greg feigned surprise. His eyes skittered around the walls, which were decorated with unframed Salvador Dali prints and a strange dangly thing made out of yellow straw and woven roots and small white feathers, brightly colored wooden beads. He said, "I like the way you've decorated the place."

She smiled. Her eyelashes fluttered and she looked away. "Neil, don't tease me . . ."

"No, I'm serious. The nest thing, with the feathers and all those beads, it's terrific."

"Come and look!"

She laced her fingers through his, squeezed hard, eagerly pulled him to his feet.

He'd guessed right. It was a nest, of sorts; a small whirlpool of straw laced with prickly strands of barbed wire. Huddled at the bottom of this still-life vortex were the bleached white bones, skull and all, of a tiny bird.

Greg said, "Jeez . . ."

"Like it?"

Greg nodded slowly, thinking about it. "Powerful," he said after a moment. "Absolutely stunning."

"You wouldn't just say that?"

"Of course not, I'm a professional."

She sipped her drink, looked up at him. "I was so excited when you phoned. I've been taking night school courses since last summer. Do you know Peter Hologram?"

Greg frowned. "The name seems familiar . . ."

"He teaches Mixed Media at Emily Carr."

"Right, right." Greg was nodding so hard he was afraid his head might fall off.

"I've been working on nests ever since I started. Such a powerful image. At first the birds were stuffed toys. Peter said they were silly and frivolous. So I went out to a farm in the valley and bought some live quail."

Greg said, "Live quail?"

"Twelve of them. A dozen. I brought them home in one of those boxes you put your cat in when you take it to the vet. Peter lent it to me."

"He did, huh. Then what?"

"Well, I guess what I did was blow out the pilot light and put them in the oven . . ."

"You *gassed* them?"

"It wasn't so bad, really." Barbara knocked back her drink, poured refills for both of them. "The worst part was plucking and cleaning them. Especially the heads, emptying the skulls." She smiled. "They're so tiny, so fragile. I don't know how many I broke before I finally got the hang of it."

Greg said, "Lots, I bet."

"Next I'm going to do a series of tiny houses, with nests in them."

163

"Houses made of little bones?" said Greg.

"Oh Neil, that's such a *terrific* idea!"

"Keep it, keep it."

"You don't mind?" She led him back to the sofa, sat a little closer to him, this time. "You should've seen Peter's face, when I told him I was seeing you."

Greg nodded, waited.

"I explained it didn't have anything to do with art, but I don't think he believed me. I should've realized he'd be jealous. I mean, he teaches art, but you're an artist. Big difference, right?"

"A world of difference," said Greg. "Peter knew my work, did he?"

"Well, obviously." Barbara drained her glass. "Can I ask you a question?"

"Yeah, sure. I guess so."

"Before you came in, did you knock?"

"Of course I knocked. I thought I heard you invite me in."

"You did?"

"I'm sure I heard a voice."

Barbara raised her face to the ceiling. "It must've been that jerk upstairs."

Greg said, "Yeah?"

"I hope you don't think I *planned* for you to see me like that."

"Never entered my mind."

"Because I certainly didn't."

"You don't have to tell me that."

"So don't get any ideas."

"I'm full of ideas," said Greg. "It's a sickness." He smiled. "I can't control myself, from time to time."

It turned out that Barbara didn't own a car because she was on a bus route to work, so why bother? Greg never drove his Pontiac when he planned to meet someone he knew, because it was a lot harder to change the way a car looked than to alter the appearance of the driver. Also, he didn't know why, but people remembered cars. They'd forget your name, whatever

164

lies you'd told them about how you made a living. But never in a million years would they forget you drove a Toyota or whatever, licence number blah blah blah.

Barbara poured him another Scotch while he used her phone to call a cab. It had started to rain – there were dimpled puddles in the parking lot outside her sliding glass door. The dispatcher cheerfully told him there was a twenty minute wait, minimum.

Barbara said, "Oh well. What can you do? Want another drink?"

As it happened, it was close to half an hour before the cab finally arrived. Greg had a couple more shots of Black Label while he admired Barbara's portfolio of water colors. Boy, did the time ever race past.

Because they were late, the restaurant hadn't held their table. The *maître d'* was one of those skinny guys with smart-ass eyes, no lips. He wore baggy black pants and a white shirt buttoned all the way to the top. His hair was blacker than a raven's heart, his skin pale and smooth as a fish's belly. He suggested they retire to the bar for a drink. Barbara smiled and said she thought that sounded like a wonderful idea. She ordered a glass of Chardonnay. Greg told the waitress he might as well make it a pair. Then Barbara changed her mind, cancelled the vino and substituted a glass of water with a twist of lemon, or better yet, lime.

Greg started to say maybe he'd have water too, but he didn't want to seem cheap. And anyhow, from the way Barbara was slumped on her barstool, he figured he had a lot of catching up to do; she was obviously looped to the eyeballs.

By the time they got a table, Greg was on his third glass of wine. He'd not only caught up with Barbara, he'd probably lapped her a couple of times.

Barbara, studying a menu the size of a small tent, said, "When you made the reservations, Neil, did you have any idea how expensive this place was?"

Greg said, "Not all artists are starving, Barbara."

"I know, but . . ."

165

"Whatever your heart desires," said Greg, "is what I want you to have."

Eventually, Barbara settled on the lobster. Greg went for the roast duck. He ordered a bottle of whatever he'd been drinking by the glass. A wicker basket of miniature loaves of different kinds of bread arrived. Greg put his jaws to work. Barbara started talking about art. She used a lot of words Greg'd never heard of, or if he had heard of them, hadn't the foggiest idea what they meant. Words like *eclectic* and *multi-media*. He ripped into the bread, theorizing that if he kept his mouth full enough, there wouldn't be room to stick his foot in it.

Eventually, Barbara ran out of wind. Greg told her if he was any judge of talent, she had a real bright future. He solicitously enquired about her lobster. Told her she was beautiful, in the candlelight. Topped up her glass, offered her a forkful of his duck.

Pampered and flattered her to the very best of his ability, in other words.

Manipulating women was something Greg was very good at. Making them feel special, feminine. Convincing them without ever directly speaking a word about it that, just as they'd always known, their lives were situated at the heart of something that mattered. A Holy Grail that only he could help them find.

Barbara passed on dessert, hesitated, and with a show of reluctance agreed to have a cognac.

By now Greg had turned the conversation to the fine art of banking, learned that she'd been double-counting other people's money for five years going on six, walked straight out of high school and into the job, the only work she'd known. While most of her friends were yukking it up at university or better yet taking a year off to backpack Europe, she was learning how to work an adding machine.

Greg said, "Ever been robbed?"

"I wish."

He smiled. "Looking forward to it, are you?"

166

"Bet your ass, buster."

Greg leaned across the table, took her hand. "I want you to promise me something, Barbara."

Barbara said, "Okay."

Greg said, "Promise me you'll be careful if it ever does happen."

"What happens?"

"Someone robs you."

Barbara leaned forward, frowned at him. He wondered what he'd said, and then realized she was having trouble keeping him in focus. She giggled and said, "Make my day."

Greg said, "It's nothing to make jokes about. You could get hurt."

Barbara spilled a little cognac on her cashmere. Greg offered her his napkin. Dabbing at the sweater, she said, "I'm going to have to take this off just as soon as we get home, aren't I?"

Greg nodded, searched for something clever to say. His throat was dry. He was remembering the way she'd looked when he'd caught her standing naked in front of the mirror.

She said, "What are you thinking, Neil?"

He smiled, reached for his wallet. The cab fare to her apartment, the restaurant. Dinner. A deuce for the hat-check girl. Another cab ride. He was looking at a hundred seventy-five bucks, minimum.

He hoped like hell it didn't take Barbara too long to fall for him, that a whirlwind romance was in the cards. Usually it was the hot pursuit that motivated him, the thrill of turning a stranger into a lover. He tended to gloss over the fact that the woman, whoever she might be, had fallen in love with someone other than himself.

As for the actual robbery, that was usually just the icing on the cake. A way of underwriting his costs. But this time out, it was different.

If he didn't break Barbara's heart in a week, he'd be bankrupt.

167

17

Willows' phone rang. He picked up. Mel Dutton said, "All set, Jack. Whenever you're ready."

"Be right there, Mel." Willows disconnected.

Parker slapped shut a file folder, put the folder away in her desk.

Willows dialled a three-digit extension. Fireplug O'Neill said, "Yeah?" His voice was wet and garbled, as if he was in the middle of brushing his teeth.

Willows said, "Mel's ready to go."

O'Neill muttered something incomprehensible and killed the connection.

Willows dialled Pat Crowthers. He gave the fraud squad detective the same message and received more or less the same response.

Parker said, "I bumped into Bernie and Cake in the cafeteria this morning. Cake wasn't too enthusiastic about the meeting."

"Said I was grasping at straws?"

"Word for word."

Bernie Adams and Pat "Patty Cake" Crowthers were a couple of old-fashioned cops, part of the last generation of detectives who'd dropped out of high school and worked their way up the ladder rung by rung, leaving a trail of sweat and unpaid overtime all the way. The new breed had degrees in criminology, sociology.

Willows cleared his desk, pushed back his chair. His phone

rang. He picked up. It was Bradley, calling from his office, less than twenty feet away.

"Your meeting still on?"

"It's all set, Inspector. Parker and I were just on our way over." Willows instinctively glanced towards the source of Bradley's voice, but the inspector's door was shut.

"You got a minute, drop by when you're finished."

Willows said, "Should be within the hour, Inspector."

"Ask Parker to come along, as well," said Bradley, and hung up.

Mel Dutton had set up a slide projector in one of the third-floor lecture rooms. Untidy rows of metal school desks faced a podium and blackboard. Someone with a minimum of talent but lots of fevered imagination had filled the blackboard with a much larger-than-life-size, remarkably immodest female nude.

Dutton said, "Nice, huh?"

Parker nodded. "Very artistic." Dutton was wearing a three-piece suit, a mustard-colored windowpane with wide lapels and full vents. His shirt was mauve, with a buttondown collar. There was hand-painted egg all over his tie. His bald head gleamed almost as brightly as the diamond in his pinky ring. He caught Parker looking and struck a peacock's pose. "Like the suit?"

"Really classy."

"I was browsing, and there it was, right at the end of the rack. Its sleeves seemed to open out to me, as if to embrace me. I went over and touched the cloth and a salesman appeared out of nowhere. How often does that happen – that there's a salesman around when you want one?"

"Never," said Parker.

"It was like a sign, a portent. When I tried it on, it was a perfect fit, almost."

"Amazing," said Parker.

Windy Windfelt and Fireplug O'Neill, Bernie Adams and Cake Crowthers were standing by the window, eating ham and cheese croissants out of a grease-stained brown paper bag, talking in low, conspiratorial tones. The chatter faded as

Willows and Parker entered the room. Crowthers and Wind-felt exchanged a look.

Willows shook hands, thanked everybody for coming.

Windfelt said, "Hey, no problem." His eyes were on Parker, who had her back to them and was energetically erasing the over-endowed nude from the blackboard. He said, "Can't you just give her a bikini and leave it at that? I mean, do you have to *wipe her out?*"

O'Neill said, "We're grateful for the opportunity to help, Jack. As I'm sure you know."

Parker finished wiping the nude. O'Neill said, "Was she somebody you knew?"

"My mother," said Parker. "I can't tell you how happy I am that you didn't recognize her."

Willows said, "First we're going to look at a number of slides lifted from security film taken at each of the thirteen robberies we suspect this guy might've pulled. The slides have been computer-enhanced, so they're going to show a lot more detail than anything you've seen up to now. No preconceptions, okay?"

"Just so long as there's plenty of popcorn," cracked Adams.

Willows said, "Bernie . . ."

"Relax, Jack. Enjoy the movie."

Crowthers picked up the brown paper bag and offered it to Parker. "Croissant?"

"Thanks anyway."

"Keeping an eye on your figure, huh? Can't say I blame you."

Dutton said, "Would somebody dim the lights?"

"As if it isn't dim enough in here already," said Parker. Adams cackled, Crowthers flushed with anger. Willows went over to the door and backhanded the switch.

The projector's fan whirred. A wash of color filled the screen. Mel Dutton adjusted the focus.

This was the perp as cross-dresser. He wore a wig like the one Jane Fonda wore in *Klute*. Lots and lots of makeup. Plastic jewelry by the pound. A cartoon bust.

"Cute," said Windfelt. "If she wasn't a guy, I could fall asleep on her pillow *real* easy."

O'Neill said, "You got a sick mind, partner."

"Damn right."

Next up, the perp looking plenty mean in short, spiky streak-bleached hair, his skin dark, tanned to death. He wore a blue-skies-and-palm-trees shirt, baggy white pants and cheap but durable Mexican sandals. He'd hidden his eyes behind a pair of mirror sunglasses. The puckered red smear of a burn scar on his left arm ran from elbow to wrist.

"Guy looks like a Club Med reject," Dutton remarked.

"You ever done that – got clubbed?" Crowthers asked his partner.

Adams said, "After I finish putting my kids through school, it's the first thing I'm gonna do. Well, maybe the second thing."

"What comes first?"

"Shoving the ungrateful little bastards out the door and changing the locks."

Dutton put the projector on automatic feed.

There was their perp at a credit union on West Tenth, in a goofy-looking duckbill cap and baggy white coveralls splattered with all the colors of the rainbow. Bushy red eyebrows and mustache, a ponytail at the back. He had a bulge on the left side of his neck, just beneath his jaw, that was about the size of a pregnant golfball. A tumor. He wore paint-splattered wire-rim glasses with untinted lenses. The computer had decided his eyes were blue.

Crowthers, losing patience, said, "If you've got it right, and all those guys are the same guy, we don't know a thing about him. And if you're wrong, and it's a whole bunch of guys, we still can't help, can we? Because we don't know anything about any of 'em."

Adams said, "Would you mind repeating that backwards, Cake?"

Crowthers wasn't finished. He said, "Me'n Bernie are in

the fucking fraud squad. Guys with *brains*, that's who we put away, not shooters."

Windfelt and O'Neill offered a round of slow motion applause.

They watched their perp limp, shuffle and prance his way in and out of ten more banks, trust companies, and credit unions.

O'Neill said, "Even if it does turn out to be the same guy, we'll never prove it. He changes his hair and eye color more often than I change my shorts."

"Or brush your teeth," said Windfelt. "Or tell your wife you love her. Or buy a round of drinks. Or douche."

"That last one's a lie, you liar."

Willows said "Back it up, Mel." Dutton worked the carousel until Willows said, "Good, perfect. Hold it right there."

After a moment Windfelt and O'Neill stopped laughing and Windfelt said, "What happened here – somebody switch channels on us?"

Bernie Adams said, "That's the bank manager, Martin Ross."

"Marty," said Crowthers. "He likes to be called Marty."

Willows said, "Ring any bulbs?"

"I got an idea we're wasting our time," said Adams. "But that's about it, actually."

Several telephoto shots of Samantha Ross wheeling her Samurai out of the driveway flashed on the screen.

Parker said, "You take these, Mel?"

Dutton shook his head.

Parker turned and stared at Willows.

Crowthers said, "Is that a gorgeous young lady, or what? She can take a bite out of my croissant any time she's hungry, lemme tell you." He grinned at Parker. "Am I a disgusting, swill-sucking pig, or what?"

"Thoroughly disgusting."

"So who's the babe?"

"Samantha Ross."

"No shit. Marty's wife?"

"Daughter."

172

Willows switched the lights back on.

Crowther said, "Like we talked about earlier, some guy walks away from a dozen scores, it ain't just a lucky streak. He's a pro, knows which way is up. Problem is, we still don't know what this guy really looks like. All that digital enhancement shit did – sorry, Mel – was give us a better look at his disguises."

Crowthers said, "You try TV, the film industry? Your perp knows a hell of a lot about makeup. Knife and burn scars, tumors . . ."

Sherman O'Neill said, "It was one of the first things we did, check out TV and the movies, the theatre crowd."

"Pinch any starlets?" Adams wanted to know.

"Dozens. But only in self-defense."

Willows said, "How soon are you going to have those stills for me, Mel?"

"As soon as possible," said Dutton. "Five o'clock, maybe. Gimme a call if you don't hear from me by six."

Willows, already on his way out the door, nodded and waved goodbye.

Bradley's door was open. He saw them coming, waved them in.

"Shut it, Jack. Sit down, both of you."

Parker sat down in a plain wooden chair. Willows leaned against the doorframe.

Bradley pushed a stack of files aside, sat back in his chair. "How'd the meeting go?"

Willows said, "Just great."

"Yeah?"

Parker said, "Everybody caught up on their sleep and left feeling refreshed and happy."

"Well . . ." Bradley toyed with the files, lining them up just so. "Got any more bright ideas up your sleeve?"

Willows said, "I've scheduled a press conference for ten tomorrow morning. Parker and I are going to review the robberies to date, Mel's developing a series of black and whites of the thirteen perps."

"Anything more on Mendez?"

"Panama's putting a file together. I don't know why it's taking them so long. We'll get it eventually, I suppose."

Bradley said, "You talked to Gordon Springway, how'd that go?"

Parker said, "He's a bereaved widower, and that's about it."

"There was something else . . ."

Parker said, "Alain Bernard, at White Shadow."

"Yeah, right."

Willows said, "He favors the kind of cigars you used to smoke when you were a kid."

"What kind's that?"

"Cheap."

Bradley winked at Parker. "It's a lucky thing we don't pay him by the wisecrack; the city'd be bankrupt inside a week." His green leather chair creaked as he leaned forward. "So – what's the plan?"

Parker said, "We're going to talk to the bank clerks, go over old ground, see if we can come up with something new."

"Hope like hell Windfelt and O'Neill screwed up, in other words. I bet they think that's a terrific idea."

Parker said, "Something we worked out – every time our perp hit a bank, the teller he picked on was a female in her early twenties or late teens."

"Somebody unlikely to have a sense of loyalty to the bank or pose a physical threat," Bradley observed. "Makes sense to me."

"Another thing," said Parker. "All but one of the women were single."

"That doesn't necessarily mean anything. If they were young, it's less likely they'd be married." Bradley checked his watch. "What about the stray?"

"Julia Vail. She's older than the others and first on our list."

Bradley took another long, hard look at his watch. "Have you eaten?"

174

"Not yet, Inspector."

"Neither have I," said Bradley, "and that's what's next on *my* agenda."

Eddy Orwell pushed away from his desk and stood up as Willows and Parker walked out of Bradley's office. There was a battered cardboard box on Orwell's desk. He picked up the box with both hands, offered it to Willows.

"What is it, Eddy?"

"A present, Jack." Orwell shook the box and a soft, shuffling noise came from within. He offered the box to Parker. "If he doesn't want it, maybe you do."

Parker said, "What's in it?"

Orwell shook the box again. "A shirt. A raggedy old shirt."

"So long, Eddy."

"And wrapped up in the shirt, a nine-mil Browning with a round up the spout and two more in the magazine."

Orwell put the box down on Willows' desk. Willows flipped it open.

Orwell said, "A bum rooting around in a dumpster in the five hundred block Alberni found the piece, wrapped it in the shirt, stuck the shirt and gun in a box, and flagged down a patrol car. Talk about irony."

Parker gave him an inquiring look.

Orwell said, "Think about it. The guy's pit-mining the dumpster, looking for stuff he can sell or eat. The Browning's worth a hundred bucks easy, and he has to give it away for free." Orwell grinned maliciously. "Asked if there was a reward. What could I tell him? Sorry, pal. Maybe next time."

Willows said, "How'd you happen to arrive on the scene?"

"Luck of the draw. The uniform noticed the hammer was cocked and the safety was off. He smelled cordite, took his hat off and scratched his head real hard, came up with a possible homicide."

"When did this happen?"

Orwell said, "Couple of hours ago." He put the box back down on his desk. "I remembered it was a nine-mil that brought down Mendez. Goldstein popped a round and put it

175

under the 'scope next to the slug we pried out of the body. Bingo."

Willows said, "Where's the guy who found the gun?"

Orwell shrugged. "Out there somewhere."

"You let him go?"

"What'd you want me to do? The dude crawls around in dumpsters for a living. His world is a four by ten steel box. He might've *smelled* something, but he sure as hell didn't see anything. Jeez, he told me he was born right here in the city, but he barely spoke English. All that bad dumpster air, I guess. On a good day, he'd have a tough time figuring which way was up."

"Were there any prints on the weapon?"

"Got a nice one off the receiver. Goldstein thinks it's probably a thumb."

Parker said, "Eddy, did you get a set of prints off the witness?"

"What for?" said Orwell, and then it was as if Parker had pulled a plug, so rapidly did the color drain out of his face.

Willows said, "You get his name?"

"Tim. He said his name was Tim."

"That's it – Tim?"

Orwell said, "We're talking about a person couldn't even afford the down payment on a shopping cart. A 'no fixed address' kind of guy, Jack."

Willows said, "Let's say we catch our perp, assemble enough evidence to take him to trial. What's the jury going to think if we can't explain the alien fingerprint on the murder weapon?"

Orwell said, "Jeez, how should I know?" He stared at the cardboard box as if he wished he could crawl into it, and vanish. "So what'm I supposed to do now?"

"Volunteer for dumpster patrol," said Parker. "You lost him – you find him. And you better organize a door-to-door, talk to people in the area. Maybe somebody saw the perp toss the gun."

"Judith's got a Tupperware party tonight. I gotta babysit. She's invited all her friends and I'm supposed to get home early, so she can clean house."

"A Tupperware party?" Willows patted Orwell on the back. "That's different, Eddy. Why didn't you say so in the first place?"

Orwell started to nod his head in relief, saw the look in Parker's eyes.

Willows said, "If Bradley finds out how badly you've screwed up, you'll spend the rest of your career cleaning out the stables for the mounted patrol. *If* you're lucky."

Outside, Parker cleared the mouth of the alley, made a left on to Hastings and then a quick right on Main. The sky was thick with cloud and it was so cold that the broad granite steps of the Carnegie Library were deserted except for a native volunteer doing a little work with a broom. She said, "How could Eddy be so incredibly dumb?"

"Genetics," suggested Willows.

She smiled. Traffic was light as they drove south on Main towards the Sky Train overpass. On the left was the old CNR station. Parker thought about how nice it would be to take a ride to somewhere far, far away, curl up in a sleeper and look out the window as miles and miles of empty Canadian landscape clicked past. Instead, if she craned her neck to look past Willows, she had a view of the filthy black waters of False Creek lapping up against the contaminated, heavy-metal wasteland of the old Expo grounds. Parker spun the wheel and hit the gas, pulled into the outside lane and signalled a left turn.

Willows said, "Why not go straight through to Great Northern Way? Make a left on Clark, and you're there."

"What's the point?"

"Saving time."

"You want to drive?"

Willows said, "I'd love to drive."

"Tough, because Great Northern Way's the most boring street in the city. But Terminal Avenue's kind of neat."

177

Willows gave her a quizzical look.

She said, "Do I have to explain myself? The brick ware-houses. Driving beside the ALERT line, the trains going by overhead. Trying to outrace that big shadow that keeps gaining on you. *Neat*."

A silver BMW with a middle-aged woman behind the wheel shot past them in the curb lane.

Willows said, "There goes one."

"What?"

"Mother, on the run from her kids."

Parker drove the unmarked Chevrolet down Terminal Avenue to Clark, made a left and followed Clark to King Edward, made a right, drove two blocks and pulled into the Bank of Montreal parking lot. She and Willows got out of the car, locked up, crossed the asphalt parking lot and entered the bank.

Parker walked up to the counter, gave her name to a woman in a black leather jumpsuit and said she was there to speak to Julia Vail.

The woman glanced at Willows, smiled. "I'll tell her you're here."

Julia Vail had been a teller when the perp robbed her, but now, eighteen months later, she'd worked her way up to chief loans officer, drove a newish Volvo, cross-border shopped at Nordstrom's in Seattle and had her own office with a parquet floor and room for a small potted plant. If the file was accurate, she was thirty-four years old. Tall, slim, and very self-possessed, she wore a dark blue skirt and a grey cardigan over a plain white blouse. A fashionably cut dark blue jacket hung on a wooden rack behind her office door. Her auburn hair was cut short in a style that was somehow both youthful and conservative.

Parker introduced herself, and Willows. She said, "We appreciate your taking the time to see us. We have a number of questions, but we'll be as quick as we can."

Willows said, "You were married at the time you were robbed, is that correct?"

178

"Yes."

"But not now?"

"The divorce came through last month. It seemed to take forever, although my lawyer said if it hadn't been uncontested, I might've died wearing a ball and chain."

"You must be wondering why we want to talk to you after all this time," said Parker.

Julia Vail nodded. "Yes, I certainly do."

Parker said, "When a series of similar crimes – such as bank robberies – is committed by one person, one of the first things we do is look for a pattern. Naturally, the longer the string of crimes, the more chance there is of a pattern developing. In this case, the only pattern we've found is that twelve of the thirteen victims were single when they were robbed."

"All of them but me."

"That's right."

Julia Vail studied her desk calendar for a moment and then smiled and said, "You must know detectives Windfelt and O'Neill."

Parker nodded.

"Then surely you understand why I found it rather difficult to discuss certain aspects of my personal life with them . . ."

"I understand perfectly." Parker glanced quickly over at Willows, motioned towards the door.

Willows said, "I think I'll get a cup of coffee. Is there a restaurant nearby, Miss Vail?"

"At the end of the next block. *Wally's*." She gave Willows a nice smile. "Turn left as you go out the door – you'll see the sign."

Julia Vail waited until the door shut behind Willows and then said, "He's been through it himself, hasn't he?"

"Been through what?" said Parker.

"Divorce."

"You're very observant."

"He seemed nice enough, but Windfelt and O'Neill put me off cops forever. *Male* cops, I mean."

Parker said, "I know exactly what you mean."

179

"I'll bet you do. Are you married?"

"No."

"The right guy never came along?"

"Came along and kept on going," said Parker.

"My husband's name was Dennis. He was a terrific, an absolutely wonderful guy. Easy to look at. Intelligent. Sensitive. Warm and loving. He dressed well, enjoyed the theatre, liked to read. He had a terrific sense of humor. He was an accomplished skier and sailor. How could any woman resist him?" She smiled. "Believe me, almost none of them did."

"He was a . . . womanizer?"

"Everyone knew it but me. I finally found out what was going on when the husband of a friend of mine told me. Dennis was in the middle of an affair with his wife. He knew all about Dennis; what a busy little prick he'd been. He asked me whether I thought Dennis should have *all* the fun."

"What did you do?"

"I had a long talk with Dennis. I made it perfectly clear that if he ever slept with another woman, we were through. Then I hired a private investigator. Dennis didn't even slow down. I walked out on him, and *then* I slept with my ex-girlfriend's husband. And a whole lot of other guys. Lots and lots of them."

"But you didn't mention any of this to Windfelt or O'Neill."

"Would you?"

"Absolutely not. Never."

Julia Vail said, "It didn't last forever. Thank God. I started thinking about what I was doing and why I was doing it. Being so self-destructive . . ."

Very softly, Parker said, "I appreciate your talking to me about this. I know how difficult it must be."

"For a while there, I never wanted to see another man in my whole life. Then I met Christopher. He was really wonderful. Handsome, charming. *Attentive*."

Julia Vail touched her ring finger, unconsciously seeking a missing band of gold. "After the robbery, I was absolutely devastated. I was off work for almost a month, had all the

180

classic symptoms – nausea, dizziness, constant migraines. I had trouble sleeping and when I was able to get some sleep I had nightmares. At first, Christopher was so gentle, so understanding. But after a little while his attitude changed, he started hinting that it was my fault, said I must have done something to *invite* the robbery. He kept asking me why the robber had picked on me. Accused me of making eye contact, flirting with the guy. I started to feel guilty, actually believe what had happened to me was my fault. Christopher turned against me. Even worse, he made me turn against myself. The bastard *abused* me, but I was too insecure, frightened and confused to tell him to go to hell."

Julia Vail dabbed at her eyes with a tissue, balled it up and threw it angrily into her wastebasket.

"Eventually he told me he couldn't stand being with me, that I was so weak it disgusted him. The bank has a counselling program, but I didn't mention Christopher until he left me. The counsellor told me to take some time off and go and visit my parents." She smiled. "I mean, he *told* me what to do, and I did it. My parents live in Calgary. I went straight back to my apartment, packed a suitcase and left town."

"How long were you gone?"

"Two weeks. I kept seeing a counsellor. The bank arranged that, too."

"Did you talk about Christopher?"

"Once or twice – not at length."

"After you came back to Vancouver, did you ever see him again?"

"No, never."

"Did you try to get in touch with him?"

"Once. I wanted to tell him what I thought of him. He'd disconnected his phone. I wasn't surprised. He was a trouble-shooter for IBM. Mainframe computers. He'd be here in Vancouver for a month or so and then he'd be off to Toronto or Halifax, wherever." Julia Vail smiled, but there was something in her eyes, a need and a longing, that Parker didn't want to acknowledge.

Parker said, "I want you to tell me everything you know about Christopher."

Julia Vail nodded, took a deep, shuddery breath. She still had that look in her eyes, of betrayal and loss, a hopeless yearning.

Parker felt ill. She wondered how long, if ever, it would take Julia Vail to recover.

18

On the way home from Barbara's, Greg dropped in at a place he knew and spent fifty bucks on a tiny anthill of Peruvian flake. He taxi'd back to his apartment on his last twenty, snorted the coke as he sat on the toilet, then prowled around all night trying to work out how to get his hands on the Mendez estate.

He woke up the next day at about the same time Parker was finishing her interview with Julia Vail. The sun hung low in a cloudy sky; thin strips of pale grey light leaked through the blinds. The sheets and pillow were smeared with makeup, hair dye, gluey bits of latex. He was hungry and thirsty, and his head felt as if it was being used for a toxic waste storage site. He headed for the fridge. The milk had curdled. Worse, it turned out the shelf life of pizza was considerably briefer than he'd anticipated. He noticed that the pizza's brown cardboard container was decorated with the universal symbol for recycled material – three arrows arranged in a circle. He wondered who'd come up with the brilliant idea of using second-hand cardboard in food containers. Probably descendants of the geniuses who'd invented the lead water pipe. He got a pot of coffee going, checked his peephole to make sure the hallway was clear, unlocked the door and walked down the hallway to the garbage chute, dumped the milk and pizza.

Back in the apartment, he locked the door, took a long, slow, very hot shower and then slipped into a pair of old Levis, suede Docksiders, a pale blue cotton shirt with button-down

183

pockets and a suede sports jacket almost the same shade of beige as the shoes.

Coffee in hand, he dialled Samantha Ross's number. She picked up on the third ring. He said, "Hi, it's the cops. Lunch was five aspirins and a glass of water. Maybe that's why I can't wait for dinner. Or maybe it's you? Interested?"

"I'll call you back in a minute."

Click.

Greg lit a cigarette. He smoked it all the way down to the filter and then the phone rang. Marilyn tried her best to sing along. Greg threw his empty mug at the cage, scored a direct hit. The canary dropped off her perch as if she'd been shot, got busy pretending to read the newspaper that lined the bottom of her world.

Greg picked up, said hello.

Samantha said, "Daddy came home early, I had to go upstairs so I could use the phone in my room."

Greg thought that one over, decided to skip the cross-examination. He asked her again if she'd like to join him for dinner.

"What a lovely idea!"

"Yeah?"

Samantha suggested a restaurant on 41st near Dunbar that Greg didn't know about. He asked her if she wanted to be picked up or would prefer to meet him there.

She told him she needed some time, a few hours, maybe a little less, was that okay? Greg said that'd be fine, he'd be there at nine-thirty sharp. She told him she'd meet him inside, said goodbye and hung up.

He had three hours, more or less. He went into his bedroom and turned on the Mac, pulled the file. Tod Erickstad smirked at him from the computer's screen. Tod's hair was combed straight back. His eyes were green, thanks to tinted contact lenses.

Greg poked at the Mac's keyboard. Tod's history floated up to the surface of the screen. Greg remembered telling Samantha about Tod's wife, how she was knocked down and flattened – turned into a tragic human pizza – by a drunk driver. Or had he added a bit of spin to the tragic tale, turned *her* into the boozer?

Greg had wiped out a lot of wives, during his career. He'd discovered that the meaningless death of a spouse was an unfailingly effective way to trigger a sympathetic reaction – that wonderful nurturing reflex that all women seemed to be cursed with. One of his several wives had been chomped by a great white shark while learning to surf during a Hawaiian vacation. A couple more had succumbed – after a long and agonizing struggle – to cancer. Another expired during a routine surgical procedure to remove a breast implant, and yet another committed suicide when a major real estate deal fell through, and she lost her job. And so on.

He played with the computer for a couple of hours, then took a bath, shaved, attacked his hair with water, gel, a thousand-watt hair dryer. He balanced the green contact lenses on the tip of his finger, slipped them into place one by one. Would a cop wear faded Levis and a beige suede sports jacket to a date with a potential informant? He slipped into a dark green silk shirt, checked himself out in a mirror and decided he looked perfect, exactly what she'd expect.

He found Samantha Ross sitting behind the wheel of a four-wheel drive white Suzuki Samurai with dark blue racing stripes. Greg was on foot, had ditched his Pontiac around the corner. The Samurai was idling in a loading zone in front of the restaurant, Lou Reed on the tape deck. In the glare of light from the restaurant he could see that she wore a fur coat, black leather gloves. The little vehicle seemed to be vibrating in time to the music – then he noticed that Samantha was bouncing up and down on the seat like a little kid. Excited to see him, apparently.

He tried to open the passenger-side door and found it locked. Samantha was smiling at him, laughing. It finally dawned on him that she might've set him up. He stood there on the sidewalk with his hands stuffed in his pockets and an idiot grin pasted on his idiot face. He was carrying Mendez's badge and a bluesteel ·38 calibre Colt revolver slung in a shoulder rig just like the cops wore on TV. More than enough incriminating evidence to put him in the slammer forever and a day.

Samantha reached across, unlocked the door and pushed it open.

Greg didn't move.

"Get in, you idiot!"

She revved the engine. The Samurai lurched along the curb. Greg got a foot up on the running board, grabbed at the door post, swung inside. He slammed the door shut and reached for the safety belt.

"Worried about my driving?"

"Buckle up," said Greg, "it's the law."

"You're working night shift? What a shame. I'd kind of hoped you were off duty."

Greg said, "Cops are always working, it's the nature of the beast." He turned the tape deck off.

"You don't like Lou's music?" Beneath her fur coat, which he was pretty sure was mink, Samantha wore faded jeans tucked into cowboy boots that looked like they'd seen a lot of miles.

"No, Lou's great."

Samantha turned the tape back on again, but lowered the volume to a whisper. She said, "'The nature of the beast'. It sounds like a quote from a training manual. I like it, though. Very masculine."

Greg said, "We going anywhere in particular?"

"Definitely."

They drove straight down Dunbar, across Southwest Marine Drive and into the Southlands, a flat, sparsely populated area of older homes and acre-plus properties that was favored by the horsy set. Greg decided it was probably best to settle back and go along for the ride, let Samantha think she was in charge. He stared out the windshield. The road was bumpy and narrow. There were ditches on both sides. Most of the houses were set well back from the road. There were hardly any streetlights. Not a lot of trees.

186

Samantha geared down, turned abruptly into an unpaved driveway. The Samurai bucked and lurched as they drove parallel to a white-painted rail fence, past a large, dark house. The headlights picked out a long, low-slung wooden building. The Samurai slowed, stopped when the front bumper nudged up against the side of the building. Samantha turned off the engine but not the lights.

A horse whinnied softly. Samantha climbed out of the car and started walking towards the building, which Greg finally realized was a stable. Her boots squished in the mud. She turned and waved to him. He got out of the car and knew with the first step he took that his suede shoes would never be the same.

Samantha was waiting for him under a covered walkway that cut through the middle of the building. She was lit by a naked low-wattage bulb. Her face was in darkness. The mink glistened silver and black. When she moved, the coat rippled as if all those expensive animals were still alive and kicking.

Greg trudged through the mud. His shoes had thin rubber soles that had been designed for use on boat decks and wall-to-wall carpet, and he had to concentrate hard to avoid falling on his ass. The air was dank, smelled of manure. Samantha opened a wide wooden door, swinging it up against a wall and killing most of the light. She disappeared into the stables. The door creaked as it started to swing shut behind her.

Greg made it under the shelter of the roof, on to higher and drier ground. He reached out and caught the door, yanked it open and stepped inside.

This wing of the stables was split down the middle with stalls on both sides. The wide concrete walkway was dimly illuminated by a row of bulbs protected by wire cages, that ran along the sloped roof above the central aisle.

A steel-clad hoof scraped on concrete. Greg peered through the open door of the closest stall, saw a wooden stool, a galvanized bucket, a heap of straw. If there was an animal in there, it was pocket-size.

187

Samantha said, "Step on it, Tod!" flashing an imperious side that he hadn't previously glimpsed and didn't much care for.

He stamped some of the mud off his shoes and walked up to her, grabbed a handful of mink. "What d'you want?"

"Look at that." In her cowboy boots, she was almost as tall as he was in his flats. He stared at her for a moment, eye to eye, then turned and peered over the top of a Dutch door, into the stall.

The horse was standing at three-quarters profile, watching him with its massive, lustrous dark eyes, the huge head slightly cocked, ears erect and its tail flicking restlessly. Greg didn't like the way the horse was looking at him, as if it was endowed with an unnatural intelligence, and was probing into his soul. Slightly unnerved but determined not to let it show, he said, "Nice looking animal."

She pulled at a steel bolt. The stall door moved an inch or two. The horse whinnied again, nostrils flaring. It did a little jig. Samantha pulled the door open wide enough to step through. She said, "His name's Panama."

Panama?

Before Greg had time to react to this titbit, she'd stepped into the stall. The horse made a low sound of welcome deep in its chest. Samantha reached into her coat pocket, pulled out the biggest damn carrot Greg'd ever seen.

"Panama, you hungry, baby?"

The horse nuzzled her, used the weight of its great head to gently push her against a plank wall. Samantha put her hand behind her back, teasing. The horse moved away, giving her room. She waved the carrot in front of his eyes and he snatched at it with big yellow teeth, missed. Laughing, she slapped him on the nose with the carrot. The stallion stomped a steel-clad hoof down on the concrete. Sparks flew. Samantha was laughing, turning to Greg and laughing. Those big yellow teeth snapped at the carrot again. The horse crowded her into a corner. All Greg could see was her lower body, the cowboy boots. She put her arm around the animal's neck, pressed

188

against him. Greg imagined he heard her say, "You want it, go ahead and take it."

The horse took the carrot, quieted, turned and stared at Greg with a thoughtful look in its big brown eyes, the massive jaws rotating slowly, ponderously.

Samantha, breathing hard, grabbed Greg's hand, pulled him into the next stall, slipped out of her full-length mink and tossed it down on the hay-sprinkled concrete as if it was an old army blanket – something that would do but nothing that mattered.

Afterwards, when she'd finished with him, Greg used the Samurai's running board to scrape the worst of the mud and manure off his ruined shoes.

Samantha said, "They'll never be the same, huh?"

"Or me either," said Greg. He climbed into the little car and slammed shut the door. Samantha started the engine. She put the transmission in reverse. The backup lights made the white picket fence look like the carefully arranged bones of a huge skeleton. Greg lit a cigarette. The Samurai's headlights swept across the shingled side of the house and then they were on their way back down the driveway, the car swaying crazily, Samantha laughing at him as he fought to keep his seat.

They turned on to the main road, drove back up the hill to Marine Drive, all those enormous ugly houses that Greg would love to burgle, if he ever changed careers.

Greg said, "That was your horse – you own it?"

"Him."

"Right, him."

Samantha said, "He's all mine."

"A present from the Panamanian dude, Mendez?"

"You're a smart cop, Tod."

"Hungry, too."

It was a straight run up Dunbar to the brick oven pizza joint. Inside, there were seven or eight tables, posters of the Mediterranean, blue water harbors crowded with white

189

sailboats. The oven was huge but the fire was small. A twisty curving chimney arched over a narrow hallway that led to the kitchen and washrooms. The place was empty except for an elderly, exhausted-looking couple with two small children seated at a window table. Nobody paid any attention to them. Greg led Samantha to the table closest to the oven.

A guy wearing a sleeveless T-shirt and lots of gold chain came out of the back drying his hands on a paper towel. He smiled at Greg, brought them menus and asked if they wanted anything to drink. Greg ordered a Kokanee Lite, Samantha a diet Coke. They sat across from each other like the strangers they were, in silence, studying their menus.

After a moment, Samantha tossed her menu on the table and said, "I'm not really all that hungry. Why don't you order whatever you would've had if I wasn't here."

"Okay." Greg caught the waiter's eye. He ordered a large green pepper and pepperoni with mushrooms, a mixed salad and two plates.

Samantha said, "Why two plates? You're all alone, re-member?"

"I thought you might develop an appetite, once the food arrives."

Staring into the fire, she shook her head. "No, if I say I'm not hungry, then I'm not hungry."

Greg said, "Okay, fine." He sipped at his beer, lit a ciga-rette. One of the kids sitting at the window table glowered at him and then said something to his mother, who turned and stared openly at him. Greg stared right back. Now both kids were watching him, and Daddy, too. Non-smokers. Greg didn't like being stared at, didn't like being noticed. He stubbed the cigarette out in the ashtray.

Finally, the salad arrived.

"Sure you don't want any?"

Samantha nodded, didn't say anything. Greg's pizza was in the oven; he could smell it cooking. He picked at his salad, used his fork to push a few thin wedges of tomato to one side of his plate. When he'd finished with the tomatoes he went to work on the onions, shoving them out of the way where they couldn't do any harm. The kid with the bulgy eyes had alerted him to the fact that there was *something wrong with this picture*. And no wonder.

Greg went over the evening's events in the slide show of his mind. The cruise down to the stables. Sloshing through the mud. The horse. Making love on a mink coat worth maybe twenty grand. Kinky – but what did it all mean?

Greg glanced up, and caught Samantha looking at him. She asked him what he was thinking.

"That for three dollars and ninety-five cents, they ought to give you more than one olive."

"You like olives?"

"Not much. I like to get my money's worth, though."

"What's it like, being a policeman?"

"Boring, mostly." Greg speared a slice of green pepper, just to give his mouth something harmless to do.

Samantha said, "What was your most interesting case?"

"The one I'm on right now."

"No, really."

"Really and truly," said Greg.

She said, "What happened – making love – I hope you don't think I planned it that way."

Greg helped himself to a chunk of cucumber.

Her hands were on the table, twisting themselves into knots. "It just happened, that's all."

"Me too," said Greg.

She gave him a quick look, fluttered her eyelashes. "You're making fun of me."

"No way."

"All I wanted to do was show you my horse. Well, I showed you a lot more than that, didn't I?"

Greg covered her hands with his. He said, "Mendez and your daddy were friends?"

She nodded, made a small sound of assent.

Greg said, "You sure as hell showed me a lot more than a horse, all right. You and Marty don't get along too well, huh?"

191

"He expects me to cook for him, keep house, do the washing and ironing. Be there when he needs company and stay out of his way when he doesn't."

The pizza arrived. Greg's mouth watered. He said, "What're you telling me, it'd suit you just fine if I found out Marty had a finger in the wrong pie, and sent him away for a few years?"

"No, of course not!"

What did that mean – that she'd wiggled her ass to save her daddy's? Greg lifted a droopy wedge of pizza off the aluminum serving plate. He chewed, swallowed. "Why'd Mendez give you the horse?"

Samantha smiled. "We were at the track. That's where I first met him. They were in the bar. Daddy was drunk." She poked delicately at the pizza, licked her finger. "Garcia saw the horse run, saw it win. He wanted it, so he bought it. And then he didn't know what to do with it. So typical. After he got to know me, he asked me if I wanted it. And I said yes."

"Who's paying the room and board?"

"Garcia paid a year in advance."

"Pretty generous guy, huh?"

"To a fault. Money meant nothing to him."

Greg bit into his pizza. He wished he'd gone for the anchovies. He said, "What was Señor Generosity doing in the bank when it was held up?"

"Talking to Daddy, I suppose."

"About what?"

"I wish I knew."

Greg said, "Yeah? Is that right? You do, huh?"

Samantha said, "While we were making love . . ."

He looked up, his mouth full.

An expression of alarm crossed her face. "God, what time is it?"

Greg checked his watch. "Eleven."

"I've got to get home!" She stood up, snatched the mink off the chair, leaned over and kissed him full on the mouth, ran towards the door.

192

Greg started after her. His napkin fluttered to the floor. He said, "Just one more question. Why was Mendez dressed up like a cablevision repairman?"

"That's how he got into the house the first time he dropped by. He had a cablevision truck, a ladder. Nobody was home. Daddy said he broke in because he wanted to poke through the closets, look for skeletons. He parked the car in front of the house, did something to the security system and used the ladder to climb up to a bedroom window. I suppose the police would call it an 'unauthorized entry'."

Greg, standing in the open doorway of the restaurant said, "Yeah, that's what we'd call it all right."

The Samurai's engine roared. The headlights bloomed and the stubby little vehicle lurched away from the curb, the knobby off-road tires squealing goodbye.

Greg said, "God *damn* it!" He glanced furtively towards the family of non-smokers but they'd crept away unnoticed, were gone. He went back to his table, sat down hard. Had she really fallen for him – could it be as simple as that? Or was she trying to find out what the hotshot cop was up to so she could cover her daddy's ass? He rolled up a slice of pizza and stuffed it into his mouth. Or did she hate her father for turning her into his personal maid?

Greg finished his beer and told the waiter to wrap the rest of the pizza, he'd take it with him.

It wasn't late but he was tired. It was time to go home, almost.

19

Julia Vail had blushed when she'd told Parker that Christopher's last name was *Smith*. In retrospect, he'd seemed so transparent, his lies so clumsy and obvious. But at the time . . .

The following morning, Parker got on the phone and started in on the list of victimized bank clerks while Willows put the computer to work on 'Christopher Smith'. Naturally there were plenty of Smiths, the majority of them dumbass aliases. But no Christophers, not a one.

Willows had come up empty.

By noon, however, Parker had a different story to tell.

"Whoever he was, it's starting to look like he went out with every last one of them, Jack."

Willows sipped at a mug of lukewarm coffee, waited. Farley Spears leaned back in his chair, openly listened in.

Parker said, "I've talked to eight of the thirteen tellers he's robbed so far. Nine counting Julia Vail. All eight stories started out differently but have identical endings. Our perp usually made initial contact while his victim was having lunch or on her way home from work. He was always extremely charming, not in the least bit pushy. The next day, he'd be back at the cafeteria or bus stop or wherever. His style is deliberately non-threatening. He comes across as shy but determined. It's a great scam – very flattering. He's making an effort and it's out of character. The message to his victim is that he's really attracted to her."

Willows said, "But the subtext is that from day one he's manipulative as hell."

Parker nodded.

Spears said, "The guy went out with bank tellers and then robbed them?"

"Made them fall in love with him," said Parker, "and then robbed them, traumatized them and dropped them. He must've been incredibly smooth. None of his victims ever knew where he lived. They'd ask and he'd put them off. Tell them he was about to move, staying with a friend, or make a joke and change the subject. If he had a phone of his own, it was unlisted. When they called him, there was rarely any direct contact. Unless it was close to the end of the relationship and he was getting ready to move, all they ever got was his answering service. It looks like he changed apartments every two or three months."

"And none of these women realized the guy who robbed them was the same dude they were going out with?"

"He's very good at disguises, Farley."

Spears nodded. "Yeah, I know, I've seen some of the tapes. The women know what they've got in common?"

"Not yet."

"So what's your next move – send a circular to all the banks and credit unions? You must have a pretty good general description, by now. The guy couldn't have worn much of a disguise when he took them out, went to bed with them . . ."

Parker said, "If they asked him how tall he was or how much he weighed, he always gave them a different answer. Sometimes he wore elevator shoes, sometimes he wore flats. Whatever helped. He wore his hair various lengths and dyed it brown, black, red, blond, and black with a grey streak. His eyes were dark blue, icy blue, sea green, pale green, dark green, and brown."

"You sure you're dealing with just the one guy?"

Parker said, "He walked with a limp because he broke his left leg in a motorcycle accident when he was a kid. Or tore the cartilage in his right knee playing high school rugby. Or

195

he suffers a partial loss of hearing because his father beat him."

"All stuff that happened to him during his youth," noted Willows.

Parker nodded. "But this is what impresses me the most. One woman described him as seriously overweight, two as average, one as kind of pudgy, and the others as very slim or skinny."

"So?"

"But not in any particular order," said Parker. "He gained and lost weight at will. One minute he's fat and the next minute he's thin."

Spears sucked in his stomach. He was down to the last two holes in his belt, and his shirts were getting tighter with every passing day. Maybe it was time to cut out the chocolate donuts, stick with plain or cinnamon flavor . . .

Willows dialled Windfelt's extension. Windfelt answered on the first ring. Willows told him what they'd learned. Windfelt swore vigorously and at length. When he finally ran out of breath, Willows picked his phone back up off his desk and gave Windfelt the names and addresses and home phone numbers from the bottom half of the list of busted banks and broken-hearted tellers.

Then he and Parker signed out an unmarked car and went to work on the top half of the list.

With the slight exception of Julia Vail, the tellers they spoke to were cut from the same cloth; all of them were young, attractive, a little unsure of themselves.

Little by little, Willows and Parker learned about the man they were pursuing. But the more they learned, the less they knew.

The perp was a jazz fan. Loved classical music, too. Especially Mozart. Or was it Beethoven? Thought it was really too bad that Roy Orbison had died, and could watch Dolly Parton sing all day long.

Ate out all the time. Loved Chinese food. Italian. Greek. Vietnamese and Thai. Or mostly shopped at the frozen foods section of his local supermarket, knew how to program a microwave oven and that was about it.

Was an expert on California wines, knew the Sonoma Valley like the back of his hand. Could knock back a mickey of gin and you'd never know it. Was a passionate teetotaller and never drank anything stronger than warm milk.

Went to church regularly. Was a Christian, a Jew, a converted Muslim. Agnostic, but wavering.

Earned a decent buck as a Porsche mechanic and had a hard time keeping his fingernails clean due to the nature of his work. But enjoyed the annual tour of the Porsche factory in Stuttgart.

Was a between-jobs car salesman.

Or he'd been a travelling salesman who sold barbed wire by the mile until, demonstrating how you could twist it every whichway and it would snap back at you, he'd had an eye plucked out of his head like a grape from a bowl. That was five years ago, and he'd worn the patch ever since. Looked kind of piratical, didn't she think?

Geneticist.

Piano tuner. Xylophone player.

What he was and perhaps all he ever could be, Parker and Willows eventually realized, was an expert at turning himself into whatever kind of man the woman he happened to be with wanted or needed him to be.

When the banks closed, they started calling on the victims at home. It was past eleven by the time they'd interviewed all seven women on Willows' list.

Parker yawned as she leaned against a field of bright orange wheat on a muddy brown background.

Canadian wallpaper.

Willows bumped his thumb up against a plastic button that glowed luminescent green. From twenty-three stories below them a dull metallic clank sounded as the elevator shuddered and came to life.

Parker said, "Priest. I'm surprised he never tried that one on for size."

197

"Maybe he did, and Windy and Fireplug'll tell us all about it."

"In the morning," said Parker, and covered her mouth with her hands as she felt another yawn coming.

"In the morning," Willows agreed.

The elevator doors slid open. They stepped inside. Parker said, "You don't mind driving me home, I hope."

"My pleasure."

Willows punched the button for the lobby. The doors slid shut. Down they went. Parker was leaning against the wall of the elevator, her eyes shut, ready to fall asleep in her shoes. Their descent was swift, and when they reached street level, the ride stopped with such abruptness that if Willows hadn't reached out to steady her, she might have fallen.

Parker did fall asleep during the drive back to her apartment, but awoke when Willows pulled up against the curb and turned off the engine.

There was an awkward silence as she unbuckled her seatbelt, got herself organized. Willows was busily weighing the risks and rewards of inviting himself up for a drink when Parker said, "See you tomorrow, Jack," and got out of the car and slammed shut the door.

Willows drove home, parked on the street. He sat in the unmarked car for a moment, listening to the quiet tick of the cooling engine. The mornings could be bad, but the nights were always a whole lot worse. It was so *disheartening*, returning to a house you knew would be dark and empty.

Maybe he should get himself a dog. A small one, that didn't chew the furniture or bark or need to be taken for walks.

He made sure the car was locked, strolled across the lawn towards the house. The motion sensor turned on the front porch light. That day's edition of *The Courier* was spread out all over the steps. He scooped up the flimsy pages of newsprint as he made his way towards the door.

The phone started ringing as he let himself in. He picked up. Parker said, "You were hoping I'd invite you in for a drink, weren't you?"

"Well, at least I'm always welcome here at home."

"Take a rain check?"

"Let it pour, let it pour, let it pour . . ."

"Night, Jack."

"Good night, Claire." Willows disconnected, checked his pockets to make sure he hadn't left his keys in the door. He went into the kitchen, turned on the overhead light and rounded up a clean lowball glass, ice from the fridge. He hauled a bottle of Cutty Sark down off the shelf, poured himself a generous double, screwed the cap back on the bottle and put it away. The refrigerator hummed.

He picked up the glass and immediately put it back down on the counter.

The refrigerator paused for breath. He was still wearing his jacket, hadn't bothered to take it off. Now, why was that?

He knelt and retrieved a stainless steel thermos from a bottom cupboard, and left the house.

There was a mini-mall at the corner of Broadway and Maple that contained the usual suspects – cheap haircuts, video rentals, takeout pizza, forty-three flavors of icecream and a Mac's twenty-four-hour convenience store. Willows went into the store and filled his thermos with hot black coffee, paid for the coffee and a couple of candy bars and a small-size submarine sandwich heated to melting point in a microwave.

It was a straight run down Maple to Ogden. The street was empty except for two or three parked cars.

The wide wrought-iron driveway gates in front of Martin Ross's house were shut but the garage doors were wide open. A strip fluorescent ceiling light shone down on a pair of mountain bikes, a jumble of ski equipment, a bright red lawn mower and Martin Ross's shiny dark blue Chrysler Imperial.

No Samurai, though. Willows drove slowly down to the end of the block, around the corner and up the lane behind the house. Still no Samurai. He continued down the lane until he hit Chestnut, made a left turn. The outsized mushroom shape of the HR MacMillan Planetarium was off to his right, the huge stylized brushed aluminum crab that reared up on its hind legs in the pond in front of the building artfully lit by submerged lights.

Straight ahead, the road dropped gently down towards the water, ended in a half-acre parking lot that serviced the Maritime Museum and the neglected A-frame building of cedar shakes and plate glass that housed the historic RCMP vessel the *St Roch*.

Willows turned on his brights and slowly cruised the length of the parking lot. A sixties-era Ford Mustang with vanity plates and steamed-up windows was parked in the far corner of the lot, facing towards the water and towering wall of light that was the West End. The only other vehicle in the lot was a battered parks board van with the city crest painted on the door.

Willows parked as far away from the Mustang as he could manage without compromising his view of Ross's house. He turned off his engine and immediately became aware of a loud, percussive thumping coming from the Mustang's stereo. He adjusted his rearview mirror so he could keep an eye on the car. If it was just some kid who couldn't afford a motel, fine. But if the Mustang's occupants were drinking, it wouldn't hurt to have a little advance notice if they decided to drop by and say hello.

He unwrapped his sub, poured his first cup of coffee, added a dollop of cream.

On the far side of the parking lot, the white-painted hull of the *St Roch* was caught in a nest of shadows and light. Years ago, he and Sheila had toured the ship with the children. The sloping wooden deck was cluttered with boxes of cargo, and the crew had been bundled up against the elements in leather and furs. There was a team of sled dogs, the frozen corpse of a sea-lion that would be devoured by men and animals alike during the course of the voyage. He remembered Annie remarking that if ghosts really did exist, the ship was exactly the sort of place they'd hang out.

Willows ate half his sandwich, bundled what was left in the

200

tinfoil wrapper. He screwed the stainless steel cup back on the thermos.

Despite the coffee, the food had made him drowsy. He rolled his window down a few inches, and as he was doing this, a low-slung black Camaro cruised silently into the parking lot, the driver killing his lights as he slowed for a speed bump.

Willows slouched lower in his seat. He rolled his window all the way down, zipped his jacket against the damp sea air.

The Camaro drove diagonally across the parking lot, brake lights flashing as it came to a stop beside the Mustang. The Mustang's passenger-side door swung open, and the thump of the bass was suddenly much louder, and then almost gone, a whisper to hide more whispering. A man with his hair in a ponytail got out of the car and leaned against the flank of the Camaro. A match flared. The Camaro's driver opened his door and leaned forward, pressing against the steering wheel so the guy from the Mustang could get into the backseat.

The Mustang's driver fired up his engine. The brake lights pulsed red as the driver tapped the brake pedal in time to the music.

The Camaro seemed to be filled with fireflies. There had to be at least six people in the car, and they were all smoking, waving their cigarettes in the air. Several minutes died in vain. Willows poured himself a little more coffee, drank it black.

Off to his right, he heard the slap of approaching feet on pavement. A group of four women dressed in Lycra and sweats trotted out of the lightly treed area around the planetarium. The group turned and headed towards the water, jogged silently across a patch of grass and then put their backs to the parking lot as they followed the limestone path that ran parallel to the narrow body of water leading towards the Burrard Street Bridge and False Creek.

Willows watched as the women were quickly swallowed by the darkness. The crunch of running shoes on packed gravel faded, and died.

Somebody in the Camaro flicked a cigarette butt out the window. Light flared as a fresh cigarette was lit.

At the far end of Ogden, a long, long block away, a car turned the corner, its headlights washing across the trunks of the maple trees in the small park that led to Kitsilano Beach.

Willows reached for his binoculars, brought the car into focus.

It was Samantha Ross's Samurai, all right. She was alone in the car. Willows continued to adjust the focal length of the binoculars as she sped down the street and pulled into the driveway in front of the house. He saw her lean forward in her seat, point at the gates, which swung open as if by magic.

Samantha Ross drove her Samurai into the garage. The door swung down and the gates swung shut. A few moments later, a light came on inside the house, in the kitchen. The kitchen light went out, and then the hall light came on and the stained-glass panels on either side of the front door lit up. Samantha was going upstairs. Now she was in the bathroom, a brighter light shining through a rectangle of frosted glass. Steam rolled from a vent hidden beneath the overhang of the roof.

She was taking a shower.

Another light came on, this time at the far end of the house, upstairs front, where there'd be a terrific view of the harbor. The master bedroom. Now Martin Ross was standing in the window, his hands on his hips, looking down at the street. The binoculars seemed to pull him right up against the windshield – Ross was so close and so clear that Willows could easily make out the repeated pattern of sailing ships on his pajamas.

Willows scanned the rest of the house, the roofline and grounds. Nothing.

The bathroom light was extinguished. A moment later Martin Ross turned from the window. He was smiling. His hair was silver in the light.

He was, Willows was sure of it, starting to unbutton his pajamas as he turned away from the window.

Willows considered getting out of the car and taking a stroll through the park. But did he really want to know what was going on in there?

Maybe not, but he wasn't quite ready to call it a night, either. He decided to stay put until the house was dark again, and then go home.

There was a sudden burst of mirthless, high-pitched laughter from the Mustang.

A dark-colored car turned the corner at the far end of Ogden. The driver swung wide, turned on his brights as he angled towards the parked cars on the far side of the road.

Willows tensed. The car was a late model four-door Pontiac, black or maybe dark blue. It looked as if the driver was trying to make sure that the parked cars were empty. Was he checking to make sure that there wasn't a stake-out at the Ross house?

The car cruised slowly down the street, headlights flooding the interiors of the parked cars in a harsh white glare.

Willows had to constantly adjust the binoculars as the car moved towards him. The driver was a white male. He was wearing a dark brown or black broad-brimmed hat, glasses, a scarf. He had a mustache, full beard. His nose was large, larger than life.

Willows widened the field of view. The Pontiac was streaked with mud. The streetlights gave everything a yellowish tinge. He still wasn't sure of the car's color. The front licence plate had been bent under the bumper and was unreadable. Willows squinted against the light as the driver made a U-turn and drove slowly back down the block.

There was more mud on the rear end of the car, and the licence plate light was dead. It was impossible to tell if the plate was local or out-of-province.

Willows scanned the car from front to rear, looking for a bumper sticker, cracked glass, a dent or scratch, anything that would help identify the vehicle.

Nothing.

Brake lights flashed as the Pontiac stopped on the far side of the street from the Ross house, in the shade of a clump of maples about fifty feet down the road from the house.

The car's lights died. The driver got out and stood quietly beside the car. He was wearing tight black jeans and a bulky leather jacket. Fine-tuning the binoculars, Willows clearly saw the orange swoosh on the sides of his Nike running shoes.

The driver's posture that of a man who was listening, tense, ready to bolt. Willows zoomed in on his face. There wasn't much to see, other than a lot of hair, the nose. The hat's wide brim cast the man's face in shadow. His features were further hidden by the scarf wrapped around his neck. There was nothing remarkable about his jacket or pants.

Willows concentrated on the Nikes. Black, with an orange swoosh. Peering through the binoculars, Willows leaned forward, blindly checked to make sure the key was in the ignition.

His quarry turned and reached inside the Pontiac. The plume of exhaust from the tailpipe faded away. The man shut the car's door and walked slowly across the street, angling towards Ross's house. Willows watched him stroll across the boulevard and pause in the shadow of one of the brick gate-posts that flanked the driveway.

The light in the upstairs bedroom was still on. He saw a shadow move across the white-painted ceiling.

The prowler was there and then he wasn't. Willows realized he'd jumped the fence.

He reached for the ignition key.

Behind him, someone screamed. A split second later there was a sound like corn popping, the dull metallic thud of bullets hitting sheet metal and then the heavy boom of a sawed-off shotgun.

Coffee sprayed across the dashboard as Willows shoved his door open, grabbed his five-cell flashlight, snatched his ·38 Special from its clamshell holster and bailed out.

The shred-the-night roar of a weapon on full auto was followed by a waterfall of glass hitting the asphalt, more screams of fear and rage, a rapid-fire exchange of pistol shots, an over-lapping burst of automatic weapon fire and a final shotgun blast, more screaming, silence.

Willows crouched low as he trotted across the parking lot, his right arm fully extended, finger on the trigger. But what was there to shoot at? The gunfire had deafened him and the dazzling fireworks display of muzzle blasts had destroyed his night vision.

In the distance, a dog began to bark, and on the far side of the harbor, over on Beach Avenue, lights flashed red and white and blue. He saw two and then three police cars on the far side of the Burrard Bridge, weaving in and out of traffic as they sped towards the scene of the gunfire. Willows waited until his night vision returned, then held the flashlight away from his body and switched it on.

A white froth of glass, dozens of spent casings and fragments of metal sparkled in the beam of light. A thin trickle of smoke leaked from the Ford's shattered rear window.

Willows inched closer, his body turned sideways to present the smallest target.

He swept the beam across the interior of the Ford and then swiftly across to the Camaro.

There were three people in the Mustang – two men and a woman, all of them caucasian. A small fire had started in the backseat where the upholstery had been shredded by gunfire.

There were five Vietnamese men in the Camaro. They were dressed like waiters, their white shirts and black pants spattered with blood.

A blue and white took the corner at the far end of Ogden with its siren wailing, headlights jabbing at the night. A second car was right behind the first. Both cars swung sharply left and tore across the grass. Three more vehicles raced down Maple into the parking lot. Another car pulled out of the alley at the near end of Ogden.

Willows holstered his unfired weapon. He raised his hands high above his head and shone the flashlight beam directly on his detective's shield.

Turning, he saw that the Ross house was dark and that the Pontiac had vanished.

20

Greg, as he made his U-turn on Ogden, saw the three cars in the Maritime Museum parking lot and felt a rush of adrenalin. Two of the cars were facing the water; the third was parked in shadow and was angled towards the street. As he spun the wheel, Greg tried to work out if the driver of the third car had a clear view of the Ross house. He decided it was unlikely. Parked. Eyeballed the neighborhood until he felt confident that he was unobserved, then eased out of the Pontiac and walked briskly across the street.

There was a light on upstairs. He could hear music, but it was very faint and he couldn't tell where it was coming from.

He jumped a low brick wall and moved quickly towards the garage. First he'd check Ross's car, see if the Chrysler held any guilty secrets. Then maybe he'd do a little breaking and a little entering. The house first, then the occupants.

He was nosing around inside Ross's Chrysler when the shooting started. He sprinted back across the street to the Pontiac. As he started the car's engine he had a quick glimpse of Samantha Ross standing naked by the bedroom window. He'd hardly registered her image when the bedroom light was extinguished. He had no idea whether she'd seen him. By the time the sawed-off fired the last round in the brief but deadly exchange of shots, Greg was long gone.

He was idling at the corner of Cypress and Cornwall, waiting for the light to change, when the first blue and white screamed past, the cop behind the wheel all eyes and jaw. If the guy was a little tense, who could blame him? He'd have been warned that multiple shots had been fired, the perps were on full auto. He'd be wishing he had his vest on, praying he wasn't first on the scene, regretting that he hadn't emptied his bladder after his last coffee break, worrying about whether he'd ever see his wife and kids again.

The traffic light changed from red to green. Greg started to let out the clutch, saw more blue and whites racing towards him, coming off the bridge at full bore. He had an idea they wouldn't pay much attention to the traffic light and he was mostly right – two of the cars laid a cloud of burnt rubber on the intersection as they took the corner at maximum speed, sliding past Greg in a controlled four-wheel drift that brought the second car within inches of his rear bumper. The third car smoked the intersection doing a hundred, easy. Another blue and white raced down the slope from Fourth Avenue, headlights jumping crazily as it ricocheted from pothole to pothole.

Greg had no place to go, so that's where he went. He yanked on the wheel and stomped on the gas, scooted into a mini-mall's lot and parked in front of an icecream parlor, turned off the engine and lights and leaned back and thought hard.

Forty-seven flavors. Okay, here we go. *Vanilla. Black cherry. Maple Walnut. Chocolate. What if they set up roadblocks?* He sailed his hat out the car window, tossed the scarf, ripped off the false mustache and the bushy prospector's beard, yanked a pink blob of latex off his nose.

A motorcycle cop cruised past, looked right through him.

There was a Ruger Blackhawk under the front seat and a Davis P-32 semi-auto with a black Teflon finish tucked away in the Pontiac's glove compartment. Greg had picked up both guns during his B&E days and had never had a chance to fire either of them. He waited until the nearest blue and white that he could see was two or three blocks down Cornwall, then grabbed the guns, jumped out of the car and retrieved the hat and scarf, stuffed his disguise and the weapons deep down into a garbage can. He screwed in the lightbulb over the rear licence plate, wiped the mud from the plate and climbed back into the Pontiac, turned on his lights and pulled out of the parking lot.

A maniac coming off the bridge at speed leaned on his horn as he stormed past in the outside lane. Greg loved that crazy Doppler Effect, but gave the maniac the finger anyway, because he had it coming. Then saw that the car was a full-size four-door model outfitted with blackwall tires and an extra antenna.

The ghost car had no time for Greg. Engine howling, it shot past him and continued down Cornwall, past the red brick elementary school and out of sight.

Greg made an illegal left turn across double solid yellow lines, headed for the Burrard Street Bridge and the downtown core. The light went from red to green as he approached the intersection in front of the brewery. A lucky sign. He drove at a sedate thirty miles an hour up the gentle slope of the span. At the crown, traffic in both directions had slowed to a crawl because of the carnival of light down by the Maritime Museum. Greg continued slowly over the bridge, cruised past the big electric torches that flickered a corny red and yellow, hit another green light at Beach Avenue.

He turned on the car radio, stabbed at the presets, worked his way up and down the dial as he tried to tune in some news on the gunfight. He was just driving into the parking lot beneath his apartment building when the radio told him that there'd been a shooting at Kits Point and a news team was live on location, please stand by.

Greg pulled into his slot, turned off the lights but left the engine running. He learned that several members of a local Vietnamese gang had attempted to sell a large quantity of cocaine to an unknown buyer, that gunfire had erupted and that the names of the dead had not yet been released. The investigation was continuing. More news at twenty past and twenty minutes to the hour.

Then – the disc jockey's idea of a sophisticated gag – the Cowboy Junkies cover of 'Sweet Jane'.

Greg turned off the engine, climbed wearily out of the Pontiac.

He smelled alcohol. Gin. He turned and Randy kicked him in the belly, the steel-clad toe of his boot sinking deep. Greg doubled over, his sails flapping. Randy spun him around and pushed hard, shoved Greg's head through the Pontiac's side window. Shiny glass pebbles tumbled across the upholstery, on to the floor. Blackbelt Randy grabbed a handful of shirt and yanked Greg out of the car and back into the real world. He punched Greg in the belly, with a left hook that came out of nowhere.

Greg's knees buckled.

Randy propped him up, drove his fist into Greg's belt buckle, cursed and sucked his bloody knuckles.

Greg tried to slip away, lost his footing. The back of his skull smacked against the concrete, made a hard wet sound, like somebody belly-flopping into a pool from a great height. Concentric waves of pain rippled through him. It felt as if he'd been run through with a lightning bolt. He cried out, made a sound like a slab of cold meat dropped on a redhot frying pan.

Randy squatted in front of him, his body perfectly still but his head moving in and out of focus. Randy's lips were moving. What was he saying? Randy broke into a smile, his teeth a white blur. A moment later, the bad news filtered through.

Randy had said, "Just taking a breather . . . not done with you yet . . ."

Greg's head throbbed. Concussion. What he needed was a plan. He tried to crawl under the Pontiac. Randy hauled him back, straddled him, pinned him down, growled like a rabid puppy with his favorite slipper. Greg wriggled and squirmed, got an arm free and drove his thumb into Randy's eye, wiped away that manic grin. He jabbed at the other eye and Randy fell away. Greg rolled over on him, punched him in the throat, hard. Somewhere inside Randy a small bone snapped with a clean, decisive sound, like a dry twig.

Greg stumbled to his feet.

Randy just lay there, staring up at the grey froth of insulation clinging to the ceiling.

Greg booted him in the kidneys. Randy's head lolled to one side. Greg kicked him a couple more times. He said, "How'd you find out where I live?" and stomped on Randy's knee. Randy didn't even blink.

Greg said, "'Scuse me, buddy, I believe I asked you a question." He placed a foot on Randy's chest, jiggled him. Now Randy's mouth was open. Time was passing and he still hadn't blinked.

Greg went quickly through Randy's pockets, found a sheet of BC Tel stationery with his unlisted telephone number and address on it, together with the name Greg had used to rent his apartment. There was also a personal note to Randy from a woman named Deb, who told Randy he owed her a big one and better pay up fast. There was a lipsticked kiss beneath her signature.

Randy still hadn't blinked. The possibility that Randy's blinking days were over slowly oozed into Greg's seriously concussed brain. He made his way over to a rusty BMW, ripped the sideview mirror off the car and dropped to his knees beside Randy, held the glass up to Randy's gaping mouth and willed him to breath.

Randy wasn't having any of it. Randy was a man who liked to go his own way. Randy was through with all that breathing stuff. Randy's breathing days were apparently *done*.

Greg said, "Well, to hell with you, then." He stood up, lit a cigarette. He walked over to the Pontiac and unlocked the trunk. Randy was a pretty big guy, but if he was folded up like a firehose, he might just fit . . . Greg grabbed Randy's belt, pulled hard. Randy's heels left unsightly black streaks on the concrete, but in a day or two, they'd be gone.

Inch by inch, Greg dragged Randy's limp body towards the Pontiac, levered upwards and pushed hard. The trunk lock opened a deep gash on Randy's forehead, but the cut bled almost not at all. Greg slammed the trunk lid down. The metal bulged where it had made violent contact with Randy's skull.

Greg drove through the downtown core, down Georgia and through the Stanley Park causeway, over the Lions Gate Bridge into West Vancouver, up Taylor Way to the highway. He drove slightly above the limit, reasoning that to do otherwise was to stand out in a crowd. He had no clear idea where he was going, except it wasn't to turn himself in. The city was off to his left and far below him; a bright grid of lights that curved gracefully into the horizon and vanished.

A horn blared. Greg saw he was straddling two lanes. He pulled over and a red sports car swept past. Somebody in the Pontiac's backseat started singing. Except there wasn't anybody *in* the backseat.

He checked the radio, twisted the knob to make sure it was off, turned it on and then off again.

The singing continued. It was an *a cappella* version of 'Help Me Rhonda'.

Greg gripped the steering wheel so tightly that his knuckles glowed a luminescent white. It wasn't 'Help Me Rhonda' that he heard, it was Randy crying *help me* over and over again.

Help me help me help me . . .

Greg had to take a peek, couldn't stop himself. He turned on the dome light, adjusted the rearview mirror. A hole big enough to let a man crawl through had been slashed in the backseat where it separated the interior of the car from the trunk. Scraps of material and foam stuffing littered the back of the car. Greg wondered how in hell the damage had been done, too late remembered the machete he'd left in the trunk.

In the mirror, Randy grunted like a pig as he lunged forward, stabbed and slashed.

Greg stomped down on the gas pedal. The car shot forward, raised a welter of sparks as it bounced off the low concrete divider that separated the highway's north and southbound

lanes. He could feel the point of the knife stabbing deeply
into the back of his seat, hear the material ripping. He risked
another look in the mirror. Randy's face and his hand
and wrist and arm to his elbow were covered in blood. He
was snarling like a large dog with a too-small bone, his eyes
wide and his teeth sharp and white, glistening with pink
saliva.

All that kept him at bay was the backseat's woven net of
steel springs.

Greg yelled, *"Get back where you belong, you stupid
bastard!"*

Unaccountably, Randy did as he was told, withdrawing
like a tame bear so far into his hole that he disappeared from
view.

Then he was back, coming out of nowhere, bigger than life
and twice as mean, the Pontiac shuddering under the force
of his onslaught as he unleashed a long scream of frustration
so high-pitched and shrill that Greg expected the windshield
to shatter.

He felt something warm trickle down the back of his neck.
Slapped at himself. Blood.

The rearview mirror was empty. Nothing there but a
raggedy black hole, spark of wire.

The singing started up again. *Help me, help me, help me
. . .* . Then, suddenly, there was a fierce animal howl of anguish
and rage that destroyed Greg's ability to think, seemed to
suck the brains right out of his skull.

The Pontiac was full out now, the big eight-cylinder engine
at maximum revs, the speedometer needle motionless against
the pin, the car vibrating as if it would fly apart.

Greg was using all of his side of the highway, both lanes.
He was barely able to keep the car on the road as he fought
the wind, a neglected wheel alignment problem, terror so
deep it congealed the blood in his veins.

The machete stabbed at him again, pricked the small of his
back.

In a voice that was not recognizably human, although a

212

trick of the imagination allowed him to hear the words reverberate in his fevered mind, Greg began to sing:

Help me help me help me . . .

And there was Randy again, returned from his sheet metal grave so abruptly that it seemed as if he'd never been gone. His teeth chattered like a semaphore as he bit at the steel wire, fought to get free of his cage. He grunted in triumph as a support bracket bent and the seat shifted forward an inch or two. He withdrew into darkness and then lunged at Greg, tried to decapitate him, chop off his head and make him die. The machete's long blade made a snaky hissing sound as it slashed the air, nicked the back of Greg's neck.

Help me help me help me.

But now Greg and Randy were both on the same page, singing the same tune.

Help me help me help me . . .

Greg kept the gas pedal on the floor all the way out to Horseshoe Bay, the Pontiac burning up the highway with the speedometer needle lying flat against the pin, the car shaking and juddering, sounding as if it was about to explode.

He kept a loaded gun in every nook and cranny of his apartment. But the Pontiac had been relatively clean; the only firepower he'd had in the car were the two semi-autos and the machete, which he'd forgotten about and in any case he had a hunch Randy wasn't about to give up.

Randy had been silent for about ten dashboard clock minutes now. Maybe he'd impaled himself. Or had a heart attack – it was his turn, for sure.

Greg ran his tongue around the inside of his mouth, lubricating himself so he could speak. He said, "How you doing back there, Randy?"

More silence, and plenty of it, thick as maple syrup.

"Mind if I smoke?" Greg managed to light up, inhaled deeply. "What's the problem – cat got your tongue?"

Randy muttered something Greg couldn't even begin to understand, that sounded like a bunch of words shoved up tight against each other after all the vowels had been yanked out. Suddenly he reappeared in the mirror, bulging eyes and snarling teeth filling the frame, bloody fingers tearing at the flimsy sprung steel cage that confined him, held him captive. He was foaming at the mouth. His left ear streamed blood. Or was it the right ear? Greg tried to remember how mirrors worked, the tricks they played. Randy's eyes were like a couple of wildly spinning, out-of-control ferris wheels. His face was the color of wet cement, and he was *spraying* sweat.

Then he withdrew into his cage, was gone.

Greg lit a fresh cigarette from the stub of the last. He had a front row seat at the bear pit, and there was no other seat to be had. The speeding Pontiac rocked from side to side. Greg heard a meaty thud. What was Randy up to now? The highway curved right. Suddenly Greg was bearing down on Horseshoe Bay. There was a ferry, a big one, all lit up, in one of the slips. Cars coming off it from two ramps.

Greg swerved into the righthand lane, away from the ferry terminal. The Pontiac's rear tires broke loose and the car went out of control, drifted across the road and on to the gravel shoulder. Cursing, Greg fought the wheel. The road had suddenly become twisty and narrow, walls of sheer rock on his right and a steep drop on the left. Randy started screaming again.

Greg yelled, "Hey, cut that out!"

The machete poked at him from the darkness, sliced a little stuffing from the seatback.

Greg yelled, "That's not what I *meant*!"

Funny.

He giggled, wiped a tear from his eye. The Pontiac was on the wrong side of the road again. Greg saw the slanting wall of rock a split second before he hit it. The impact jerked the steering wheel out of his hands. The splintered remains of a small tree skittered across the hood. The car was off the road and then back on it again, spun in tight circles across slick black asphalt. A few more trees died, and then the Pontiac was cruising down the road at fifty miles an hour, and a dogleg turn was coming up fast.

Greg took his foot off the gas pedal, hit the brakes. Up ahead, on the far side of the road, there was room to pull off – a tourist viewpoint made safe by a four-foot-high stone wall.

Greg spun the wheel. The Pontiac shot across the highway, skidded to a stop in a rising cloud of dust. Greg put it in reverse and stomped on it, drove the rear end into the stone wall. His head snapped back and his spine bottomed out. He drove forward thirty feet and stopped, found reverse gear and floored it, slammed into the wall again. And again. The rear bumper fell off. The tail lights shattered but the wall held. One more time.

And again.

Sheet metal crumpled. The trunk lid popped open. Randy didn't take advantage, though. All that bouncing around, he'd have been turned to mush even if he'd been packed in an American Tourister hardshell suitcase.

Greg got out of the car. He lit his last cigarette, tossed away the empty package. Walked around to the back of the car and raised the trunk lid a little higher, for a better look inside. Randy snapped wearily at him with the stumps of his teeth. One of his eyes had gone and the other was focused on the doorbell to hell.

Greg hauled him out of the trunk, managed to shove him over the wall. In the dim light from the ferry he could see Randy rolling and sliding towards the ocean, gathering a crowd of loose stones as he continued to lose altitude.

When he finally rolled to a stop, he was a long way down, and his body was sprawled across two shiny parallel lines of steel.

A railway. Greg was sure of it, because there was the train, half a mile or more away, barreling down the tracks.

A few minutes later, Randy's body was bathed in the un-romantic glow of five thousand candles. The shriek of the train's whistle ripped the night air like a stone hurled through a window. Randy's leg twitched. Or was it a trick of the light? The whistle howled again, and the hard-packed gravel shook beneath Greg's feet. Randy seemed to float up into the hard pure light, and then the light swallowed him whole.

Greg counted eighty-seven cars. No caboose.

21

Homer Bradley said, "That isn't the way I heard it, Jack."

Willows was exhausted. It had been a long night, and it wasn't over yet. Bradley and Claire Parker had both believed that Willows had been shot in the Maritime Museum parking lot. Bradley was restrained, but furious. Parker was more furious than restrained. Willows, his hands deep in the pockets of his leather jacket, leaned against Bradley's office wall as if it had been built specifically for his convenience.

Bradley wasn't finished, wouldn't let go of it. He said, "I heard something entirely different. I heard you almost got yourself shot."

"Nobody was aiming at *me*, Inspector." Willows was on the defensive, and he was a little annoyed. Bradley knew damn well that the shootout had been between Vietnamese gang-bangers and a couple of half-bright kids from the suburbs who'd tried to buy a lifetime's supply of coke with two hundred and fifty thousand dollars printed on a Canon laser copier. Willows said, "I doubt if they were even aware that I was in the parking lot."

Bradley said, "I'm not talking about the punks and dealers, Jack. The shot I'm referring to was fired by the female narcotics officer who put a round through your flashlight. Which, correct me if I'm wrong, was resting on your head at the time said round was fired."

"Put my lights out, didn't she?" Willows smiled, but Bradley didn't join in. The officer had been one of the group of joggers he'd seen earlier, huffing and puffing their way across

217

the park from the Planetarium. Bradley would never know how winded the narc had been, the way the muzzle of her revolver had wandered across the city's skyline as she struggled to catch her breath, the look on her face when she accidently pulled on him.

Bradley said, "Very funny, Jack. Make a pretty good headline, too, wouldn't it? *Cop shoots cop.*" He flipped open the Haida-carved lid of his cigar box, didn't like what he saw. "The point is, what the hell were you doing there in the first place? Nobody authorized you to camp out on Ross's front porch."

"I was working on my own time, Inspector."

"Sure you were. But what if that cop *had* shot your lights out? Who pays the freight then?"

Willows leaned a little harder into the wall.

Bradley said, "There are guys around here who make a point of keeping track of this kind of stuff. Five years down the road, all they've got to do is push a button and sit back and wait for the printout. It'll all be there, Jack. Every single time you've screwed up, every last detail. So I'm telling you, don't put in one more minute of unauthorized overtime, understand?"

Willows nodded. Almost as an afterthought, he said, "I came this close to nailing him," pinching thumb and index finger together.

Bradley gave him a cold look. "Almost nailed who?"

Willows told him about the Pontiac that had turned down Ogden Road just before the shoot-out.

Bradley said, "You saw the guy walk across the road and jump the fence into Ross's yard?"

Willows nodded. Parker was staring at him. This was news to her, too.

Bradley said, "Why didn't you bust him then?"

"Because the way I saw it he was going to keep right on jumping fences."

"Break into Ross's house."

"That's what it looked like, Inspector."

218

"You think that would've been smart, to let him go inside? Especially when you're alone – no backup. The guy carries a gun, he's a killer. Christ. You could've had a hostage situation, anything . . ."

There wasn't much Willows could say in his defense. Bradley was right, and he'd been wrong.

After a moment, Bradley said, "Okay, the shooting spooked him and he split. What's done is done. He see you?"

"No."

"You're sure?"

"Yeah, I'm sure."

Bradley said, "By now he's found out the shooting was about a drug deal that went all sour and curdly, nothing to do with his little scam. Think he'll be back?"

Willows nodded. "The guy's hit at least thirteen banks, thirteen tellers. Scored every time. What he goes after, he's used to getting."

"Yeah, but he does *banks*, not houses."

Willows said, "As far as the bank is concerned, Ross is clean. So far, we haven't worked out what Mendez was doing in Ross's office. But the fraud squad is positive Ross hasn't been operating a laundry for Panamanian drug money. I don't know what Mendez had in that briefcase – maybe it was only his lunch."

Bradley checked the contents of his cigar box again. He smiled at Parker.

Willows said, "The way I see it, loverboy's shifted gears. He's after the daughter. Some way of using her to get at Ross's money. She fits the pattern – single, about the right age, easy to look at."

"You think he might try to snatch her?"

Willows said, "He's a heartbreaker, not a fighter. Being pushy isn't his style, not with women."

Bradley said, "So what was he planning to do once he got inside the house?"

"I don't know, Inspector."

Bradley thought about it for a moment and then said,

"Okay, assuming the guy you saw is the guy we're after, and that he'll be back, how do you want to set it up?"

"Get rid of Ross and his daughter, fill in for them."

"Think he'll go along with the idea?"

"What choice does he have?"

"None, from my point of view. Let's hope he's smart enough to see it our way. When are you going to talk to him?"

"We're on our way."

Bradley took another look in the box, selected the cigar he'd had his eye on all day long. "This time," he said, "make sure you've got adequate backup."

Willows drove a pale green Caprice from the unmarked car pool. Parker, sitting bolt upright in the passenger seat, watched a two-ton delivery van pursue a chocolate-brown Mercedes through a red light.

"Know what I'd like, Jack?"

"Mandatory capital punishment for any moving traffic violation."

"That, too. But also a partner who let me know what the hell he was up to."

Willows said, "Look, I'm sorry. I got home last night, the house felt so *empty*. I poured myself a drink and I had this sudden thought – here I go again. You know what it's like, Claire. I had to get out of there, *do* something."

"Find a parking lot somewhere," said Parker, "hang out." But Jack was right – she knew how bad it could be, walking into an empty apartment at end of shift. Maybe he had held out on her. But all he'd really wanted to do was kill some time.

Willows parked in the customer lot behind Ross's bank, lowered the sun visor so the POLICE VEHICLE card was clearly visible.

Getting out of the car, Parker said, "How do you want to handle this, Jack?"

"With tact, diplomacy and guile."

"And if that doesn't work?"

"Naked threats."

220

Martin Ross was in his office, crouched behind a desk littered with paperwork, staring out the window. Willows rapped the door frame with his knuckles. The banker kept right on staring out the window. Willows knocked again, so hard it made his knuckles sting. Ross blinked, turned his head. He stared at Willows and Parker but gave no indication that he saw them.

Parker said, "Mr Ross."

Ross took a deep breath. He turned and glanced out the window again, as if there was something on the other side of the glass that fascinated and terrified him.

Parker said, "Mr Ross, could we talk with you for a few minutes . . ." She stepped into the office, Willows trailing along behind her.

Ross smiled blankly up at the two detectives as they approached his desk. He adjusted the knot of his blue and gold striped tie, smoothed his silvery hair. From a distance, he didn't look too bad. But up close, his skin was pale and slack, and there was a redness in his eyes. Ross had been crying, and recently. Parker was sure of it.

Willows walked right up to the banker's desk, leaned over him. Ross didn't object – hardly seemed to notice the intrusion.

Willows said, "You're aware that there was a shoot-out in your neighborhood last night, Mr Ross?"

The banker nodded, but didn't look up from his desk. "Yes, I read about it in this morning's paper."

"Surely you heard the gunfire?"

Ross hesitated.

Willows pressed harder. "The shooting occurred half a block from your front door. More than a hundred rounds were fired. Eight people were killed. Do you expect me to believe you didn't *notice*?"

Ross's face betrayed a mixture of anger, resentment, fear. He said, "What are you getting at, what's any of this got to do with me?"

"Narcotics officers were in the area at the time the shooting

221

started, Mr Ross. They had advance notice that a buy was going down. There was intensive surveillance of the parking lot."

Parker said, "Do you know anyone who drives a late-model dark blue or black Pontiac four-door?"

Ross's red-rimmed eyes shifted from Willows to Parker and back to Willows. "No, I don't. Why do you ask?"

"One of the detectives on duty last night observed a vehicle of that description cruise slowly past your home shortly before the shooting began. The driver made a U-turn at the end of the block, came back and parked across the street from your house. He got out of the car and entered your yard. He was observed attempting a break-and-enter of your home."

Ross said, "I'm not sure I understand what this is all about."

"It's about your daughter, Samantha," said Parker.

Ross's eyelashes fluttered. His skin suddenly had a yellowish, freshly lacquered look. Willows had a feeling that the banker's suit was the only thing that held him together.

Ross said, "How did you find out?"

Parker and Willows exchanged a quick glance which Ross, staring down at his desk, failed to notice.

Parker said, "It was an accident, really. We just got lucky, I guess."

Ross shuddered, his upper body twitching as if a long-buried charge of dynamite had exploded somewhere deep inside him.

Willows said, "Want to tell us about it?"

A crystal-clear drop of sweat fell from the banker's chin to his desk, smeared his signature at the bottom of a typed document. Ross wiped his face with a blue and gold striped handkerchief. He said, "It isn't Samantha's fault. She's hardly more than a child. Mendez was such a charmer. He told her . . ." As he spoke, Ross refolded his handkerchief and put it back in the breast pocket of his suit. Now he took it out again, wiped more sweat from his face.

"Told her what?" said Willows.

"That he was divorcing his wife, and that's why he was

222

squirrelling money away in Canada, because he didn't want her to get her hands on it."

"How much money?" asked Parker.

"I have no idea."

"Did you know Mendez was a narcotics officer, back in Panama?"

"No, certainly not."

"How did your daughter meet Mendez?"

"He tried to involve me in his schemes. I made the mistake of telling her about it. Then, by chance, they happened to meet. But the attraction was strictly personal, believe me."

"Was Samantha helping Mendez launder his cash?"

"*What* cash? This is all conjecture, isn't it?"

"We found a ledger in his hotel room," Willows said. "Believe me, Mr Ross, there's a lot of money out there somewhere."

"Well, Samantha didn't have anything to do with it. She's a headstrong young woman, but she isn't stupid."

"But if she *was* handling his money, she'd be a very wealthy young woman, now that he's dead, wouldn't she?"

Ross's head came up. There was a snarl in his eyes. For the first time, Parker and Willows glimpsed a hint of the tiger crouched behind the pinstripes.

"What are you implying, exactly? That my daughter hired a *hitman* to kill Mendez?"

"Not at all," said Parker smoothly.

Willows said, "The thing is, the man who shot Mendez and grabbed his briefcase may believe that either you or Samantha has access to the money. I asked you if you knew anyone who drove a dark blue or black late-model Pontiac. We believe the car is owned by the man who shot Mendez."

"He was at my house?"

Willows nodded.

"My God, she . . ."

"The house is under surveillance."

Parker said, "Do you know where your daughter is now, Mr Ross?"

223

"No, I'm sorry, but I have no idea."

"Attending classes?"

"She dropped out in the first month of the semester, told me she was bored."

"And you don't know what she's been doing with her time since then?"

Ross said, "I was afraid to ask."

"What we'd like to do," said Parker, "is set up a stake-out at your home. You and Samantha would spend the next night or two at a downtown hotel, at the city's expense. How does that sound to you?"

Ross fiddled with his Rolodex. After a moment he said, "Fine. It sounds just fine."

A small brass carriage clock on Ross's desk chimed the quarter-hour. Parker glanced at her watch, saw that she was running a little fast. She smiled.

Better to be quick than slow.

22

The morning after his joyride, Greg slept late but woke up in a hurry when the freight train muscled its way through the bedroom door, lathe and plaster flying, tons of iron and steel roaring and clattering down on him, the air filled with diesel fumes and smoke pierced through by an incandescent white light.

His eyes popped open. Nightmare. Whew! But being wide awake wasn't a whole lot better. Randy had really worked him over. It hurt like hell, just thinking about what had been done to him.

He eased out of bed, stood up and checked himself out in the cheap full-length mirror fastened to the back of the bedroom door. He wouldn't have believed it possible, but he looked even worse than he felt. As if he'd spent all night making love to a barbed-wire fence. The area around his kidneys was badly swollen and was the color of an overripe plum. He had a plum-sized bump on the back of his head where he'd bounced off the concrete. His foot, the one he'd used on Randy, throbbed painfully. He was pretty sure he hadn't broken anything, though, and it was just as well, because if there was one thing a man on the run didn't need, it was a broken foot.

And Greg would soon be on the run, his mind was clear on that much, at least.

He took a long, slow bath, dressed in a soft flannel shirt and black cords, black Nikes. In the kitchen, he popped a couple of waffles in the toaster, made a pot of coffee. By the time he finished breakfast he felt wide awake, was thinking with both sides of his brain.

He was pouring his third cup of coffee when Randy leapt up at him from the steaming black hole of the pot. Greg hit him with a left hook, struck him right between the eyes, drove his fist right through Randy's forehead and out the back of his skull. Randy frowned, and went away.

Greg knew damn well that you couldn't make a genuine flesh-and-blood person dematerialize with a left hook, no matter how powerful the blow. He'd beat Randy to a pulp and watched him fall down a cliff, get sucker-punched by a locomotive, mushed by eighty-seven railroad cars. The guy was *dead*.

But so was Greg – he was dead on his feet. The wall clock over the fridge insisted it was only a few minutes short of noon. The idea of falling asleep terrified him. Who knew what evil lurked in dreamland? But wasn't it a lot smarter to take a nap in broad daylight? He went back into the bedroom, stretched out, aimed the remote at the rented Hitachi television squatting malevolently on the bureau. The range of entertainment was sparse. News. Game shows. Soaps. Soft-porn music videos. The real-estate channel, the shopping channel. And then he was listening to a deliriously happy guy on a massive yacht crewed by large-breasted women in small pastel bikinis assure him that he too could be a millionaire, if only he had the *guts*.

Greg needed an omen, and there it was. He turned up the volume. The yacht was replaced by a house large enough to qualify as a mansion. There was a Rolls-Royce parked out front, a pool big enough to park the yacht out back. The babes were there too, smiling in a friendly way but silent, not even looking as if they had something in mind that they'd like to say. Full bikinis, empty heads.

Cash cash cash! All you needed was the guts to take a chance. *Chance chance chance!*

The guy was giving a series of seminars. He was a believer in free enterprise, and he wanted to spread the word. Soon, lucky for Greg, he'd be in Vancouver. The name of a suburban hotel flashed on the screen in big, easy-to-read block letters. The seminar was three hours long and it was free. *Free free free!*

Now the guy was back, grinning at Greg from behind the wheel of a redder-than-hell Ferrari. A black Porsche 911 squatted beside the Ferrari, and beside the Porsche there was another Rolls, a white convertible. In the background were palm trees the color of money and a blue-chip sky. But where were the babes? Right there, dozens of them, popping up in the Ferrari, the Porsche and the Rolls, all eyes on the happy guy as they waited for him to finish his pitch and get back to having lots and lots of *fun fun fun!*

Back on the yacht, the happy guy told Greg again that getting rich wasn't all that tricky – *all you needed was guts guts guts!*

An omen, definitely.

Greg slept all the rest of that day and deep into the night, woke up in darkness at twenty past ten. He turned off the TV. The red light on his answering machine was flashing at about half his pulse rate. He stared at it awhile, then rolled out of bed, went into the kitchen and snatched the last beer out of the fridge.

Another omen. When you were out of beer, it was time to move on. He drank half the bottle, wandered into the living room. It entered his mind that if the cops showed up he'd tell them Randy had broken into his apartment and beaten him up and stolen the Pontiac.

But he'd abandoned the stolen Pontiac several blocks away, poured gasoline over it and burnt it to a crisp. So – here's a good question – how did Randy make it to Horseshoe Bay?

Well, come to think of it, Randy *and a pal* had come to his apartment and knocked him silly and stolen his car.

Another question – what did Randy's pal look like?

Greg formed a fairly accurate mental picture of Paul Newman. No, that wouldn't do . . . He imagined a washed-up biker type, a chunky dude with thinning hair, salt-and-ketchup beard, round eyeglasses with copper-tinted frames perched halfway down a button nose, too much chest hair, a *vinaigrette* smile, stubby fingers squeezing a Camel cigarette to death. Great, but the cops would bust the apartment manager the minute they laid eyes on him. So what *did* Randy's pal look like?

All I saw was his fist, officer.

Greg drank some more beer and lit a cigarette. He had a few grams of coke hidden somewhere in the apartment but couldn't remember where. He started poking around in the living room, found a Charter Arms ·44 tucked under the sofa cushions, a Hi-Standard ·22 long semi-auto hidden behind the stereo system, and a stainless steel ·357 Colt revolver in a vase full of dead flowers next to the fake fireplace. He stuck the Hi-Standard in the waistband of his pants and then went and stood at the window with the stainless in his right hand and the Charter Arms ·44 in his left, the dead weight of the guns stretching his arms to the limit, ruining his posture. People had no idea how heavy a large-calibre handgun was, or what a nuisance it was to have to pack one around – the wear and tear on your clothes, for instance.

He thumbed back the hammers. The Charter Arms was brand new and the action was stiffer than he expected; the hammer started to slip away from him before engaging the sear. But he recovered nicely, no shots fired. He went into the bedroom, rooted around for his coke until the answering machine caught his eye. The little red light was blinking in sequences of three – indicating the number of messages waiting for him.

The first message was from Hilary. She sounded at first as if dumping him had been a big mistake. Then, suddenly turning into judge and jury, she told him it was almost midnight and Randy was way overdue. Then she went all melancholy again, her voice dripping with regret as she said goodbye. Didn't ask him to call her, Greg noticed.

The second message was a blind call from a carpet and upholstery cleaning company. Windows and chimneys, too, could be swiftly dealt with.

Greg lit a cigarette, adjusted the Hi-Standard in his pants so the front sight wasn't as intrusive.

The third and final message was Hilary again. She sounded frantic, right on the edge. She was positive Randy had gone to Greg's to get his pictures back. Where was her pretty boy? What had Greg done to him?

Had she really said that? *What have you done to my pretty boy?*

Greg rewound the tape and played it again.

Yup.

He took a last hit on his cigarette, squashed the butt into the carpet with the heel of his shoe.

He picked up the phone, punched Hilary's number. She answered on the fifteenth ring, her voice blurred, as if she'd been counting logs or sawing up sheep.

Greg said, "I wake you? What happened to that fun-loving insomniac I used to know so well?"

"Randy?" Hopeful. Perky.

"Once-upon-a-time, honey. But not any more."

"Greg?" Depressed. Disappointed. Deflated.

Greg said, "Just returning your call."

"Have you seen Randy?"

"Not since the last time." *Or was it the time before last, when I caught the two of you in the sack?* He said, "What makes you think he might've been here?"

"I don't know . . ."

Whew!

"I've been phoning around . . ."

Greg's voice, when he spoke, was tough as a cowboy's leathers, slippery as wet silk. "Oh baby," he said, "I miss you so much."

Hilary sighed deeply into his ear. Slammed down the phone.

Greg spent some time lurching around the apartment,

kicking the furniture and muttering vile oaths. After a while he ran out of steam and collapsed on the sofa.

In the bedroom, the telephone rang three times and then the answering machine picked up.

Greg smoked a cigarette, checked the message. It was Samantha. Daddy was out of town on business. Could he come over and play? About midnight would be nice.

Greg resumed his search of the apartment and found eleven loaded handguns and a sawed-off twelve gauge Purdy shotgun he hadn't realized he owned, a box of shells, enough coke to fuel another twenty-four hours in the fast lane. He packed a duffel bag with his makeup and then gathered all his other possessions that were of value and couldn't easily be replaced, stuffed it all – including the Mac's software and files, a wire coathanger and a brand-new roll of duct tape, in a single black canvas flight bag.

Except for a few clothes, everything else he owned, rented or leased went down the garbage chute or into the dumpster via the service elevator. Soon the apartment was empty except for the larger pieces of furniture; the sofa and bed, a coffee table and a few other odds and ends, all those cracked and shattered mirrors. Everything was rented under the name of the dead guy who technically owned the Pontiac. The collection agency hounds would find nothing to chew but a heap of dusty old bones.

Greg snorted a couple of lines of low-cal energy and vacuumed the hell out of the carpets, wiped clean every surface that might conceivably take a fingerprint. He moved after every caper so it was a familiar routine, one he'd performed a dozen times before. When he was done with his chores he stripped and took a long, hot shower. Then he hauled the duffel bag into the bathroom, slapped an eight-inch scar diagonally across his throat, taped his ears flat, gave himself a little more chin and a slab forehead, bushy eyebrows. Finally, he doubled the width and breadth of his nose and carefully applied gold foil to his upper left front tooth.

Whoever he looked like, it was someone else. The face that

230

smiled back at him from the fractured depths of the mirror belonged to anybody but him. But then, wasn't that always the case?

He dressed in a three-piece Hugo Boss black silk suit, sparkling white dress shirt and shiny grey silk tie, black lace-ups, an Yves Saint-Laurent trenchcoat. He admired himself in the hall mirror and then gave the glass a vicious kick, broke himself up.

It took him fifteen minutes to walk the five blocks to the nearest bank with an ATM. There was a bus stop within twenty feet of the machine. Greg lit a cigarette and mimed waiting for a bus. Half an hour and two buses and three burly male ATM customers later, a woman in a white Toyota pulled up against the curb.

Greg watched as she got out of the car, not bothering to turn off the engine, and hurried across to the ATM. She was in a rush, apparently. Too much of a rush to take a quick look around and make sure nobody like Greg was waiting to pounce.

She punched in her four-digit security code, fingers dancing across the ATM's keyboard.

Greg said, "You must be a secretary, huh? Do a lot of typing?"

Startled, she glanced over her shoulder, registered the weird-looking dude in the Yves Saint-Laurent. A tad nervous, she peered up and down the street.

Greg moved right up to her, slipped his arm around her waist. "What's your limit, sweetheart?"

"Get away from me!" It was a whisper of denial, not an outraged shout.

"In a minute, okay?" Greg told the ATM he wanted five hundred dollars. The woman squirmed and wriggled in his grasp. He said, "You trying to turn me on, honey?" She became very still. The ATM screen informed him that five hundred exceeded his limit. He tried for three. The machine's grim steel mouth clanked open and it spat a wad of twenties at him.

231

Greg asked the woman what her name was. Lorraine Flaviani. Greg said he was pleased to meet her. He put away the gun, grabbed his duffel bag and the flight bag and duck-walked Lorraine back to the Toyota, opened the driver's door and shoved her right across the seat, tossed his baggage in the backseat and climbed behind the wheel. He said, "How d'you adjust the seat, Lorraine? Never mind, I got it." He gave himself as much legroom as possible, put the Toyota in gear and hit the gas. The little car's acceleration surprised him, snapped his head back. Grinning, he said, "Peppy, huh?"

Lorraine stared out the windshield, making a point of not looking at him.

Greg said, "You married?"

She shook her head, no.

"Live alone?"

This time, her head moved in a vertical plane. Her hair was auburn, with reddish tints. He said, "Where do you live, Lorraine?"

She yanked at the door, kicked it open. The Toyota was doing 55K, the legal limit. Greg made an unscheduled lane change as he grabbed a handful of hair, pulled hard, reached across her and slammed shut the door. She tried to bite him on the wrist.

Greg showed her his big one, the Colt.

"Ever see any *Dirty Harry* movies, Clint Eastwood and his three fifty-seven magnum, can blow up whole buildings or knock an airplane out of the sky with one shot?"

She nodded, rubbed her shoulder where the frame of the door had bruised her.

Greg said, "Here's the deal. Why should I want to hurt you when I don't even know you? I need your car for a few hours – but I don't need you. So what am I gonna do, take you down to the beach and bury your head in the sand? Wouldn't you rather be tied up in the comfort and safety of your own home, Lorraine?"

She blinked. Crying a little, but otherwise holding up

232

pretty well, considering. Tough cookies, secretaries. A wild bunch, all in all.

Greg said, "You got a VCR?"

She nodded, still peering out the windshield, almost as if hoping to divine her future, somewhere up the road.

He said, "I'll slip in a movie, you'll probably fall asleep watching it." He smiled. "You can look at me if you want. What're you thinking – that I might bump you off so you can't identify me? Relax. I'm wearing a ton of latex, a wig." He took her hand. "Push your finger against the tip of my nose, Lorraine. See what happens? Now I look like Karl Malden, don't I?"

Lorraine lived in a ground-level suite in a house on West 19th, just off Cambie. Greg checked the bathroom, let her freshen up and then used almost the entire roll of duct tape to fasten her to an oak rocking chair. He made a noose of the wire coathanger, slipped it around her neck and tied it to the back of the chair, explained in lurid detail how she'd be putting herself at risk if she struggled. Finally, he asked if there was anything else he could do for her, would she like a cookie, glass of milk . . .

Apparently not.

Greg knelt beside her, rested a hand lightly on her knee. "Relationships are built on trust, Lorraine. Will you promise not to yell for help, the minute I'm gone?"

Lorraine thought about it for a moment, weighing the risks, trying to figure him out.

Greg said, "Think about it, okay?" He used the last of the duct tape to seal her lips, then turned the TV on and inserted a tape marked *The Cosby Show* into the VCR, got it rolling, adjusted the volume.

While Lorraine watched the Huxtables, Greg went into the kitchen and laid out a couple of fat white lines on the counter. He inhaled the coke, his nostrils feeling like they'd turned into afterburners, bent and licked the counter clean. Mr Huxtable was funny as only Mr Huxtable could be, but Lorraine didn't seem even slightly amused.

233

Greg said, "You seen this already? I could fast-forward."

Lorraine ignored him. Caught up in the plot, maybe. Laughing on the inside, perhaps. He let himself out of the apartment, locked the door behind him. Things were looking up. He had a bundle of twenties, a Toyota with a full tank of gas, a heavy date and a plan.

What more could a guy ask of life?

23

At six o'clock, when the bank closed for the day, Martin Ross handed Willows the keys to his Chrysler and took a taxi downtown, checked into the Ritz and headed straight for the bar. Several hours earlier, Samantha Ross had been intercepted by an unmarked car within a few blocks of her home. Parker arrived on the scene within minutes and briefly explained the situation. Unlike her father, Samantha turned down the offer of a paid hotel room. She told Parker she had friends at Whistler, a ski resort about ninety minutes north of the city, that she'd been meaning to visit for months.

Willows had driven to Ross's house in the Lincoln, confident that loverboy wouldn't be able to identify him through the car's tinted windows even if he was watching the house. Willows parked in the garage next to Parker's rented Samurai, deliberately left the garage's automatic door open.

Parker was already inside the house. Together, she and Willows went through the building room by room, made sure all the doors and windows were shut and locked, and that the security system was functioning. Later, Parker raided the fridge and put together a plate of cold roast beef sandwiches while Willows made a pot of coffee. In the Maritime Museum parking lot, Orwell and Oikawa were concealed in the back of a Parks Board pickup truck, crouched down beneath a blind made of boughs slashed from a fir tree. Across the alley from Ross's house, Farley Spears had taken a concealed position in a neighbor's garage. Both Orwell and Spears were in radio contact with Willows and Parker.

Parker and Willows ate their sandwiches in the den. The TV flickered, but the sound had been turned off. Parker's gun lay on the arm of her overstuffed leather recliner. Willows was reading *People* magazine. The house was quiet. Parker watched Willows as he paged through the magazine, the way his eyes moved, the play of shadow and light upon his face.

It had been a long day, and it was going to get longer. There was nothing Parker wanted more at that moment than a hot, leisurely shower. Was loverboy going to show up, or were they wasting their time? The ensuite bathroom in the master bedroom had recessed lighting, gold fixtures, a gold dish full of scented soap in the shapes of small birds, fish. She wondered how Jack would feel about a shower, if she asked.

In the back of the pickup truck, Oikawa seemed to have fallen asleep. Orwell hoped he was just resting, that his fellow detective was ready to leap into action at a moment's notice. It was cold and damp down there by the water. He'd zipped himself into his sleeping bag. Now he was snug and warm in his red plaid cocoon. But the zipper had jammed, trapping him. Orwell knew he should get Oikawa to help him with the zipper, but he also knew that the detective would never stop laughing, if he found out Orwell was stuck. Cops. Every last one of them had money troubles, and a twisted sense of humor.

On the far side of the alley behind the Ross house, Farley Spears sat on a fat bundle of newspapers he'd found near the rear of the garage and packed over to the open doorway by the lane. He was reasonably comfortable, except for a stray cat that had fallen for him, wouldn't leave him alone. Spears had an allergy. Dogs were fine but cats drove him crazy. He'd pick the cat up and forcefully hurl it into the alley and a couple of minutes later it'd be back in his lap, lashing his face with its tail.

Spears' eyes could have watered a lawn. His nose was running fast enough to qualify for the Olympics. Each time he tossed the cat into the alley, he put a little more effort into it.

236

The cat couldn't seem to get enough of Spears. The animal was endlessly playful and very smart, kept coming at him from different directions. The last time it had sneaked up on him, it'd crept along the rafters over his head and dropped on him from about eight feet up. He'd *yelped* with terror, grabbed the creature by a hind leg, spun it around like a discus thrower and flung it high into the darkness.

That had been ten minutes ago, a record, and Spears was starting to have second thoughts. Was a runny nose worth killing for? So he had an allergy, so what? The cat was only trying to be friendly. And now, poor helpless creature, it was lying out there somewhere with a shattered spine or lethal internal injuries, wondering what in hell it had done to deserve such a horrible fate.

Spears' knees creaked as he stood up. He stepped out of the shelter of the garage, knelt and whispered, "Here kitty kitty, puss puss puss . . ."

The cat was somewhere behind him, in the garage. It meowed softly. An eye glinted, a tooth gleamed. Spears picked up his MAG-LITE, flashed the beam quickly around the garage. He said, "Kitty kitty kitty . . ." and then the beast leapt straight at him, into his face. Spears raised his hands to intercept its flight.

Greg hit him right between the eyes with the heavy barrel of his Charter Arms ·44. The detective dropped as if he'd been shot. Greg grabbed a handful of coat and dragged Spears' limp body across the oil-stained floor of the garage. Kitty kitty played with the detective's shoelace as Greg relieved him of his revolver and walkie-talkie, extremely thin wallet, a gold Mont Blanc pen that had to be worth a few bucks.

Exhausted by his labors, Greg slumped down beside the unconscious or possibly dead cop. His skull bouncing off the concrete during his tussle with Randy must have left him with a priority one concussion. Now it felt as if there was a high-speed motorboat race going on inside his brain. All those propellers churning the grey matter into froth sure made it hard to concentrate.

237

He flipped open the wallet. The cop was carrying six dollars in cash and an expired American Express card with a bunch of holes punched through it. Well, what did he expect, mugging a cop. To get rich?

He tried the flashlight. It cast a beam bright enough to illuminate a surgery. He unzipped the duffel bag, rummaged around until he found his scalpel, slashed Spears' overcoat into strips and bound and gagged him. Then, just for laughs, he spent a few more minutes on the unconscious cop – gave him a little something to remember Greg by.

Finished, he stuffed the tools of his trade back in the duffel bag. This one, Farley Spears, was gone for the night. The cop hidden under the pile of shrubbery in the pickup truck was no threat unless Greg waltzed up to the front door and rang the bell. Would there be more cops waiting for him inside the house? It was hard to think clearly with all those motorboats racing around in his head, but he thought probably there were. Samantha wouldn't set him up. There'd been a spark between them, he was sure. But her daddy was different. Daddy was the kind of guy who'd mortgage his soul if the price was right. So, yeah, there'd be a couple of cops in there, waiting.

The way Greg saw it, he still had the advantage. He knew where they were – but they didn't know where he was.

The element of surprise, that's what he had going for him. Plus a ruthless nature. And plenty of charm . . .

Greg knew he should blow Samantha a kiss, turn around and walk away. Problem was, the happy guy was right – if you wanted to get rich you had to have *guts guts guts*. And there was the fact that he sensed he was running out of time and luck. Despite everything, he was in a cheerful, careless frame of mind. It was the concussion and he knew it, but somehow knowing didn't help. If he didn't break into the house, what would he do instead? He had no idea. He found the plastic bag containing his stash, spilled the contents into the palm of his hand, pinched a nostril shut and snorted hard, whinnied like a horse.

Inside the house, Willows checked his watch, frowned. He reached out, turned the walkie-talkie towards him and verified that the battery warning light was off. He said, "What time have you got, Claire?"

"Quarter past."

Willows picked up the radio, thought it over for a minute, and then pressed the transmit button and softly spoke Spears' name.

"Farley?"

A burst of static, then silence.

"Farley? You there, Farley?"

Nothing.

Parker said, "You want dependability, I'd rather have a length of string and a couple of empty soup tins. See if you can raise Oikawa."

Willows pressed transmit. "Danny, you read me?"

Oikawa came back immediately. "Loud and clear. Want me to take a look?"

"I'll do it." Willows watched his Seiko beat ten seconds to death, then tried Spears again.

More silence.

Willows drew his snubnose ·38. He swung out the cylinder and checked the load. Parker followed him out of the den, down the hall and into the kitchen. She said, "Take it slow, Jack."

Willows nodded, used his left hand to open the front door. The ·38 was in his right fist, pointed in front of him and down. He said, "Be right back," and reached out and lightly touched her arm. Then he was gone.

The two-car garage attached to Ross's house was so wide that the outer wall butted up against the neighbor's fence. Greg scrambled up on top of the fence, waited until his head cleared and then hoisted himself up on the garage's gently sloped roof of cedar shingles. He stayed low, straddling the ridgeline, as he made his way towards the frosted-glass window that he figured would give him access to the

239

second-floor bathroom. As soon as he'd finished crossing the roof, he leaned towards the gutter and was violently ill.

Sitting on the roof with his back against the wall of the house and the flight bag and duffel bag in his lap, he turned his head slightly and looked across the street and empty park towards the city. How strong the wind must be, to make the highrises shift and sway like that, as if they were dancing.

Dancing buildings.

Greg suddenly remembered why he'd frisked the cop who thought he was a pussy cat.

It was because he was out of cigarettes, damn it. He stared bitterly at the dancing highrises, then gasped with delight as a two-hundred-foot monster suddenly broke free and rose slowly above the skyline, hovered for an endless moment and then accelerated, a blur of light that veered into blackness, dwindled and was gone.

Greg sat there on the roof, eyes full of pupil, mouth agape. Was it the coke, or the blow to his head – was he hallucinating? Maybe, but somehow he doubted it.

Down in the alley, Willows almost shot the cat as it rushed him from the darkness of the garage. Oblivious to its brush with death, the animal tried to wrap itself around his leg.

Willows slowly moved deeper into the garage. He had a pocket flashlight, but didn't want to risk using it for fear of giving his position away. The cat stayed right beside him, the roar of its purring loud enough to wake the dead. His foot bumped into something that was soft and yielding. He switched on the flashlight. Farley Spears' eyes were shut tight. His skin was the color of a new moon, and a trickle of blood had run down the side of his head into his ear. Willows aimed the flashlight beam a little lower. Farley's throat had been slashed from ear to ear; torn flesh shrinking from the perimeter of a slit trench overflowing with blood.

In the house, Parker curled up in the overstuffed leather chair in the den. The walkie-talkie lay in her lap and her finger rested lightly on the trigger of her second-best friend.

The bathroom window was double-glazed, in a cheap aluminum frame. Greg opened his bag, shoved the spreadsheets to one side, found his all-purpose scalpel and went to work on the window until he felt the tongue of the lock, then pushed upward, steadily increasing the pressure. The metal bar started to slip, then suddenly popped right out of the socket. He pulled the window open as far as he could, tossed the flight bag and duffel bag inside. Another highrise was launched into the heavens. Spectacular, but distracting. He took a deep breath and half-dived and half-fell through the window, into the house.

The first thing he noticed was that the bathroom door was shut. Good, fine. He hauled himself to his feet, rested a moment and then swung shut the window and turned on the light. The bathroom had all the warmth and charm of a train station. The thought gave Greg pause. Maybe it would be best if he abandoned his plans, moved on. Somewhere, there had to be greener pastures. And if the ugly truth were known, he couldn't even remember what he was doing there, what his plans were. Grab Samantha and the money and run. Was that it? Greg peered into a bronzed mirror over the sink. He looked pretty good for a strung-out, doped-up, terminally concussed killer.

He swung open the medicine cabinet door. Aspirin. 222s. Industrial-strength Tylenol. A vial of little yellow pills, a smaller vial of red and blue pills, a medium-size vial of orange and black pills striped like a barber's pole. He helped himself to four or five of each, washed the lot down with a mouthful of tap water and then, bobbing and weaving, went to work on his face.

The fighter, the pug. Rodeo rider. Norman Mailer. The postman, the beggar and the blind man. Cop. The *artiste* and bus driver. Liquor store clerk. Motorcycle racer. The guy who worked in the gas station and had a face like a cobble-stone road; covered in warts the size of marbles. Working furiously, Greg tried them all and couldn't get any of them right.

He pulled an auburn wig from his head, tore bubbles of

latex from his face. Ripped blue contact lenses from his eyes. Latex, artificial blood, and a dozen wigs lay scattered on the tiled floor. The bathroom looked like a slaughterhouse for small animals. Greg yanked a handful of hair from his head. His scalp stung. A trickle of blood ran down into his eyes. His fingers clawed at his flesh. The coke had filled him with manic energy. The aspirin and red and blue and orange and black and yellow pills had killed the pain, numbed him.

His hands slapped at his face. Did this face belong to him? Was *this* his face? He couldn't quite remember what he was supposed to look like. He tried to conjure up an image of his features. Bits and pieces of various adopted personas floated in the mirror. Such a weird sensation. He remembered that he wanted Mendez's money, Samantha, a cigarette.

And not necessarily in that order, either. He drove his fist into the mirror, head-butted the silvered glass until it shattered.

Outside, Willows' head came up as he heard the mirror break. He was fairly sure the sound had come from inside the house. Switching off the flashlight, he made his way out of the garage and across the alley.

Take it easy, take it slow.

He stayed close to the fence as he moved through the backyard, checked the narrow, dimly lit space between Ross's house and the neighbor's. Cautiously, he worked his way around to the garage. Had the top-floor bathroom light been on earlier? He didn't think so. It seemed to take him forever to find where Greg'd scrambled up on the garage roof, his weight bending the aluminum gutter out of true.

Willows yelled at Oikawa and Orwell. Oikawa drew his revolver and ran towards the house.

In the house, Parker heard the bathroom door swing open, thought for a moment that it was Willows returning but then remembered that the door was deadbolted and that Willows didn't have a key. A moment later she heard what sounded like someone falling down a flight of stairs, and then a shouted oath.

242

Out on the front porch, Oikawa threw himself at the door, grunted in pain. Willows sprinted for the parks board pickup. He started the motor and backed across the driveway and swung wide on the lawn. Eddy Orwell, still caught up in his sleeping bag, rolled helplessly off the back of the truck and into a flower bed.

Inside, Parker was half out of her chair when Greg suddenly appeared in the open doorway. He held on to the doorframe with both hands, as if for dear life. Rivulets of blood slithered down the white-painted wood. Parker bisected his chest with the front sight of her revolver.

Greg said, "Hello there, Samantha."

Parker said, "What?" The guy was slurring his words, and no wonder. He looked, at best, dead on his feet.

Greg said, "I want the money, honey."

Parker said, "What money?"

Greg frowned, scratched his scalp. There was blood beneath his fingernails. He'd worked everything out but it was hard to remember how it went. After a moment he said, "Your daddy was working for Mendez, laundering all that Panamanian drug money. Mendez dropped by the house one night, didn't he?"

Oikawa jumped clear of the porch as Willows slammed the gas pedal to the floor. The truck bounced up three steps. The right front fender hit the door. The fender crumpled but the door held.

The house shuddered. Greg glanced over his shoulder, turned back to Parker.

She waited.

Greg said, "Met Daddy's little girl and decided he'd rather have her do his wash. Fired Daddy."

Greg leaned heavily against a wall. He wiped his nose with the back of his hand and blood – or something that looked like blood – spurted. He said, "Tell you what."

Parker said, "What?"

"Gimme a cigarette and we'll call it quits."

Parker said, "I don't smoke."

243

"Be reasonable, Samantha!" Greg lurched towards her. His left ear had been hanging by a thread. Now it fell off.

Parker stared at the ear lying there on the carpet.

Greg said, "Gimme a cigarette, dammit!" Piqued, he stomped the ear into the rug.

Parker said, "I'm not Samantha."

"Oh, sure."

Parker said, "What *happened* to you?"

Greg smiled. "I got into a fight with a freight train."

Parker believed it. She believed it all.

"Eighty-seven cars," bragged Greg. His vision was watery and badly blurred because he'd scratched a cornea trying to pluck out a contact lens that wasn't there. He squeezed the damaged eye shut, stared in amazement at what he saw and then said, "Who the hell are you?" as he fumbled under his ragged clothes for the Charter Arms ·44.

Parker yelled, "Drop it!"

Greg said, "My gun's bigger than your gun."

The house shook again, as if struck by a giant fist. Wood splintered and glass shattered. Greg risked another look behind him. A very serious-looking guy was running down the hall towards him. The guy pointed a pistol and screamed, "Freeze!"

Greg reached under his jacket for the ·357 magnum. He was trying to thumb back the ·357's hammer when Willows and Parker tackled him and knocked him down.

Out on the front lawn, Orwell shucked his ruined sleeping bag and turned towards the house. Farley Spears stepped out of the shadows. Orwell's mouth fell open.

Spears said, "It's okay, it's me."

Orwell, staring at him, said, "Jeez, what happened to your neck?"

Spears said, "Nothing, why?" His hand touched his throat. What the hell kind of allergic reaction was *that*? His fingers gently probed the wound. He pulled hard.

The thing made a rubbery, snapping sound, and then let go.

244

Orwell said, "What is it, some kind of leech?"

Spears held the stretchy rubber thing up to the light streaming from the shattered doorway. He said, "What's the matter with you, Eddy – don't you know a *gaping wound* when you see one?"

Willows read Greg his rights while Oikawa frisked and handcuffed him. Parker phoned for an ambulance. Spears and Orwell joined the throng. Spears retrieved his gun and wallet. Greg told him about the apartment buildings that had blasted into space, how beautiful they were.

Orwell said, "That's missing persons, pal. Nothing to do with me."

Greg made eye contact with Parker, and told her that she was an extraordinarily beautiful woman.

She thanked him for the compliment and smiled sweetly at Willows.

Greg asked her if by any chance she happened to work in a bank or credit union or trust company.

24

The bar closed at one. Martin Ross knocked back his sixth or seventh martini, fished around in his pocket for the key to his room, checked the number, signed for the drinks and an over-generous tip with an uncharacteristic flourish. He took the elevator up to his floor, paused by the ice machine. There were no buckets, so he carried half a dozen melting cubes to his room in his cupped hands. Inside, he unlocked the bar fridge and emptied a two-ounce bottle of vodka into a glass, added some ice.

He thought about Garcia Lorca Mendez, and then he thought about the derelict, and the animal sound the man made as he was separated from his hand.

He thought about how quickly the Panamanian had died, the animal look in his eyes.

He thought about his gambling debts, how Mendez had taken care of them, but at the same time put him deeper in debt than he had ever been.

He thought for a long, long time about the restless, hungry way Mendez had stared at Samantha, the first time he saw her.

He thought about the way his daughter had stared back at the Panamanian.

Later, when the two men were alone, Mendez dropped heavily to his knees, took Ross's hand and begged for permission to ask Samantha out. Martin Ross didn't want his hand chopped off, so he hadn't said no. Pretty soon he didn't need to worry about laundering Mendez's money any more, because Samantha was taking care of it.

When Mendez was shot and the briefcase containing the monthly statements were taken, Ross had panicked, but Samantha had remained calm and poised, assured him that the spreadsheets were useless, numbers in a void. She'd told him that the money was all hers, now, and that she intended to keep it.

He told her about the machete. He told her Mendez was nothing but a small cog in a very large machine, that soon a replacement would arrive and that the money had to be in place.

Samantha had laughed at him, told him he had a pretty lively imagination, for a banker.

She seemed to believe Mendez was the only Panamanian in the whole wide world.

By the time the phone started ringing Ross was well into his third miniature vodka bottle, and loss of motor control had considerably slowed the pace of his drinking. He fell across the king-size bed, grabbed the receiver and mumbled hello.

"Daddy, is that you?"

Ross mumbled his assent.

Samantha said, "Have you been drinking?"

"Jus' a little . . ."

Samantha said, "I'm supposed to be up in Whistler, visiting friends. But I'm not."

Ross struggled to digest the information, divine its meaning.

His daughter said, "I've decided to tell the police everything."

Ross said, "About what, honey?"

Samantha's voice suddenly changed. For the first time in years she sounded unsure of herself, vulnerable and very young. She said, "You know. Everything."

Ross said, "Baby, you *promised* . . ."

"Everything you did." She was crying. He saw the tears

247

falling down her cheeks, trails of slime, her face red and swollen. Distorted. Ugly. She said, "I was your little girl. *Just look what you did.*"

Ross said, "Baby, listen to me . . ."

She slammed the phone down hard, cutting him off.

Ross knelt in front of the bar fridge, helped himself to the last of the vodka. In the bathroom, he sipped at his drink as he stood in front of the mirror, fiddled with his tie and then brushed his silvery hair until it was exactly right. When he was finally satisfied with his appearance, he slipped into his suit jacket and then, still carrying his drink, left the room and walked down the corridor to a door marked "Fire Exit. Do not enter – alarm will ring".

He yanked open the door. Directly above him, a red light flashed and a bell rang shrilly. He stepped out on to the rusty metal grid of a staircase. He was twelve floors up – close to a hundred and thirty feet. The air was cold and damp. He heard voices and turned and glanced behind him.

An elderly man in red and white striped pajamas said, "For God's sake, don't do it!"

Ross stepped over the railing. His shoes slipped on the rusty steel. He lost his balance and fell, twisted through blackness, all that screaming and the blurred jangle of the fire alarm fading as he tumbled, helpless and disoriented, into the void.

He was still trying to figure out which way was up when he hit the asphalt.

25

Bradley pushed his window wide open and then did the unthinkable – lit a cigar. Much to his surprise, neither Parker nor Willows objected.

He blew out the match and said, "Loverboy's looking at thirteen counts of armed robbery, the Mendez shooting, kidnapping, assault and battery, possession of various unregistered firearms, arson, break and enter, whacking a guy with a freight train . . . Is that it, or did I miss something?"

"*Fourteen* counts of armed robbery," said Parker. "You forgot about Lorraine Flaviani."

"Right, right." Bradley chewed on his cigar, blew a stream of smoke out the window. "How's the suicide note look?"

"It's authentic," said Willows. The undated note had been found in a locked drawer in Martin Ross's office desk.

Bradley said, "Okay, let's say Ross writes and signs a suicide note in which he apologizes for his sins, and leaves everything he owns to his daughter. Then he takes a header off a five-star hotel in front of a small but select group of witnesses. *What sins?*"

Willows said, "We don't know."

Bradley peered out the window, looking down, flicked an inch of ash into the street. "What's Ross's daughter end up with?"

Parker said, "She gets the house – the mortgage was insured – plus about two hundred thousand in stocks and bonds, six hundred thousand from Ross's life insurance policy."

"Lucky girl. What'd she say when you asked her about the phone call she made to her father from Whistler, only a few minutes before he jumped?"

"That he was drunk and seemed depressed."

"That's it?"

Parker nodded.

Bradley said, "How much time did you spend with her?"

"As much as her lawyer would allow."

"She pretty broken up?"

Parker said, "Not really, no. Ross's wife died when she was eleven years old. Ross never remarried. Jack and I talked it over. We don't have any hard evidence and we can't prove anything, but we agree that there was more than one heartbreaker involved in this case."

Bradley destroyed an inch of cigar mulling over the possibilities.

Willows said, "It's just a guess, but I wouldn't be surprised if Samantha and Mendez had something going. It'd be a way for her to get back at daddy. Right now, she's staying in a four hundred thousand dollar Whistler condominium that's owned by a numbered company. Might be interesting to find out who or what's hiding behind the numbers."

Bradley said, "Speaking of numbers, has anybody managed to decipher the spreadsheets yet?"

Willows shook his head. "Fraud took a peek. Joey Chang said there's no way of knowing what the numbers represent. It could be bank account balances or a numerical code for barbecue sauce. Without bank branch or account numbers it'd take them months to find out."

Bradley said, "If they had the time. Which they don't. And by then the accounts – if that's what they are – would probably have been cleaned out anyway. Right?" He turned to Parker. "Claire, anything you want to add?"

"Martin Ross wasn't pushed – at least not in a legal sense. I say let's call it a wrap."

Bradley stared out the window. His jaw rose and fell as

he took his frustration out on the cigar. "What's new from Panama?"

Willows said, "*Nada*. Mendez was an ace cop. No way he could have been over here laundering drug money."

"That's their story and they're sticking to it?"

"For now. They mentioned that they'll probably fly a couple of Mendez's vice squad pals over for a closer look, to make sure he wasn't up to something they didn't know about."

Bradley nodded thoughtfully, spent some more time looking out the window. Finally he said, "So what was Mendez doing in the bank? Why was he wearing the cable repairman's coveralls?"

Parker said, "We talked to Ross's neighbors. There was a cablevision truck parked in front of his house the day before the bank was robbed. A man answering Mendez's description was seen entering the house. We think he was putting some kind of pressure on Ross – blackmailing him, maybe. Trying to involve him in his money laundering schemes. If Samantha was involved with Mendez and Ross knew about it, it'd explain why Ross took such a risk to hold on to the briefcase during the robbery."

Bradley said, "Okay, I'll buy it. What else have you got on your plate?"

"Lunch," said Willows.

Parker wanted to try a new Hungarian restaurant on Broadway, off Main, that a friend had recommended. At Main and Eighth, she braked hard and pulled the unmarked Caprice up to the curb. Willows rolled down his window, and the thin blonde woman in fish-net stockings and red leather shorts turned towards him, smiled a crooked smile.

Willows said, "How you doing, Honey?"

Honey cocked a hip, scratched an arm. "Real good, up until now."

Willows hit the gas, eased the unmarked car into the noon-hour traffic. He gave Parker a rueful grin. "Tell me something

– why is it that the only things that don't change are the ones that should?"

Parker said, "Maybe because that's the way we want it, Jack. I mean everybody. Even you and me."